ALSO BY STELLA HOLMES

THE
PATIENT

ALSO BY STEENA HOLMES

Finding Emma

Emma's Secret

The Memory Child

Stillwater Rising

The Word Game

Saving Abby

Abby's Journey

THE
PATIENT

a novel

NEW YORK TIMES & USA TODAY BESTSELLING AUTHOR
STEENA HOLMES

Text copyright © 2019 by Steena Holmes
All rights reserved.

Published by Lake Union Publishing, Seattle

www.apub.com

Amazon, the Amazon logo, and Lake Union Publishing are trademarks of Amazon.com, Inc., or its affiliates.

ISBN-13: 9781542040389
ISBN-10: 1542040388

Cover design by Shasti O'Leary Soudant

Printed in the United States of America

To my husband.
The crazy cycle is over.
But I still don't want to cook.

In a Wonderland they lie,

Dreaming as the days go by,

Dreaming as the summers die.

—Lewis Carroll, *Through the Looking-Glass*

Chapter One

THURSDAY, AUGUST 15

How do I admit this? Disclose that I've held this secret out of fear? I think about the words I need to say, unsure that I can voice them. Admit my shame, my failures, my . . . suspicions.

I look at myself in the car mirror, barely recognizing the woman who stares back. I need to speak the words out loud to myself, make them real, before I can tell them to someone else.

"I think . . ." My voice sputters, splits, spirals into silence.

It's hard to vocalize. What I'm about to say feels like a betrayal. What if I'm wrong? What if I'm making a mistake? What if . . .

I take a deep breath and try again.

"I think one of my patients is a serial killer. I just don't know which one."

Chapter Two

ALMOST TWO WEEKS EARLIER
SATURDAY, AUGUST 3

The moments before a book is opened, before a page is turned and the words leap out—those moments are my favorite.

Even when I know the words. Even when I've read them over and over and over again.

"Seriously, Danielle? Another *Alice in Wonderland*? Don't you have a bazillion copies of that same book on your shelf at home?"

Only an ignorant person would say something so foolish to a hard-core Alice addict like me.

"It's an 1883 hardbound edition of *Alice's Adventures in Wonderland.*" I couldn't believe the blank look on Tami's face.

"How are we even friends?"

"You tell me." She nudged my shoulder and gave me that you-know-you-love-me smile of hers before she shoved the book she held in my face. "You should read this one. I heard it was good."

I looked at the cover and title and didn't give it a second glance. "A thriller? Seriously?" She knew I didn't read those. I preferred fairy tales and old classics.

"Yeah, but it's Kimberly Belle."

Like I knew who that was.

"Unless Stephen King wrote a novel about twisted fairy tales, I'm not interested." I pushed her book aside and focused on the one in my hand.

The Rabbit Hole Goods was an antique store in the heart of Cheshire that sold everything from old silverware to hand-carved furniture. There was also one small section beside the cash desk with a rack of the latest novels, probably the only things in the store that weren't used.

I preferred the old tomes. The ones that showed their history, revealed their treasured finds within the pages.

Like the one I held. I needed to own it regardless of the cost.

"You're honestly going to spend over three hundred dollars for a book?" Tami rested her chin on my shoulder and *tsk*ed in my ear when she saw the sticker price. "Do you have a stash of cash and other buried treasure in that basement of yours I don't know about?"

I wanted to laugh, but she knew how I felt about that basement.

"Feel free to take a shovel and see what you can find." I wrinkled my nose at the idea.

"Oh, the things we'd discover." Tami rubbed her hands together in glee. "I've always wanted to go treasure hunting. Maybe the past owners didn't believe in banks and kept all their money in a box down there? We totally need to check it out."

I snorted. Like that was going to happen. The last time I'd headed down the stairs, I'd walked into a huge spiderweb. I hadn't been back down since.

"I have a few rookies who could go down for us," she teased. "Give them something to do other than flirt with all the weekend tourists."

Tami was a detective in our sleepy town of Cheshire and had more time on her hands than a retired substitute teacher.

"Because I love you so much," she said as she nudged a box at our feet, "why don't I get my hands dirty and see if there are any other Alice books in here? Although I think you have enough, don't you?" She set the thriller down on a table and sat on the floor, going through each book while I looked on. I didn't tell her I had already gone through the lot and was holding the only one I'd found. I rather enjoyed watching her shove her fingers through her messy hair and leave dust streaks.

"Enough? Never." Alice was my childhood, my comfort blanket, my anchor when life got messy. Wonderland was the world I'd wandered into whenever my parents fought, when I got anxious or too scared.

"Can I help you with something?"

At my side stood an older man in worn jeans with black suspenders over a red plaid shirt. He pushed his sleeves up as he stood there, a funny look on his face. In all the times I'd shopped there, I'd never seen him before.

"I was just admiring this classic." I showed him the book in my hands.

He studied me for a moment before he glanced down at Tami.

"You a buyer or a browser?" Gruff and to the point, he held out his hand as if he expected me to relinquish my hold.

That wasn't about to happen.

"It's an 1883 edition. Out of your price range." His fingers grabbed the book, but I pulled back.

"Don't mess with Dee when it comes to her Alice." Tami's voice was full of laughter.

"Technically it's not mine yet," I reminded her.

She gave me one of those like-that-matters looks, and I smiled.

"Technically it's mine and not for sale." He jerked it out of my hands with a grunt and walked away.

"Hey, wait." I stood there like a frozen mannequin, shocked at what'd just happened.

"Did he honestly just take that from you?" Tami brushed her hands on her shorts and grimaced at the dirt. "What kind of customer service is that anyhow?"

"Um, sir?" I trailed after him as he wove through the store. "Sir, I'd like to buy that book."

He didn't stop until he reached the back counter. He set the book down, picked up a pipe, and placed it between his lips. I waited to see if he'd light it up, but he didn't.

The pipe looked to be as much a part of him as the suspenders.

"Hey, Dad, can you help me with this . . ." The curtain behind the man moved, and out walked Alicia, the owner. She wore a gray apron over her sundress and tugged an old suitcase behind her. "Oh, hey, Danielle. I see you've met my father." The smile on her face beamed brighter than the canary yellow of her dress.

"Ah, you found the Alice book." A hint of disappointment trailed in her voice.

"Who said we were sellin' my book?" Her father scowled.

Alicia ran her fingers lightly over the cover. "We did, remember?"

I stood there, a silent spectator to the family discussion. I wanted the book and didn't want to walk away quietly, not if I could help it.

"Sorry," Alicia said to me. I knew she meant it. "I know you collect these books. I'll keep my eye out for another."

"This belongs in a collector's library with someone who appreciates what they have." He turned his grumpy frown toward me. "Not for sale." He took the book, yanked the curtain open, and disappeared.

The disappointment must have been evident on my face.

"Sorry, Dad is a bit of a . . . well, he's a book collector, and . . . sorry," she repeated. "There's really no excuse. He comes in sometimes to help out but rarely ever deals with customers." She had the decency to look apologetic.

"Maybe he'll reconsider?" Tami suggested.

"I promise, I'll keep an eye out for another like it and put it aside for you," Alicia said.

The bell over the door jingled, and the sounds from a band filled the store.

"Come on," Tami said. "I've only got a bit of time before I have to dress up and join the parade."

Every Saturday, the town of Cheshire had a small midday parade where the high school band marched, the children's theater dressed up, and all the characters from the Wonderland books walked the streets, waving to the crowds.

"Did you say dress up?" Once outside, I looked down the street and was shocked at how crowded the sidewalk already was with lawn chairs and groups of families.

"Yeah, I picked the short stick and ended up being the department mascot." Tami tried to frown. She worked really hard at it, I could tell, but the edges of her lips tilted until she laughed.

Tami in a white rabbit suit. I could see it. Hopping around the street, handing out suckers to the kids, waving at everyone . . . she'd love every second of it.

Me, on the other hand—my plan was to huddle inside my house and wait for the crowd to disperse before I ventured out again.

Something about the throngs of people jammed together like sardines in a can . . . I wouldn't say it gave me a panic attack, but it was close.

I like people. I like talking and creating relationships with people, but one-on-one. Too many, and the air gets sucked out of the room and I'm swirling in a vortex of dizziness.

No thank you.

"Why don't we head down to the tea shop?" I asked. "I keep wanting to introduce you to Sabrina, the owner." Tami was a coffee addict, not a tea lover. Every time I'd attempted to get my two friends to meet, something had always come up.

Tami glanced at her watch. "As much as I'd love to, I'd rather grab an ice cream before I'm in that sweaty costume. How about another time?"

I should have expected the excuse.

"I'm going to make a cheesecake and have you both over. Enough is enough. I really want you to meet her. I think you'll love her."

Tami's eyes lit up at the word *cheesecake*. It'd been forever since I'd made one, and it was her favorite dessert.

"Chocolate chip?" she asked.

"With chocolate ganache on top." I amped up the temptation.

"Can I look at my calendar and let you know?"

I shook my head. "You'll find some excuse to not come and then pop over the next day for leftovers."

"I won't. I promise." She held out her pinkie finger, and we did our childish pinkie-swear custom with wide smiles.

We stopped at the ice cream shop next to the antique store and grabbed our cones before Tami and I went in different directions. Rather than watch the parade, I decided to meander along the park pathways, maybe stop at the library until I could be sure most of the downtown crowd had dispersed. I should have been at the parade, where I could chat with the different families and wave at all the Alice characters, local shop owners, and school clubs that walked by. It was what Sabrina would have encouraged.

I had only two close friends here in town, and they couldn't have been any more opposite.

Tami never pushed, prodded, or poked me to do something I wasn't ready for. Instead, she waited, knowing eventually I'd break, bare my soul, and be ready to step out of my comfort zone.

Sabrina, on the other hand, always pushed, prodded, and poked, believing I needed to be dragged into situations whether I was ready or not.

Despite being so different, they were exactly what I needed in my life.

Tami knew I couldn't handle being at the parade, that the crowds and noise would be too much to handle, but if Sabrina knew I'd escaped an opportunity to grow, she'd be more than a little disappointed in me.

~

I found my way to a park bench that overlooked the children's area across from the main steps of the Cheshire Public Library.

The weathered gray steps that led to the open doors were crammed with families enjoying the sunny day. Popcorn littered the ground around a portable machine run by a woman dressed as a clown, with birds scooping up the discarded kernels.

Off to the side in a grassy area, a dozen children circled around one of the library staff members, who had a stack of books by her side. In her hands was a large picture book, one where the words were written on the left side with the image on the right. Her fingers tracked along with what she read, and she smiled at those who shouted out the words they recognized as they read with her.

The children were a mixed group. Short. Tall. Skinny. Round. Girls. Boys. Quiet. Loud. Some sat on the grass with their legs crossed while others bounced on their knees, barely remaining on the ground. A few shy ones hovered at the back, their interest barely overcoming their hesitation.

All but one child.

She sat far off to the side, hands clasped tightly in front of her, gaze never straying from the woman who read from the book. She was close enough to hear the story but not close enough to participate when the storyteller asked the children to read out a word with her.

She'd take one step forward, closer to the group, before stepping back, too afraid to be so close.

I wanted to cross the park, take that child by the hand, and join the group. I wanted the storyteller to notice, to include the child. I wanted to find that child's mother and discover why her daughter was sitting so far away from the others.

In the end, I did nothing. Maybe she was like me, and crowds weren't her thing. But I could tell, even from where I sat, she wanted to be with the other children.

I couldn't hear the words from the storyteller, nor could I make out the images in the book, but the sounds from the group filled me with a peace that reached deep inside and wanted to curl up for a long stay.

I sat on the bench until story time was over and saw that before the group dispersed, the storyteller handed out bags to the children. A few whooped with surprise and then ran to their parents, while a few others dug into their bags and held out books they found inside with pride.

The only one who didn't take a bag was the young girl I'd noticed earlier.

"Robin, let's go." Her mother had appeared on the steps. The little girl looked up with a half-hearted wave and got to her feet. She took a few tiny steps in the direction of her mother before she glanced back to the mass of children, now a chaotic circus, with disappointment.

"I said now!" The woman clapped her hands together, her voice testy.

The storyteller noticed. "Don't forget your bag," she called out to the child, who stopped.

"Robin, get your ass over here right this instant." The mother stood there, arms crossed over her heaving chest, purse slung over her shoulder, and the death glares she sent the librarian's way had me almost on my feet.

The child warred with herself. Listen to her mother or run to get the bag of goodies being held out to her?

"Are you deaf? Am I raising a stupid, dumb child?" the woman screamed as she stepped off the concrete steps and headed toward her daughter. "Get your ass over here." She pointed to her side as she marched across the grass. Spit flew from her mouth. Her steps were heavy, shoulders pushed back.

A giant prepared to fight a small creature. Goliath versus David. A mother against a child. Didn't she see how wrong that was?

My fingers curled around the edge of the bench seat, nails digging into the wood as I watched.

Everyone parented differently; I understood that. My patients had told me stories of abuse and horror, of parents who never wanted their children, of families torn apart from anger.

For every action, there was a reaction.

But to be called offensive names . . . that wasn't right.

Robin's chin rested on her chest, her shoulders bowed. Her hands hung at her sides, but even from where I sat, I caught the slight fisting motion.

My heart lifted at her tiny display of anger.

"Good for you," I whispered.

"You ungrateful little shit, just wait till we get home."

I popped to my feet at the same time the storyteller left her mini horde of munchkins and ran to the little girl, reaching her before the mother did. She bent at the waist, looked eye to eye with the child, and offered the bag.

I couldn't see, but I imagined the sweetest of smiles gracing both their faces as the child took the offered bag. No doubt she whispered *thank you*, and her eyes must have shone with happiness, longing, a desire to read, and a wish for a different life.

I had no idea if any of that happened, but deep down, I hoped it did.

It was the wish for a different life, whether the child knew it was there or not, that lodged a pinecone-shaped ball in my throat.

The mother grabbed the bag from the child's hand and looked inside. "We aren't paying for this. Take it back."

The look of dejection and disappointment on that child's face as she took the bag back was heart-wrenching.

I couldn't hear the young woman's reply, but the mother's face went bright red. She grabbed her daughter's hand and yanked as she marched across the grass to the parking lot.

If I were that mother, I'd feel humiliated and even ashamed for how I'd acted.

In her rush to keep up, the child lost her grip on the bag, and items fell, some rolling beneath parked cars. The little girl tried to get her mom to stop.

I imagined the child's eyes open wide, tears rolling down her cheeks, and sobs reeling through her tiny frame as she climbed into the car.

I should have moved.

I should have run, crawled crablike beneath the vehicles for the items that dropped out of the bag. I should have rushed to hand them to the mother, smiled at the little girl, let her know everything would be okay.

There are a lot of things I should have done, a lot of things I could have done, but in the end, I didn't do any of them. I just sat there and watched.

Thankfully, someone else moved. Someone else ran to pick up those items and return them to the child.

Someone else was stronger than I.

There was something I'd learned through my practice. Something I'd realized years ago after seeing countless patients with histories so different from my own.

Not every woman deserves to be a mother.

But every child deserves to be loved, to feel loved.

My goal was to help those children understand that they were loved and could live different lives from what they had been shown growing up.

But to be honest, I failed way too often.

Chapter Three

I sat at a window table of Sabrina's tea shop, the Mad Hatter's Tea House, and stared out at the street as people strolled by, some with bags in hand, others as they chased their toddlers, a few who meandered without a care in the world.

I watched but didn't really see. All I could think about was the scene from yesterday and that small girl's face as her mother yelled, screamed, lost her shit for no reason at all.

It had bothered me all night.

A million emotions rolled through me. Anger that someone would treat their child that way, shame that I hadn't stood up and defended the girl, and a feeling of helplessness.

I think it was that feeling that surprised me the most.

I was a trained therapist. My job was supposed to be to help others. So why was I such a failure?

"Phew. I didn't think I'd ever get a chance to come on over to say hi," said Sabrina, who plunked herself down in the seat across from me and pushed a plate of freshly baked squares my way.

"Tell me what you think of these Nanaimo bars." She took a pot of tea a server handed her, opened the lid, and settled her nose over the steam, inhaling deeply.

"A new shipment came in, and I've been dying to try this mandarin green tea," she said, continuing to ramble. "That's not what you're drinking, though. Yours is special, picked with you in mind. Did they tell you the name of it? Alice's Dream. Isn't that perfect?"

Rather than answer, I lifted my cup to my lips and sipped. "There's hints of orange, vanilla, and . . ."

"White chocolate." Sabrina beamed like a child, finishing my sentence for me.

"Ah, that's what I was tasting." I blew the steam away before I sipped once more. I liked it.

"What's going on with you? You've sat here, staring out that window and frowning, ever since you walked in."

I looked around the room. When I'd first walked in, only a few tables had been available, but now only a few tables were full. Rush hour must have been over.

"I saw something at the library yesterday that bothered me. I regret not doing anything about it."

"What happened?"

I told Sabrina about the mother and child—the venom in the mother's voice as she spoke and my frozen state as I just sat there and witnessed it.

"I always thought if I saw a child being mistreated, I would step up, step in and stop it, but I didn't. I did nothing." That was the crux of the issue, my lack of response.

I couldn't read the look on Sabrina's face. Was she disappointed in me too? I've always had a hard time reading her. Her hair was up in a messy bun, her glasses were perched on the edge of her nose, and she reminded me of a librarian, how they have that look when they watch you.

"Verbal abuse is hard to listen to," Sabrina said as she took off her glasses. "If you know what it's like to live with that, then it's understandable if you froze."

"I'm a trained therapist, Sabrina. I should have been there, talking to the mom, offering help and support."

Sabrina nodded. "True. You probably should have. But it sounds like the librarian stepped up, which was probably better, since you were only a bystander."

Despite the truth to her words, I couldn't let it go. I played with my cup, turning it in circles, leaving tea stains on the napkin beneath it.

"Stop beating yourself up, girl. Okay, so you messed up by your standards, but learn from it. Realize how not reacting has affected you, and don't let it happen again, okay?"

That was one thing I loved about Sabrina. She was no-nonsense all the time.

"You're right," I admitted.

"Of course I am." A wide smile spread on her face before she winked. She looked around her café and sighed. "Today was a madhouse. The crowds keep growing each weekend, it seems. I'm afraid of what our annual summer fair is going to be like."

"I might escape town for that weekend." I glanced out the window again as I spoke.

"You will not." Sabrina slapped the table with her hand. "I can't believe you. You should be out there, handing out your business cards so you can grow your clientele. Interact with the community more. You've been here two years, and you have only, what . . . three clients?"

"I didn't realize you were keeping track." I tried to keep the smile in my voice, but it had more bite than anything. "My three patients are all I need at the moment. I see them weekly, and not having a large base means I can focus on them more. Don't compare me to others, please."

"Sorry." Sabrina held up her hands. "I didn't mean to upset you."

I shook my head. "I'm just off," I explained. "I probably overreacted."

"Is there something else bothering you, Danielle?"

I wasn't sure how to answer this.

"I'm exhausted," I finally admitted. "I haven't slept well the past week, so I'm a little more on edge than I should be."

"Have you tried warm baths? Turning off electronics? Chamomile tea? Going for a long walk before bed?" Her suggestions flew at me one after the other before I could comment.

"Yes on the baths and the walks. No to the tea, but maybe I should lay off my after-dinner coffee."

She rolled her eyes at me. "Coffee? I thought I had you off that crap."

I laughed. "Never," I teased, happy to be on a topic less serious. "I don't mind the occasional cup of tea, hot or cold, but I will never give up my coffee."

"What are you doing tonight?" Sabrina asked.

Inside, I wanted to groan. Sabrina was forever trying to get me to commit to some committee or group or to meet some people. She thought I didn't have a life, that I hid at home too much.

What she didn't understand was I quite liked my life just fine.

"Probably crawl into bed early, why?"

She frowned.

"I haven't slept well all week," I reminded her.

The frown lifted a little as she poured herself another cup of tea.

"Fine, I'll give you that," she said. "A group of us are starting a walking club in the evenings. It might be good for you to join. Might even help you sleep better at night."

I liked the idea of a walking club in theory, but if I joined, it would be purely for social reasons, and I really wasn't in the mood to be social.

I was tired, weary to the point of exhaustion, and if I didn't get a good night's sleep soon, I wouldn't be any good to anyone.

"Or not," Sabrina said when I didn't respond. "Just think about it, okay? We're going to meet at the entrance of the park at eight o'clock."

I'd think about it, but I doubted I'd change my mind.

All I wanted to do was sleep. A nice long rest, after which I'd wake up refreshed and ready for tomorrow's patient.

Chapter Four

PATIENT SESSION: TYLER

I set the timer on my phone to one minute and worked on my breathing exercises. In through the nose, hold to the count of three, then out through the mouth until all the air disappeared. Breathe in, hold, exhale. Over and over.

And over again.

I'd woken up with a massive headache and dark bags under my eyes. I was lucky if I'd gotten three hours of sleep last night. After today's session, my only goal was to crawl back into bed.

Tyler was scheduled to sit on my red couch, and while I waited, I looked over my notes, walked through our last session, and read over the red-penned comments that it was time to go deeper.

There was a timid knock at the door.

"Come on in." The smile on my face carried my professional look—warm, caring, interested.

Some might think Tyler quite handsome. With a friendly face, gentle brown eyes, and a smile that drew you in, he'd probably make most women's hearts go pitter-patter the moment he focused on them.

I never let his charm fool me. I saw through his easy smile to the fears deep in his heart.

"Dr. Rycroft, I'm sorry if I'm late." Tyler held out a warm, sweaty palm.

"You're right on time."

I turned to a fresh page in my notebook while Tyler settled in. He hugged a pillow to his chest and stared at the box of tissues on the coffee table in front of him.

"How are you feeling today?" I was ready with my pen to scribble notes, curious to see which direction we would take.

"Not good." He let go of the pillow, setting it to the side, and clasped his hands between his thighs. He sighed, the sound similar to the wind that blew through a haunted forest. Eerie. Heavy. Dreadful.

I waited for him to continue.

"I know you said to try meditating, that it would release the war raging inside me, but it's not working."

His big brown eyes pleaded for understanding, for help.

"Did you try setting a timer for one minute?"

His head bobbed.

"Did you do the exercises when all your thoughts struggled for attention?"

Rather than reply, he looked around the room, taking in every single item.

"What are you looking for, Tyler?"

"There was a photo of you on your bookshelf. The one where you were reading in a park. You said it was a favorite memory. What happened to it?"

I had moved it after noticing Tyler kept looking at it session after session. It made me uncomfortable. Now there were no personal photos in the room.

"I've been wanting to change things up a little." I shrugged, pretending his attentiveness wasn't an issue for me.

"I focused on my breathing," he said, returning the conversation to his meditations. "Just like you told me to. But the thoughts were louder. You told me they wouldn't be."

I leaned forward, my arms crisscrossed over my knees, and covered the pad of paper in my lap. "I believe my words were that eventually they wouldn't be." I looked him straight in the eye, daring him to lie but silently hoping he'd tell me the truth.

"What are the thoughts?"

He shifted in his seat.

His head moved side to side. "I repeat your words over and over as I go for walks by myself. I notice things too."

Interesting. I made a few notes about his avoidance of my question before I gave him a gentle smile, one I hoped he'd take as encouragement to continue.

"What do you notice?"

His eyes brightened with the question, and excitement radiated from him.

"I keep a journal with me, just like you suggested." He was so pliable, like a puppy. "I walk around town and see things most ignore. Who moves in or moves out, who likes to go for walks and when, who has pets, who has no concept of personal space, and those who air their business for everyone to hear and don't care. I see the homeless, the sluts on the corners, the weak men who give in for a quick rut against a dirty alley wall . . ."

I held up my hand to stop him.

"I brought it. Do you want to read it?" His need for approval was obvious as he pulled the notebook from his back pocket.

It was small, and when he opened the pages for me to see, the scribbling was barely legible. I took it to appease him, looked through the last few pages, able to read only a few words.

What I read was focused solely on *her*.

I sighed heavily, the sound coming from deep inside me. I didn't bother to even hide it from him.

There was nothing in there about conversations, something we'd discussed in the past. "Have you had coffee at the shop close to your home yet?"

The crease between his eyes deepened as a flash of irritation passed through his gaze.

"No. Why would I? People look down on me—you know that. I can hear their whisperings." He rubbed his hands together, leaving white marks on his skin from the pressure of his fingers.

"What are they whispering?"

He wouldn't look at me.

"Tyler?" I didn't need to prod. I could go back through my past notes and read what he believed people he'd never talked to thought.

He was weak.

He was worthless.

He didn't deserve to be loved.

"Sometimes I don't think they even see me." He pushed himself to his feet, and his long frame towered over me.

"You feel invisible?" Tyler had sat on my couch for more than eighteen months now. In all our sessions, that aspect of his paranoia had never come up. Why today?

Tyler's silhouette cast a shadow that arched over my couch as he stood in front of the window, his hands jammed into his pant pockets, his shoulders slouched as his body gave off an air of dejection.

"Do you like living here? In front of the park, I mean?" he asked.

Avoidance. I underlined that word since it seemed to be a constant theme.

"I do." I hesitated to admit that as I rarely shared much of my life with Tyler. He was the type who could become easily . . . attached . . . and that wouldn't be healthy.

The park across the street was what I loved most about my house. I loved to walk around the paths in the early mornings and later in the evening as the sun set. There was one park bench I liked in particular. It was off in a corner of trees, sheltered from the sun and noise of any nearby traffic.

"Have you ever thought how ants feel surrounded by so many humans? We don't notice them, step on them with little thought, careless in our actions. We destroy so many lives, and yet we never even think about that."

"You are not an ant."

He shook his head, his shoulders slouched even further. "No one sees me. I'm right there, in their faces, and they don't recognize me."

Depression covered him like a dark haze of buzzing flies.

"I stand in *her* shadow, you know? But no matter how hard I try, I can't reach her."

He had never once said her name to me. I'd asked multiple times, but he clammed up each time, almost to the point of being skittish, and changed the subject to something abstract and insignificant. So I'd stopped asking. One day, when he was ready, he would tell me.

Due to his paranoid delusions, the thought that he overexaggerated his issues with *her* was always there, in the back of my mind.

He returned to his seat, hands clasped tightly around his knees.

"Have you tried to talk to her about how you feel?" It was a simplistic approach, but it always amazed me how many patients believed simply talking to someone was out of the question.

"It wouldn't make a difference." His voice dropped an octave, and the pain behind his words tugged at my heartstrings.

"You might be surprised."

"It won't make a difference," he repeated, but this time, I heard a questionable hope in his voice.

"Why?"

"You know why."

Avoidance. I underlined that again.

"I have a role," he muttered. "We're all here for a reason—we've discussed that. My role is to support her. But talking to her, trying to get her to change her mind or look at other options . . . she gets angry." He balled his hand into a fist.

This was the first time I'd seen him show anger while talking about *her*. It was a good emotion for him to experience. Healthy.

"Yes, we've discussed the roles we all play. For instance, I believe I'm here to help those who struggle."

He snorted, the force clearing his nostrils, leaving a mark on his hands, which he rubbed on his pants.

I handed him the box of tissues while trying not to gag.

"So you are saying you're here for me."

I nodded.

"I'm here for her. That's it. That's my role."

"You're more than that, Tyler," I said, but his quick downcast glance told me he didn't agree.

That was what made our sessions difficult. That was where I was left feeling all I'd done was fail him over and over again as his therapist.

I wished he had more self-confidence, more trust in himself, more . . . just more.

He fidgeted in his seat, his attention diverted from me to every possible item placed in the room.

"She's changed, you know? Every time I reach for her, she's not there. Not emotionally, at least. When she looks at me, it's as if she sees a ghost, unrecognizable. But I'm not the one who's changed. It's her. I don't know what to do anymore . . ." He scrubbed his face with the palm of his hand. "I know you think I jump to conclusions, that I tend to make things out to be worse than they are, but it's true. It's all true."

Yes, those were thoughts I held, but I'd never actually said them to him.

"Tyler, I believe your truth is very real to you, and I would never suggest otherwise."

He eyed me as he thought about my words. I saw the thought process all over his face.

"I thought we worked together, worked well," he said, not addressing my comment. "But where she used to be loving, now she's cold as stone . . . and I'm . . . I'm scared," he whispered. "She . . . she doesn't like that I'm up all the time, at all hours. She says it's not good for me, not healthy, that I need to sleep, so she gave me something, but I can't take it. I won't."

"Did you bring it with you today? Whatever it is she's giving you to sleep?"

"No. I can't. She'd notice and ask me why. How would I explain that to her? She doesn't like it when I accuse her of something, so I try not to, even when I know . . ." His voice trailed off to the point of silence, which stretched on longer than it should have.

"Tyler? What is it you know?" He was stuck in a loop, and we danced around it in every session. It was as if a brick wall had been built directly in front of him, and he couldn't find a way around it.

"She's different. Not the same anymore."

"Everyone changes. It's okay. We've discussed this." I was getting tired of butting my head against that brick wall.

"You don't. You can't understand. I want . . ." He clutched one of the decorative pillows I'd recently bought tightly to his chest and rocked back and forth, back and forth, as if that would protect him from whatever imagined demons he faced. "I can't." He shook his head. "It's not safe. Not here."

"You're perfectly safe here, Tyler. I promise."

He looked around wildly, a mad glint in his gaze.

"Nowhere is safe. Not from her. I want to be someone she considers an equal. But she doesn't."

"How does she react when you try showing her that you are?" I asked. "Her equal," I clarified.

His shoulders hunched. "Haven't you heard a thing I've said? She gets angry. That's why I can't talk to her, why I have to blend with the shadows. I've stopped watching for her. I can't do it anymore. What she's doing is . . . I just can't. Instead"—he swallowed hard and ran his hand over his face—"instead, I just watch her."

What did he mean, he stopped watching for her and instead just watched her? That one word made a world of difference. Was it a slip of the tongue or intentional?

I leaned forward. I couldn't help myself. "What do you see?"

He wouldn't say. He just tightened his lips, his fingers white as they clenched around that pillow.

Tyler continued to rock there for nearly ten minutes, pillow clutched tightly to his chest, like a small child.

"Tyler? Ready to talk?" I gently nudged him.

He blinked. One, two, three, four long seconds passed. His tight grip on the cushion relaxed, and his chest expanded as he took in a deep breath.

"I'm okay." His smile, full of trust, looked innocent but felt as fake as the Rolex on his wrist. I heard it in his voice. He'd donned a mask, become something or someone he thought I wanted him to be. He wasn't okay; we both knew that.

"I know you are. I just want you to remember, this will always be a safe place for you, Tyler." I played along. "How about we go back a bit and talk about . . ." My voice drifted as he reached for the glass of water I'd left on the coffee table. He sniffed at it, and his nose wrinkled before he set it back down.

"Is something the matter?" I asked.

"The water . . . it . . . it . . . smells funny."

I reached for my own glass and took a sip before I pointed to the water jug on the side bar in my office.

"The water is infused with cucumber." I'd left a few slices in the water.

"Cucumber?"

"Is there an issue with the water?"

"You're not trying to poison me?" His voice rumbled like a lawn mower in the middle of summer.

I held my hand out for his glass and sipped, careful to not leave a lipstick stain before I handed it back.

"It's safe to drink, Tyler. I promise, I'm not poisoning you."

His gaze never strayed from mine as he sipped, not until half the water was gone.

"Maybe that's what she does," he said slowly, as if the idea that he wasn't actually being drugged caught him off guard.

The claim of being drugged to sleep wasn't new, but it was the first time he seemed to be open to the idea that he could be wrong.

"You don't think she's drugging me?"

Paranoia. Since the beginning, I'd believed Tyler suffered from PPD, paranoid personality disorder, where suspicion and mistrust of others colored every aspect of his daily life.

I let that idea sit with him for a bit as I made notes.

"But why do I feel all groggy when I wake up?" he asked.

"How often do you wake up feeling that way?"

The look on his face gave me the response I needed.

"All the time."

I set my notepad down beside my water and leaned forward, my elbows resting on my knees to create a more relaxed yet serious pose.

"Tyler, your sleep patterns are erratic, and your body simply cannot function properly. Sleep is so important to your mental health and physical well-being. It's possible that once your body knows it can rest, you're simply waking up too early or from a deep sleep. I'd suggest not setting your alarm and allowing your body to wake up naturally when it's ready."

No matter how minuscule these steps seemed, each one made a world of difference.

"Are you sure?"

"Have you kept your sleep journal up to date like I asked? Do you ever find yourself jolted awake?"

He nodded.

"That's you waking from a deep sleep, and your body can't make the adjustment as quick as you need. I think that's why you're groggy, unfocused, unable to concentrate, and feeling like you could sleep all day."

"Next thing you're going to tell me is I don't need to be following her. But you don't know her like I do. I know the real her. The control freak, the—"

He stopped himself; a hand rose to cover his mouth, as if he could physically block the words from being spoken, then dropped back to his lap.

His mouth gaped like a fish desperate for air, but no sound came out. He tried again but with the same results. The desperation in his eyes punched my heart.

Tyler was a man stuck in the cycle of emotional and mental abuse by his girlfriend, and yet, no matter how much we'd worked on his self-image and self-worth, he wouldn't leave her.

He said he couldn't. I told him it was his choice to make. He claimed to have no choice.

I couldn't make him. That wasn't my role. My patients came to me for help, to be built up, to learn strategies so that when they were ready, they could move on.

"Tyler, in all our sessions, you've never mentioned why you've stayed. Is it love? Does she add something to your life you couldn't get on your own?"

His lips tightened, and I caught a flash of anger on his face, but it was gone in an instant.

That glimpse forced a shiver of fear through my body.

"Let's discuss the anger I've noticed today."

Crack-crack-crack-crack. He cracked his knuckles, one bone at a time.

"I'm not angry."

Riiiight.

"Do you love her?"

There it was again. That look. The tightening of his lips, the way his nose flared, the twitchy vein in his cheek.

What was I missing? Was this the true Tyler? The one he'd never shown me until now?

I glanced at the clock on the table behind where he sat. It was only a slight flicker of my gaze, but Tyler noticed.

"Is there somewhere else you need to be?" He issued a challenge with his gaze.

I met his challenge and didn't back down.

"Sorry," he conceded. "I just . . . you must be tired of me by now, listening to me talk about my failings over and over." He sounded so contrite, but the look in his eyes was anything but repentant.

"Do you love her?" I asked him again.

"Love doesn't matter. Not with us. She needs me. She *needs* me," he repeated, this time with more conviction.

He leaned back on the couch, his legs sprawled out, and he played with a button on his shirt.

"What about you, Tyler? Do you need her?" I noticed the quick change in his behavior and reactions. From anger to confidence to uncertainty.

"I think . . . so." He hesitated. "I mean . . . things have changed or . . . are changing, but . . . it's a two-way street. I can't survive without her, but . . . I'm trying to be the man I used to be. The one she wanted before . . . just . . . before."

"Before what?"

He looked away.

"How does it make you feel to go back to that man you once were?"

He swallowed hard but still wouldn't look at me. "Scared. She's the type of person who feeds off that fear, and I need her to start respecting me." He rubbed the back of his neck.

This was all new. Deeper than we'd ever gone before. I wanted to believe it was real, that he'd finally let down the facade that had been hiding emotions from me, but a part of me wasn't so certain.

Respect and trust were two issues that continued to pop up. There was this innate need in him to be both trusted and respected.

The bell on my phone sounded, alerting us both that our session was over. I was tempted to prolong our time, but he jumped up from the couch.

"I . . . I need to go. I promised her I'd be back. I . . ." He worried his hands together and swallowed hard.

Before I could say a word, he slipped past me and left. He looked back once, and I noticed him hesitate, as if debating whether to come back in so we could continue discussing this fear he'd revealed. But then he turned and disappeared from view.

Chapter Five

I needed to escape.

That driving force washed over me until I was drowning, dying, caught in a riptide, unable to breathe, and my lungs were crushed from the burning weight of that need.

Sometimes following my sessions, the emotions were too much for me to carry, and I needed to get out.

Like today. Tyler's session had suffocated me. His energy was monstrous, like a growing shadow that crept along a wall as the sun inched farther in the sky, its shape looming over me until I was as tiny as an ant.

Tyler complained of feeling invisible, but right then, I wished I were.

Ants, despite their size, are surprisingly strong. I wished I had that strength, not physically but emotionally.

I was going to meet Tami for coffee. She'd bring the coffee, and I'd bring the dessert.

The park, where I tended to escape most days, provided a sense of serenity, solitude, and a stillness I craved.

Tami called it my sanctuary.

Instead of walking, as I normally did, I needed to run. Instead of peace, I was on the cusp of a panic attack.

Tonight there was no sanctuary, no safety net as I entered the park. I couldn't shake off the sense of dread as I passed beneath the Wonderland arches over the entrance.

Wonderland was my escape. It had always been my escape, ever since I was a small child and found an old book with a gold-embossed rabbit on the cover in a box my father picked up at a garage sale. When my parents would argue, I'd take that book, climb a tree, and read for hours nestled between branches. Alice and all her adventures were everything I'd wished for my own life back then.

I'd learned that simply existing wasn't enough for me. In order to live life the way it was meant to be experienced, I had to push past my own boundaries and embrace every adventure that came my way.

If I were living a safe life, I wouldn't have moved to Cheshire, away from everything familiar, all because I knew I was needed here.

Growing up, the life lessons became invaluable, and I'd tried to impart the things I'd learned to my patients. For Tyler, it was the idea of pushing past our boundaries and not living in the past. For Ella, it was accepting who we are and living with that acceptance rather than hiding from it. For Savannah . . . she was the epitome of Alice herself. Her refusal to live within the lines others had colored for her, her willingness to try new things and to dream bigger than was societally accepted—that made her the modern-day Alice in my book.

The park was full of walking paths, hidden alcoves with park benches, flowering bushes, and *Alice in Wonderland* character sculptures.

Rather than head directly to our regular meeting place, I took my time, focused on my breathing exercises. I clenched and unclenched my fists in rhythm to my breath until the tension in my body left. When my nostrils no longer flared, when my jaw and chest weren't as tight, I slowed my pace and took in the scenery around me.

Everything from the Mad Hatter to the Cheshire Cat was hidden between the bushes and trees of the park.

You had to look to find them, but they were there.

I wound my way through the circular pathways until I came to Alice.

She always waited for me, her statue pointing the way to my favorite secluded place.

Normally I smiled in greeting, but today I caught the look on her face as if for the first time.

A warning carved in stone.

She may as well have spoken out loud, with a caution to be careful—a warning that the direction I was about to take wasn't the direction I was looking for.

Tyler's face flashed in my mind, and his voice was on repeat. *I need you please I need you please I need you please.*

The need to purge myself of Tyler's draining energy was strong. I couldn't let him affect me like that. It wasn't right.

Something about him had been off today.

His emotions had been all over the place, his thought pattern frantic, rushed, fearful. His need for love, to be noticed, to have a purpose, blinded him.

We all had our own demons. I faced those demons with my patients on a daily basis. All but my own. My demons were stifled, stuffed so deep inside they were silenced by the force of my will.

Today, those demons noticed a crack through the flash I saw in Tyler's eyes, their shouts of joy and victory deafening after years of defeat.

I had to fill that crack before it grew even more, and the only way I knew was thanks to this park. This park and Tami.

Tami, my port during the roughest of storms, waited for me at the end of Alice's journey with the Cheshire Cat looking on. Her head was bowed as she stared at her phone, her forehead knotted so tight I winced from the headache she must have. She didn't notice me as I walked up.

With her there, the anxiety that had pushed me just moments ago, heavy and wider than the Rocky Mountains, relaxed to the size of a mustard seed.

"Why do I have a feeling," I said as I tapped her shoulder, "I didn't bring enough chocolate?"

She rubbed her forehead, her fingers trailing along the deep lines, and she sighed.

"For days like today, there will never be enough chocolate." She handed me a cup she'd set to the side.

"I added something to our coffee," she said. "Figured we could both use it."

I inhaled the waft of fresh beans along with a hint of Baileys and smiled. This was exactly what I needed. Fresh air, my friend, chocolate, and spiked coffee.

I pulled a container out of my bag that held some cheesecake bites dipped in chocolate I'd pulled from the freezer.

"God, I love you." She took the container and popped one of the bites into her mouth. "I also have a surprise for you." After she finished off another cheesecake bite, Tami handed me a small item wrapped in soft-pink tissue paper.

My eyes lit up as I took the gift and unwrapped a silver spoon with the rabbit from Alice's book on the handle.

"I love it!" I leaned over to give her a warm hug and squeezed hard. Sabrina had these spoons in her shop, and I'd always wanted to buy a few.

We sat in silence as we sipped our coffee, Tami slurping as she did so. She said it enhanced the taste, something she'd learned once from a coffee master.

"Rough day?" I leaned back and relaxed my neck, my head tilted toward the sky. The stretch felt good.

"That doesn't even begin to describe it. The tip line is going crazy, and I've spent way too many hours chasing after ghosts and any little thing that scurries off into the night. Some people have the craziest imaginations." Tami pocketed her phone. "All I want to do is crawl back into bed and attempt to wake up from this nightmare."

"What are you talking about?" I asked.

"The recent murders." The look on Tami's face said she couldn't believe I even had to ask. "Have you not been watching the news?"

"I knew you had a case, but . . ." I pursed my lips and blew before I took another sip. "Sorry, I should have paid more attention."

It was a small thing, but I felt guilty. I should have known. We were best friends, lived blocks from one another. I had no excuse.

"You've been pretty preoccupied lately," she said.

Regardless, I still felt bad.

"I'm listening now if you need to work something out." I half turned toward her and gave her my full attention.

Tami tented her fingers, brought them close to her lips, and blew hard. She measured her words, deciding how much to reveal and what shouldn't be told. It was a tell for when she was about to say something that she knew would bother me.

"It's happened again."

A ball full of pins lodged in my throat, the tips piercing straight through my windpipe. I immediately knew what she was talking about.

"When?"

"Last night."

I felt sucker punched and realized if the pain I felt was that bad, then what Tami must be dealing with had to be excruciating.

"The whole family?" I choked on the words, bile rising until my throat was scorched from the acid, the liquid leaving invisible scars.

I'd gone home with my college roommate one Thanksgiving during our sophomore year to find emergency responders outside her home. Her father had died from a massive heart attack. I remembered watching the stretcher bring out her father, holding her as she crumbled when she realized she'd never gotten to say goodbye . . .

Some moments in life leave lasting impressions. That one will forever haunt me.

"No," Tami said, aware of my roommate and her loss. "The child slept blissfully unaware." After a pause, she continued. "Watch the news tonight. Mother and father killed in their beds, throats slashed while their child slept a few feet down the hall, just like the murder last month. It's disgusting and horrific. Middle of the night on quiet streets, so of course no witnesses. We opened the tip line, and as expected, all the crazies come out."

"That's . . ." A chill swept through me as I imagined that sweet child waking up to find their parents dead, everything covered in blood.

I hadn't known about the first murder, either, not when it first happened. Not until Tami told me. I didn't like to listen to the news or read the paper. There was too much negativity in the world, and I didn't need to surround myself with it. I'd tried being on social media once, but it was easy to be sucked into the vileness of what was happening in our world.

"Are you okay?" I reached out, touched her arm. A mask of exhaustion and edginess mixed with extreme sadness settled over Tami. She shook her head.

"We need to find the killer before they strike again."

The weight of the murders draped across Tami like a wet wool sweater, and the need to take away the worry and fear she carried was strong.

Her pain called out to me.

Not everyone knew their reason for being, but I knew mine.

I was never more complete than when I was able to help those in need. To listen, to carry, to create peace when life fell apart. I discovered that in college with my roommate. She'd once told me if I hadn't been there for her, she never would have survived that holiday. Before those words, I'd been undecided, unsettled, and unsure of what I wanted to do, only knowing I wanted to do something.

"I'm here." I placed all my love for this woman who was a dear friend into my voice. "If you need to talk, you know I'm safe."

Tami reached over and rested her hand on mine.

"You might regret that," she said, clarifying what I already knew. She needed me. "I haven't dealt with murder cases like these in a long time." She breathed in deeply through her nose, then slowly exhaled through her mouth. "I'm worried I can't handle it, that I'm not strong enough."

"What?" *Impossible.*

Of all the people I knew, Tami wasn't the type to let stress get to her.

"You have that gift of being able to separate your work life from your personal life better than anyone I know—even myself."

"What are you talking about?" she asked. "You're the master of being levelheaded. Why do you think I hang around you so much?"

Levelheaded? In my dreams, maybe. Every minute of the day, my mind raced with thoughts, with ideas, with emotions that at times were unrecognizable.

"Free counseling sessions, of course." The sarcasm in my voice was more teasing than truthful.

"Thank God for that." The tight lines around her mouth disappeared. "Do you honestly think I can afford private therapy on a detective's salary? Come on now."

We shared a smile that spoke more of our close friendship than anything else.

"Seriously, I'm here." Three simple words, and yet I meant them with everything I had.

I caught the slight tremble of her hand as she lifted the coffee to her lips.

"There's something more, isn't there? Something you haven't told me?" I asked.

A shadow covered her face, her darkened silhouette foreshadowing. I braced myself.

"I've never told you about my first murder, have I? It's not something I like to talk about. I was a rookie." She inhaled sharply. "So many firsts back then shaped who I am today."

The stories she'd told me over bottles of wine and pints of ice cream about her first partner as a rookie were disgusting. He was of the generation where newbie female cops needed to learn the hard way that they were the weaker sex when it came to the minds of criminals. Every chance he had, he'd forced this belief in her face, time after time after time.

"I had to prove myself, you know? Prove I was better than him, than what he gave me credit for. I couldn't let him under my skin because I knew if I did, I'd lose my shit, and I'd never make it. I'd never be where I am now.

"That first murder, though." She paused, her face etched with all the pain she'd never confessed. "I almost walked away. That was my first and only time doubting who I was as an officer."

"You've never told me that before."

"Not really my proudest moment." She closed her eyes. "I always thought I'd be able to handle my first dead body. It wasn't like I'd never seen one before in the morgue, but those cadavers were cleaned up." She rubbed her face, and I'd never seen her look so old. "My first real murder, there was nothing clean about it. It was a mother and child, but we didn't know that at first." She shuddered. "The husband went crazy—like banshee crazy—with a chain saw and hacked his wife into pieces. We figured she'd been hunched over their newborn, trying to protect it, but . . ." Her voice trailed off, and she gulped her coffee down. "The body parts were spread all over the house, blood everywhere. We found him out in the garage. He'd impaled himself on his saw while it ran. Back then, there were no automatic safety stops, at least not on this saw."

Images of the scene flashed through my mind, and my stomach churned as I understood the damage the saw would have done to his body.

"I puked, Dani. I couldn't handle the sight, the stench, the savagery. I puked, and my partner laughed. After that, every murder case he'd hand me a paper bag and make a comment about my weak sensibilities." Her fingers tightened around her cup.

My stomach churned, and it was all I could do not to heave.

"Tami, you are one of the strongest women I know." I cleared my throat. "You reacted like any normal human being would. Why are you so hard on yourself?"

Her mouth opened and closed.

"Because I . . ." Her forehead creased as she thought about what I'd asked. "I really don't know how to answer that," she finally said.

"Exactly. You're so hard on yourself when you don't need to be. Hell, Tami. I would have run as fast as I could in the other direction. There's no way I could have handled something like that." I nudged her leg with mine. "I would have quit that day. That's the difference between the two of us. I hope you saw someone about it, though? Talked it through?"

"And prove once again just how weak I was? No."

I hated that mentality when it came to therapy. I'd heard it all too often.

"That's not a sign of weakness. It shows your strength in understanding your own emotional needs and being in touch with your feelings."

"And that, my dear friend, is why you are in my life, and I'll never let you leave," Tami said.

My heart bloomed from the love in her voice. Other than Tami, I'd never really had a close friend, a girlfriend to bond with, to talk things over and just be my real self with. I was very thankful that Tami was in my life. And Sabrina too. We all had issues, had struggled with our pasts, but they'd never expected me to have all the answers, to know what to say in those hard moments. In fact, most of the time, it was the other way around; they were my confidants.

"So, then, talk to me," I urged. "Technically, I'm the only therapist you see on a regular basis, so you know everything is confidential."

She rolled her eyes.

"So far there have been two cases, roughly a month apart. In both, the parents were killed and the children spared. There's no sign of forced entry, and we're still processing the fingerprints from the first crime scene, but there are too many similarities for these to not be connected."

"Two separate attacks? You're thinking it's the same person."

Tami nodded.

"Don't say it," she warned me.

Don't say it? How could I not?

"There's a serial killer out there, isn't there?"

Her expression reminded me of my mother's after she'd realize I was in the room when she swore.

"That's what it's looking like, as much as I hate to admit it."

Tami's job had always fascinated me. Or, rather, she fascinated me. She was different from most police officers I knew. She could be detached as needed, but there was still a gentleness about her, a vulnerability she would never admit to. I'd watched her build a wall around her heart each time she was on a case, but just as quick as she was to build that wall for protection, she'd have no problem dismantling it if it helped those around her.

I kept waiting for her to crumble under the pressure of getting too close, but she never did.

I would have crumbled a long time ago in her shoes. I felt like an impostor as it was, a little girl playing dress up, especially lately.

"You'll be okay." The words were rote, I said them without thought, but they were the truth.

The look on her face, in her eyes, the way she smiled at my words . . . she knew she'd be okay too.

"What about you, though?" Tami cocked her head, her eyes full of concern.

"What about me?" The indent between my eyes deepened, and I rubbed the area to relieve the beginning of a headache that was forming behind my eyes.

"Are you going to be okay?"

I shrugged. "I'm fine," I lied, whether for my own benefit or for Tami's, I'm not sure. She didn't need my fragile emotions to add to her already heavy load. "I just . . . Those poor kids. The horror of finding their parents dead . . ." I choked, unable to put into words the pain in my heart. I teared up, and it took everything inside me to squash that sentiment down. I hated crying. I tended to end up with a headache that knocked me out.

"It's horrible." I struggled even more to push back the tears.

Tami played with her coffee cup. "We received an anonymous tip. I swear I've listened to that voice over and over until I'm sure I'll hear it in my sleep. It's the murderer." Her shoulders tensed up, and she shivered.

"What was said?" I shivered too. I couldn't help it. "No, don't tell me. You probably shouldn't." To listen to the voice of a killer . . . I'd have nightmares.

"It's not something we're making public, but the call was basically telling the responders to be careful of the child," she said.

So many thoughts raced through my mind at her admission.

"How can I help?"

I knew she needed answers, or insights at least. And that I could help with.

"Can you tell me who the killer is?" She leaned forward, eyes closed, and rested her elbows on her knees. "Why here? Why Cheshire?"

I wished I had the answers. I really did.

"The fact they called shows a sign of remorse as well as an unusual desire to care for the children. It shows a protective side you wouldn't necessarily equate to a murderer."

"What does that mean?" Tami asked.

"It means there is a reason the murderer is protecting the children."

She palmed her forehead, leaving indents from the force of her fingers.

"Either children are precious, or they know the children personally is what you're saying," Tami clarified, realization seeping into her voice as she mulled over my words.

My gut instinct believed that to be the truth.

"It could be either one or both, or it could have nothing to do with the children, but that's my first thought, for what it's worth," I said.

"It's worth a lot and tells me I'm on the right track."

"You've gotten that phone call both times?"

She nodded. "The voice is muffled, as if a cloth or the palm of a hand is covering the mouthpiece, but it's the same voice. We have it being analyzed to see if it's male or female."

"Unless it's a man in touch with his paternal instincts, it's a female." I was confident about this revelation, but I wasn't sure why. "It could be someone who recently lost her child or is unable to go full term with her pregnancies," I suggested. Now I was guessing.

"So you're a profiler now, are you?"

I knew she teased—I heard it in her voice—but I bristled all the same.

"I'm kidding, Danielle. Thank you. I really appreciate your help and insights. Honestly," she said before she yawned. "I'm exhausted and ready to crash. Walk out with me?"

I sipped my coffee, which was now almost cold. "I'm going to sit here for a bit." There was a lot I needed to process before I went home.

There was something about these murders, about the children and the little details Tami shared, that bothered me.

Why were these families targeted? Why were these parents killed? Why leave the children alive? If the murders weren't ones of passion but rather premeditated, then there was a reason the children had been spared. The children had been not only spared but protected—the murderer took precious time to call the authorities and ensure they knew the children were alive.

Why?

In my mind's eye, an image flashed of a bedroom, pink and full of teddy bears. I held a stuffed animal in my hands, brought it up to my nose, and inhaled the sweet scent of a bear that had been loved. An eye was missing, an ear half torn off, but the love for this teddy bear filled me with warmth.

Had this been my bear as a child? I couldn't remember. But for me to think about it now, to recall it . . . it had to be important.

I just wished I knew how.

Chapter Six

PATIENT SESSION: ELLA

Today was all about Ella.

She was my first patient here in Cheshire, and in fact, she was my first patient ever. When she'd told me she was accepting a new position in a new town, I'd been in the midst of my own life change. I had just ended a relationship, was living in an apartment full of roaches, and was tired of the bustle of big-city living. My grandmother used to live here, and I had a few precious memories of summer visits with sun-kissed lemonade, s'mores over a firepit in the backyard, and repeated attempts to learn to crochet. She'd passed years ago, and as the only one left in the Rycroft dynasty, I inherited her home. It hadn't been a big stretch to follow Ella and continue with her sessions.

Ella and I had made a lot of progress over the past four years she'd been seeing me, but it had been slow going.

When she finally arrived, her dry, mouselike hair hung over her face, covering her eyes. She wouldn't look at me.

Not when I opened my office door.

Not when she handed me a container of homemade almond tea cookies.

Not when she sat down on the couch, hands wrapped around the fresh cup of tea I'd just poured.

This wasn't new, though. It was our regular routine. Ella came in every Tuesday morning and Friday afternoon, or at least those were her scheduled times.

"It's good to see you, Ella. I worried when you didn't contact me after missing your last appointment. How are you?"

Her hands trembled, and the spoon in her cup clinked.

"I thought maybe you'd been called into work, or perhaps you were reading." It wouldn't have been the first time—or the last, knowing Ella—that she'd missed our session because she'd been lost in a book.

Still no words, but she did look up, and I caught the red-rimmed eyes she tried to hide.

"Do you feel like talking about what made you cry?" I asked.

She shook her head back and forth, back and forth, back and forth, like a raggedy doll being tossed by a young child.

Without saying a word, I picked up one of my older copies of *Alice's Adventures in Wonderland*. I'd found this edition years ago, and it had since become a favorite. The green cover was faded, the gold lettering muted, but I'd known right away that it had been gently loved by its owner due to the multiple handmade bookmarks left inside.

But it was the handwritten note on the inside cover that sealed the deal.

To Anna. May you always live with the wonder and joy of an adventurous soul. Love, Mommy.

I didn't know Anna, but I knew she was loved, joyful, and exuberant, and I felt a kinship with her through our mutual love of Alice.

"Should I pick up where we left off? For, say, five minutes?" Nothing calmed Ella like being read *Alice's Adventures in Wonderland*.

"But I don't want to go among mad people," Alice remarked.

Despite the uplift in my voice, I stopped and looked at Ella from the corner of my eye. I should have skipped this part, but then, knowing Ella, she'd call me on it. Most days, as I read, her lips moved as she said the words with me.

"Oh, you can't help that," said the Cat: "we're all mad here. I'm mad. You're mad."

"How do you know I'm mad?" said Alice.

Another glance toward Ella, and sure enough, her lips were moving.

"You must be," said the Cat, "or—" I stopped and hesitated long enough to see if she'd finish the sentence for me.

"Or I wouldn't have come here," Ella said, changing a word to make it personal. "I cross-stitched that onto a sampler and framed it." Her childlike smile was contagious when she finally spoke to me. "It reminds me that I'm no different than anyone else. We're all just on different paths."

I set the book down on the table and picked up my notepad. It was a rare day that Ella was ready to talk so quickly.

She held her teacup between the palms of her hands and blew at the steam. The look on her face was one of the reasons I'd bought the set of cups from Sabrina. Her smile was full of warmth, and her eyes glittered with happiness. "Did you know, I'm actually reading this to our preschoolers during our reading hour at the library?"

"Then it's good they have a librarian like you," I praised her.

She beamed with a confidence I rarely saw, her cheeks a nice rosy shade.

"Being lost in books is my sanctuary, and . . . I'd die if I couldn't do this anymore."

This wasn't the first time this train of thought had come up, but it had been a while.

"Ella, you live a full life, and you've been through so much. It would be hard, but you would survive."

Her lips compressed into a frown that also wrinkled her forehead.

"You survived ten years in prison. I doubt there is very much that would destroy you now." I needed to remind her of where she'd been and how far she had come since those days.

She swallowed more of her tea, her back straighter than a ruler.

"I only survived because of the books."

The tap-tap-tap of my pen against the notepad brought a flush of red to her cheeks. It wasn't a loud sound, but it carried a message that said I knew she wasn't being truthful—with me or with herself.

Ella didn't like to discuss her time in prison. Each time we skimmed the surface, she retreated, withdrew from me, from the life around her, and lost herself in a book.

She liked to become a character within the story she read, and despite our twice-a-week sessions, there had been times when it was a week before I saw her again.

She would say the world she lived in now, our world, our present reality, was fictional, a facade she maintained in order to live with freedom, but her reality was found within the pages of any book she read.

"You don't understand, Dr. Rycroft," Ella said. "The person I was before I started to work in the library at the prison was horrible." She shuddered. "Evil. Bad. I didn't like being her, but I was lost. It was like I was waiting to be reborn, to become new, but all that anger and hatred continued to build until I—the real me—was brought into being."

Ella stared off into the distance, not seeing me, the wall, or anything else.

This was the most she'd revealed on a personal level about her emotional displacement, and I wasn't about to interrupt.

"Spending hours each day alone in that library, poring through the books on those shelves, discovering help through the nonfiction section . . ." She pinched the bridge of her nose. "It saved my life. Literally." There was a naked truth in her gaze. "I would have ended up dead or killing anyone who got in my way. Instead, I found healing."

Fixated on death. I jotted that down.

"I swore I would never be that person again." Ella's voice turned whisper soft. "I can't."

Her smile was mixed with both sadness and sympathy, except I wasn't sure who the sympathy was meant for. Herself? I couldn't imagine her being the way she described herself in prison. Evil? Bad?

Not my Ella.

Regardless of her past, the person she was today—so different.

Her revelation surprised me, and I was filled with pride. For her. For her growth.

"Ella." I needed to bring the conversation back, to retain the flow of truth between us. "You've used a lot of destructive words today." I glanced down at my notepad and repeated the ones I'd made note of. "Destroy, death, evil, bad, killing . . . Would you like to talk about what was wrong earlier?"

Ella went through the motions of pouring herself a fresh cup of tea, added in a sugar cube, and stirred it round and round and round.

"Have you been watching the news?" she asked. "It's horrible, isn't it?" She continued to stir. "Parents murdered in their own beds . . . and their children so close by? How is anyone safe anymore?" She hugged herself, squeezing tightly, her eyes closed.

"You're safe, Ella." I waited until her hold loosened, her eyes opened, and the scared look on her face disappeared.

"I need to tell you a secret," she whispered, her voice barely audible, "but you can't tell anyone. You can't."

I remained silent, not giving voice to the anticipation that built like a stoked fire. I expected this would lead back to her time in prison, to the reason she'd been sentenced, and a nervous expectation settled in my stomach as the seconds ticked on.

If she told me what I hoped she would, I'd be thrilled. She held so much guilt and condemnation while at the same time attempting to pretend those feelings didn't exist.

Except they did.

I squashed down the excitement, gave her time to think about her words, to build up the courage to face a truth that had always been there, right beside her, just waiting for her acceptance.

"I have a confession to make."

Chapter Seven

WEDNESDAY, AUGUST 7

PATIENT SESSION: SAVANNAH

Some days I just wanted to crawl back into bed—covered in blankets, lights off, curtains closed—and hear nothing but silence. Sweet, blissful silence.

Some days the pain was too much, too draining, too strong.

For the past six months, I'd had more headaches than I could count. Some days the pain was generalized, like a regular headache, one that made me cranky and irritable, but given enough coffee and water, I could plow through.

Today, the pain was more than I could handle, but it was the one day I needed to ignore the pain the most.

Savannah was coming. I had once made her a promise that I would never reschedule our sessions. I hadn't broken that promise in the past nine months, and I didn't plan to.

With a glass of water in hand, I people-watched from the window in my front office. It was a gorgeous summer day, and the park was full of those taking advantage of the weather. I didn't blame them.

Looking out at the park, you wouldn't know a killer was terrorizing my town.

From my window, I watched families with little ones who crawled around on blankets. Older couples walked hand in hand through the gardens. Teenagers zipped through the bike lanes on their skateboards, not caring who was in the way.

My phone buzzed with a text from Tami, her third check-in this morning. She'd just left, not twenty minutes ago, with fresh soup from the deli.

Cancel your session.

I'm fine. I even added a smiley face that proved my point.

No, your not.

You're, and yes, I am.

Stop correcting my texts.

Use proper grammar and I will.

O.M.G. Just promise you'll go back to bed afterward then, Tami replied.

If not for the pain pulsing in my head, I would have rolled my eyes.

Yes, Mom.

Despite my sarcasm, I appreciated her looking out for me.

By the time Savannah arrived, I was on my third glass of water. Hydration was supposed to help when it came to headaches. My poor bladder might say otherwise.

The front door opened.

"You around?" Savannah called out.

She asked that every time, and every time I wondered if she secretly hoped I wouldn't answer.

"I sure am," I replied, and held my office door open with a warm smile. I noticed her clothing along with the soft smile on her face and knew today would be a good session.

One thing I'd learned early on with Savannah was her outfit tended to indicate her mood.

We used a number system.

Goth was a three, angry and on edge.

Normal teenage attire was a five. That would be a mixture of tights and a baggy sweater or ripped jeans and tight shirt.

Nightwear was a one. Depressed, exhausted, and once upon a time, suicidal.

The safety plan we'd put in place had helped her to move past suicidal thoughts to depression.

Today, by the look of it, she was a four. Tight, ripped black jeans, hair in two braids, skull earrings, black plaid top, but with a gray tank beneath.

"You look like shit." Disgust mixed with pity spread on her face.

She definitely was not one to hold back, which was something I'd learned to appreciate.

"I've got a headache."

If I wanted honesty from her, she expected it in return. Even if it meant she knew I wasn't at my best.

"I hear green tea is supposed to help." She made her way to my side counter and turned on the kettle. I watched as she made us a pot, something I normally took care of before she arrived.

"Have any whiskey?" Her eyes twinkled with mischief as she glanced at me over her shoulder. "I hear it goes nice with green tea."

I smothered a snort and winced in the process.

"Doesn't hurt to try." She played with the end of one braid, the hair twisted in her fingers, as we waited for the kettle to boil.

Once the tea was made and she was comfortable on the couch, I asked the question she'd waited for.

"Why would a seventeen-year-old know about adding whiskey to green tea?"

The smothered grin of hers told me more than her words would.

Nothing about Savannah surprised me anymore.

All our sessions started with casual talk. She led. I followed. There was never a set destination to our journey, and our only time frame was the clock. The goals were understanding, strength, and moving one step forward.

Some weeks we retreated more steps than I cared to admit.

But we always regained that ground.

She fiddled with her hands, played with the cushion on the couch, and made small talk about finally reading the latest Stephen King novel before she handed me a letter her school had sent about a fight she'd gotten into last month following an exam.

"How come this is the first I'm hearing of this fight?" I asked.

The look on her face was one hundred percent teenager.

"It wasn't that big of a deal, and you didn't need to know," she mumbled. "I don't get why everyone is making such a fuss. Mom said I had to show you. She didn't say anything about me talking about it."

I laid the letter on my lap. "Savannah, if she asked you to show it to me, I'm pretty sure she'd like us to talk about it."

"I don't see why."

"Why don't you tell me about the fight, and I'll decide if we need to explore it a little deeper."

Her sigh almost resembled a growl, but I ignored it.

"Community service in exchange for charges tells me this isn't something we should be ignoring." Did it surprise me Savannah had gotten into a fight? No. What surprised me was her unwillingness to discuss it.

"I was just defending myself, okay? No big deal. I don't deal with bullies, and now she knows it."

I didn't say anything. She hadn't really given me much of a reply. In my experience, the less you said to fill the silence, the more the other person let slip. In my line of work, being uncomfortable in a place of safety was a good thing for the patient to experience.

"Fine," Savannah said as she rolled her eyes. "The bitch told me to fuck myself and said my parents must have been drugged out of their skulls to not abort me. She called me a psycho and said I'd be the first in our class to land in jail for being a terrorist and killing schools full of kids."

Her hands balled into fists at her sides. The anger was still there from the altercation. What part of it was she angry at the most?

"Like I'd kill kids. That bitch had it coming." Savannah spat out the words like spitballs through a straw.

"Says here," I said as I looked down at the letter, "you caused a cornea laceration from the skull ring on your finger, a broken nose, permanent loss of her two front teeth, broken fingers, and other bruising and cuts."

"I went easy on her."

I covered my laughter with a cough that had bells ringing in my head.

"What type of community service will you be doing?"

"Weeding in the park gardens and around the library. It's lame, but whatever." She tapped her long black fingernails on her leg.

I thought about saying more, but I had a feeling it would come up later and didn't want to push it.

"Savannah, how are things at home? Last week you were at a two. We discussed ways we could bring that up to a four, which, by the look of things, you were able to do. How did that go?"

51

Our number system wasn't just for clothing. We used it for everything in her life she struggled with.

The scowl on her face, along with the way her hands clenched as she hid them beneath her legs, hurt. It felt like a brick had dropped on my heart.

"Out of all the things we discussed, which did you find worked the most?" I didn't need to look at my notes—I'd memorized everything in her file—but I still reached for it.

"None of it," she answered before I even started to ask the questions. "I didn't call a friend and see if we could hang out. I didn't leave the house when I should have. I didn't call you like you told me to. I didn't do any of the things you suggested." She pulled her hands from beneath her legs and slapped her knee. "I didn't do any of those things you suggested for one simple reason. I. Didn't. Want. To." She slapped her knee again with each word. Hard.

"Well then." The click of my pen ricocheted. "Maybe we should come up with some ideas that you'd like to suggest? If I remember correctly, we came up with those together, but . . ."

"No," she grumbled. "I just didn't *want* to do any of those things." Her lips turned into a pout. "It wasn't that I didn't need to—I just didn't want to."

At least she was being honest. Savannah could be a brilliant-but-petulant toddler some days.

"What did you do instead?"

Again with the shrug.

"So . . . you just stayed in the situation? Did you keep quiet or mouth off? Did you state your opinion or say what was expected?" I could probably ascertain the answers myself, given what I knew about her, but she had the capacity to surprise me when I least expected it.

"Yeah, right," she scoffed. "Have you seen my parents when they're both drunk? When my mom is higher than a kite thanks to the antidepressants her doctor has no idea she's buying on the side? She's either pissing herself from laughing at the imaginary ladybug who talks to her or she's crying in bed because my dad didn't kiss her goodbye before he left for work."

"Savannah." I fought hard to keep the exasperation out of my voice but apparently failed, judging by the sudden fold of her arms. "Your mother isn't on drugs."

She snorted. "She's a good liar."

Savannah claimed to hate her parents based on imagined offenses, whether it was drugs, physical and emotional abuse, neglect, or any other type of charge she imagined.

I pulled out a drug test from the file I'd recently received.

"Like I believe that." She kicked out her legs and crossed her ankles on the table as if to prove she couldn't care less about anything I said.

"You haven't trusted any of the tests she's taken, correct?"

Her right brow rose to the edge of her hairline, but she didn't respond.

All right—a different tactic, then.

"What would it take for you to believe your mom is telling the truth?"

Her face transformed from an average teenager's look of disgust to one of raw hatred. "I know what I saw. I know what I experienced. Your question tells me one thing—you think I'm lying." She unfolded her arms and leaned toward me. "Perhaps the question isn't what it would take for me to trust her, but what will it take for you to believe me?"

I dipped my chin toward my chest, not wanting to feel the hurt her words caused.

"You know better than that," I said.

I knew that Savannah trusted her warped truth to be real. Those were lies she believed to be true. There are terms for this: *Delusions. Pathological liar. Narcissist. Pseudologia fantastica.*

"What happened during the week? How about we start there?"

Savannah's paranoia could hit extreme levels. To her, everyone was out to harm her, one way or another.

She'd even gone to the police with accusations of physical harm at the hands of her parents. I had been asked to step in after child services found no such evidence; otherwise, she'd have been put under psychiatric care within a facility. Thankfully, with our weekly sessions, we'd been able to keep her at home.

"I don't want to talk about it."

"Sometimes it's better to talk things through," I said, repeating the words I'd said to her countless times. One day she would hear them.

At least I hoped so.

"Why? Why is it better?" She popped to her feet and walked around my office. She ran her fingers along the spines of books I'd collected and bought for patients to read. "You say that over and over, just like my mom. What does talking do? Nothing. It's never done a damn thing."

I just smiled. Not a one-day-you'll-learn kind of smile. More like a I-know-that-you-know-you-don't-mean-that kind of smile.

"I hate her. You know that, right? That hasn't changed. That will never change. We can talk for the rest of my life, and I will always hate my mother. I'll sit on your fucking bloodred couch and spill my guts until you and everyone else is satisfied I'm okay, but I promise you one thing. You will never convince me to feel anything but hate for them." With the speed of a police chase on Highway 101, the words rushed out of her mouth as she stood there, statue still, as if daring me to tell her any different. "God, I wish I could kill them," she mumbled.

"You're right," I said, my voice calm, as if I weren't concerned about the words she'd uttered. The shock, surprise, and suspicion on her face said that was the last thing she'd expected me to admit.

"What do you mean, I'm right?" Her left hand trailed along the top of my *bloodred couch* before she sat back down.

Sometimes I forgot she was only seventeen years old. She was a hormonal, emotionally immature young adult who struggled to find her identity in a messed-up world. When I looked at her, I didn't see the face of a teen but rather the mind of a woman who had been through too much. Her eyes were the first thing that caught my attention. Always. She was an old soul.

"I'm not going to argue with you. Your feelings are your feelings," I said. "You're the only one who can change how you feel toward your parents, and then it's only if you want to." I kept my tone conversational, like a friend. "If you'd rather spend your life hating them, by all means, do that. Let all that negative energy that swirls around you suck you dry." I dropped my voice an octave, crossed my legs, and leaned myself toward her. "Personally, I'd rather use my energy for something else, but hey, this is your life, and you'll make your own decisions and mistakes as you see fit."

She was off guard—I saw it. Inside, I smiled like the Cheshire Cat from the Wonderland books on my shelf.

"What do you know about hating someone?" The challenge in her voice made my grin even wider.

There was a tenacity within this girl, a spirit that couldn't be quenched no matter how hard life tried.

"I know what it's like to go through life wishing things were different, that you were different." An image of a girl—alone in a room, wishing for someone who could help her understand what was happening—flashed in my mind.

I squashed that image, that memory. Squashed it like a piece of paper in my hand until it was a tight wad, and tossed it into a box with no bottom.

"Different? I'm beyond that. I don't just want things to be different—I want change."

I grabbed my notepad and wrote that word down. *Change*. It wasn't a topic we'd often discussed in the past.

"What would you like changed, Savannah?"

If this were a staring contest, she'd walk away with the gold trophy.

Blame it on my headache or her youth or . . . gah, it didn't matter how she won, she just did. Her eyes were made of ice.

The look sent shivers along my arms, and the muscles along my shoulders and neck tensed.

I wasn't going to like her next words.

"Have you heard about the murders?" she asked.

"Yes."

She nodded, as if my answer said more than I'd intended.

"I'm jealous of those kids." She sounded like a little girl who not only asked for a pony but expected to get one too.

"Jealous? Why is that?"

She fiddled with her hands. Her thumbs twirled round and round.

I gave her the time and space to answer.

"I know that's wrong to say, that I should feel sorry for them. I mean, they just lost their parents and are orphaned, but . . ." She pulled her lip inward and bit hard.

"But . . ." I urged her on.

The truth, no matter how hard to admit, was best said out loud. Once you spoke it, there was no turning back—those words gave birth to the feelings and beliefs harbored inside your heart.

No matter how much it hurt, the truth was always worth it.

"This is a safe place, Savannah. Your truth is safe with me. I promise."

I should have known better than to make a promise I couldn't keep.

"They are better off now. Those kids. I wish . . ." She puffed a breath of air from her lips, unclenched her fingers, and rested her hands in her lap.

"I wish," she said again, this time with less hesitation and more determination, "that I was strong enough to kill mine."

Chapter Eight

THURSDAY, AUGUST 8

I bolted upright from the couch.

The sound of a closing door had woken me.

It hadn't been a hard slam or even a soft click but more of a thud.

I threw the light blanket off my body, and the cobwebs in my head slowly fell to the ground, but it was a sluggish process.

"Hello?" I called out. "Tami? Are you here?"

If she was, it was with coffee, because the scent was strong and called to me. Maybe that's what had woken me, that she came in, saw I was asleep, and left.

I uncurled my legs and winced at the throbbing pain that shot up my ankle when I tried to stand.

I collapsed back on the couch. My ankle was swollen, with slight purplish marks formed around it and an ache that increased each time I touched it. I must have slept on it wrong or twisted it earlier in the day and not realized it. Unless it was a spider bite.

The thump-thump-thump-thump-thump-thump pain in my ankle beat a steady rhythm, similar to my heartbeat but not in sync. It pulsed and throbbed and hurt more than I wanted to admit.

What the hell had bitten me while I slept?

It was too swollen and discolored for me to notice any marks. It was lumpy to the touch like a balloon full of soft, wet gel capsules. If Tami were here, she'd tell me to see a doctor.

If Tami were here, I'd tell her to go to hell.

I had enough Benadryl in the kitchen to fight whatever bug had bitten me, if indeed that was the issue. I didn't need to see a doctor to tell me the same thing.

I hobbled into the kitchen, where the relaxing whiff of fresh beans was strong.

I tried to recall if I'd started the coffee before dozing off or not. It wouldn't have surprised me if I had and forgot about it. It wouldn't be the first time. Especially with the headache that had my stomach rolling like a bowling ball. I'd hoped sleep would have tamed the migraine, but it was still there, just muted.

I rooted around the cupboard for a bottle of aspirin to dull the pain and help the headache.

Things felt off. They had since the moment I'd woken up and smelled the coffee I couldn't remember making.

When I was younger, I used to sleepwalk. My parents would find me out in the driveway or in the field behind our house in the middle of the night. Or on the toilet holding a toothbrush.

After a plethora of doctor visits, blood tests, and sleep tests, I was told it was all stress related. Stress, lack of sleep, and simple exhaustion—my three familiars.

The last time this happened was before I moved to Cheshire. I'd been found in the middle of a street carrying a bag full of groceries I'd taken out of my own cupboards.

I grabbed the cup I'd left on the counter and noticed a folded note beneath it.

A part of me hesitated to open it.

You know a killer.

My hands shook as I reread the note.

Someone had been in my house. They had gotten past my locked door and alarm and left me a note while I slept. My privacy was destroyed, security demolished, safety defeated. Chills ran along my skin. The sensation of being watched crept up my back like a slithering snake, and I shuddered.

Was I being watched? How had someone broken into my house without my knowing? The idea that I had slept through the invasion had panic skidding down my spine, the feeling coiled around each vertebra until it hacked through my stomach like a Japanese star blade.

The note in my hand wobbled while I reminded myself to breathe. I reread the words, and the panic lodged in my heart like a boulder blocking a stream, bumped it into a staggered run.

I did know a killer. But no one knew that. Not Tami. Not Sabrina. Not anyone. Who would have sent this? Who would know?

How had they found out about Ella? I'd been so careful when it came to her, and I knew she'd been as well. What connection could they have discovered between her alias and her prison record?

My chest shook, and I gasped as a single thought boomed in my head.

This was bad. Really bad. Ella's deepest fear was that her past would be discovered. It would destroy her.

My mind raced with thoughts, questions, and realizations.

Ella's life as she knew it was over. It was why she'd moved here, to Cheshire. To escape the whispered gossip, to break from her past, to run from the judgment of others once word got out.

I felt sick inside.

None of this made sense. I wanted to call Tami. I needed to talk to her.

My hands shook like a swing in a storm when the realization hit that I couldn't.

I had promised to protect Ella, and I couldn't break that promise. I couldn't do that to Ella, not even when that wasn't the reason why I needed Tami.

I no longer felt safe in my own home.

Chapter Nine

THURSDAY, AUGUST 8

KILLER

The minutes before death are my favorite.

Everything is right.

Everything is still.

So still the huff of my breath sounds louder than the thwack a gavel makes as it strikes a judge's desk.

I stand before the wall of family photos, sneering at the fake smiles.

You'd think this family perfect. But it doesn't take much to peel away the thin veneer of lies, to notice the cracks, the jagged edges, the potholes of pain.

A fever of hatred spreads through me faster than fire in a forest.

Seeing the parents' fake smiles staring back at me almost destroys my resolve. I want to heave each frame off that wall to the floor, erasing those picture-perfect, smothering smiles until all that remains is the innocent—the child I came to protect.

But I don't.

I can't make any noise.

I climb the stairs, my hand on the knife. I rub the pad of my thumb along the blade. Not enough to cut. Just enough to remind me of what is to come.

I've spent countless evenings outside this house, preparing for this night, watching the family, learning which room is little Robin's.

She'll be adopted. Loved. Treasured.

I make sure she's fast asleep, one hand tucked beneath her cheek.

This is how I'll always remember her.

Sweet. Innocent. And now, for the first time in her life, protected.

That's who I am.

The protector.

The avenger.

I avenge the children. Protect them when their own parents fail.

Her parents don't deserve her.

They deserve to die.

The condemned are drugged, asleep in their beds, with no idea their sentence is about to be delivered.

Tonight there is no courtroom, no judge, no jury.

Tonight there is only me. And I offer no mercy.

Children are always so innocent when they're asleep.

Angelic.

Like a Precious Moments figurine, her porcelain skin, light-brown hair, little button nose, and heart-shaped lips.

Right here, right now, I am calm.

Calm and full of peace and a sense of rightness.

Children are the real and true victims in this world. They have no choices, no opportunities, no way to discern who they are meant for and who to avoid. If there is a God, they're ignorant of the value God has placed on their small heads.

The Bible says something like, *Let the little children come unto me, for the kingdom of heaven belongs to them.*

If there were a God, those who are unable to love would never be gifted with a child who needs love.

If there were a God, those who are unable to think of others would never be given a child who needs to be thought of.

If there were a God, those who are unable to put themselves last would never be given a child who needs to come first.

I have learned that there is no God. Not one who loves unconditionally.

There is also no such thing as unconditional love. It's a lie, a facade, a tale told to romantics so they believe they have hope.

I look around her room, and sadness leaks out of me. There's not much here. A few dolls scattered about and family drawings tacked to the wall.

The rooms downstairs are magazine worthy. Cold, characterless, and clutter free. There should be toys and books and crayons lying around. This house should be screaming *A child lives in me,* but it doesn't.

How sad this little one must feel. How alone. How unloved.

There is one thing that brings me hope.

Tucked beneath her hand is a fairy-tale book. Is she dreaming of glass slippers and talking candlesticks? I hope so.

Very gently, I pull the book from beneath her hand and replace it with another. One that has been gift-wrapped with a note inside especially for her. One that will get her through the next few nights, the next few weeks, the next few years, as she learns what it's like to truly be loved.

I have one more task to complete before I leave this home. One more act of love toward little Robin.

I look in on her parents and smile.

After, their slashed throats remind me of the deep-red smile on a clown's painted face.

Chapter Ten

MEMORY

A wood fire crackles with sparks like red fireworks around the burned bricks. Smoke dances with the wind, swaying one way, then the next, searching for a partner but never finding any.

I pretend it's calling to me, but I say no.

I'm not allowed too close to the fire.

My fingers, my lips, and my cheeks are sticky with marshmallow goo, my smile wider than the mouth of Niagara Falls, something Daddy always says to me. I laugh because I'm happy.

The fire whispers to me, shows me pictures that seem magical. I know not to touch it. My palm still bears the pink imprint of fire from when I was three. It still hurts sometimes too.

The sky is lit up with diamonds, and the moon is so bright, I can see the man's face, thanks to Mommy pointing him out.

Mommy and Daddy are whispering to each other. They smile at me, but I know something is wrong.

Sometimes I like to play a game. See how long I can be as quiet as my teddy bears. Sometimes I can be quiet for hours, and everyone forgets me. Other times, there's a tickling feeling inside me, and I can't keep the giggles in.

I want another marshmallow. I've had three so far. I was only allowed two, but no one said anything when I toasted the third one with the long stick Daddy gave me.

The fire crackles more and more, and the whispering stops.

Daddy leans over and adds another piece of wood to the flames.

"Doing okay there, princess?" The smile on his face lies, but I nod and am a good girl.

I notice a lot of things. Things they say I'm too young to see and hear. But I'm a smart whippersnapper, as Daddy says, and I'm starting school soon. I notice more than they think.

Like how often Mommy cries.

Like when Daddy fists his hands in anger, then hides them behind his back when he sees me looking.

Like when they slam the cupboard doors. I'm not allowed to do that when I'm angry, so why are they?

Like the yelling when I'm supposed to be asleep.

I don't like when Mommy and Daddy are mad at each other. Or when Mommy is extra sad and the tears fall out.

I always make sure I give Mommy extra hugs when Daddy's not around. I tell her I love her and that she's the best mommy in the whole wide world.

She always gives me a kiss on the head and says thank you. Sometimes she says she tries as hard as she can. Other times she says she doesn't deserve a little girl like me.

Mommy lets out a really long sigh and gets up from her chair.

"I'm just going into the house for a minute, love. Are you cold yet? Do you need a sweater?" She rubs her hands down my arms, her touch tickling me.

I shake my head. The fire is warm on my skin, and I pretend it's giving me a suntan.

"What do you think, should we see how high we can make this fire?" Daddy leans forward, really close to the flames, and pokes at them with his

stick. "I think we can add more wood, don't you?" He turns to look at me, but his eyes are looking over my head, watching Mommy.

Bright lights sweep across our grass.

A truck is turning into our driveway.

Black dots swim in my eyes from looking at the truck. When I close them, the lights dance, moving around like a disco ball.

"Who would come out here at this time of night?" Daddy mutters.

He stands to see.

The truck door slams.

Daddy swears.

He leaves me there, sitting by the fire, alone.

I'm all alone now. I'm never allowed to be alone at the fire.

I pull my legs up under me to get as far away from the fire as I can.

If Mommy were here, she'd be upset and yell at Daddy.

I want to get up and run to him, but I don't know who is here.

I don't like strangers.

I sit here, all by myself, and I'm scared.

Daddy talks with someone, their voices low but not friendly.

Our house door slams, and Mommy comes rushing out. I think she's running to me because she knows I'm here by myself in front of the fire and that I'm scared.

When she runs past me, my eyes hurt like there's sand in them. I had sand in them last week when we went to the beach. I want to cry, but I'm a big girl now, and big girls don't cry.

She calls out a name and wraps her arms around the person who drove up in the truck.

Daddy's swearing because it's Uncle. Daddy doesn't like Uncle.

I want to get up off my chair and run into the house, hide myself in my closet beneath my blankets so no one can find me.

I can't get off the chair, though. The wind makes the fire dance my way, the flames reaching out past the brick walls Daddy built around it. He said *those bricks will keep the fire inside the circle, but those flames aren't staying where they're supposed to. They're coming my way.*

I curl my toes in as far as I can, pull my legs up to my chest, and push my face into my knees.

Maybe if the fire doesn't know I'm here, it'll forget all about me.

Maybe I have a superpower no one but me knows about.

I'm Invisible Girl.

Mommy and Daddy come back to the fire. So does Uncle.

I wait for Mommy to get upset at Daddy for leaving me here all by myself. Any minute now she's going to scoop me up in her arms and have me sit in her lap. Her arms will be tight around me, like a big soft bear hug, and I'll be okay.

I won't be alone anymore.

But it's not Mommy who scoops me up from my chair.

She's not the one who digs her fingers beneath my arms, hurting me.

She's not the one who holds me in her lap, wrapping her arms around me.

She's not the one who is kissing the top of my head or running her hands down my arms.

She doesn't even see my frown. Or notice how quiet I am. Or that I don't want to be here, in his lap.

My daddy does, though.

He has his angry face on.

He holds out his arms to me, and I fly into them, ignoring the way the other man laughs.

"Oh, don't be like that, love." Mommy has a big smile on her face, but her voice says she's upset with me.

"Don't you worry, princess. I've got you," Daddy whispers to me as he sits down in his chair and holds me close. "How about we do another marshmallow?" he says.

"I think she's had enough." Mommy is now frowning. "She'll be up all night, hyped up on sugar."

"One more won't hurt." Daddy's voice is strong. Strong like a bear. He'll protect me.

I nod my head, not saying anything. Maybe if I don't speak, I'll be forgotten about again.

I would like that.

"You know you can stay as long as you need," Mommy says.

I stare at the fire but stay really still so I can hear what he says.

I don't want him to stay long. I hope he doesn't.

Even Daddy thinks so, the way he mutters while handing me his branch. I stare at my marshmallow and hold it as close to the flames as I can.

Daddy helps to keep it steady, because I keep dipping the branch into the fire, and my marshmallow keeps going up in flames.

"Whoa, be careful there, princess," Daddy says softly. So softly that only I can hear. "We don't want it to get burned, now. The secret to roasting the perfect marshmallow is to hold it close enough to the fire but not too close. You want it to turn toasty brown."

The man beside Daddy starts to laugh.

"Nah," he says. "Let the girl burn her treat. The crispier it gets, the more she'll learn. She's getting to be a big girl now, aren't you?" He leans over and touches my knee.

I jerk it away.

"Don't you remember me, princess?" he says. "I'm your favorite uncle. The only uncle who loves you more than anybody else in the whole wide world." He winks over at Mommy, and they both laugh.

"I love you more than anyone ever could," Daddy whispers into my ear. "Don't you ever forget that."

I hold up my pinkie and wait for him to promise. A pinkie promise is the most important promise ever.

"She needs to go to bed now," Mommy says.

Daddy pushes me off his lap and tells me to go get ready, that he'll be there to tuck me in.

The Patient

I walk back to the house, the grass tickling my legs and feet. I brush my teeth, wash my hands, get my pajamas on, and sit at the top of the stairs, waiting.

I wait forever, but no one comes. In my room, I can hear them fighting. Daddy doesn't want Uncle here. Mommy does. She says he can watch me, and she can get a job. I don't want Mommy to get a job. I don't want Uncle to watch me. I want Daddy to come and tuck me in and tell me everything will be okay.

But no one does.

Chapter Eleven

FRIDAY, AUGUST 9

It was midmorning, and I hadn't showered, eaten, or even brushed my teeth. All I'd done was stare at Ella's file while curled on my couch.

I wrestled with Ella's declaration that she had a confession to make. We'd never gotten around to that confession because the timer had gone off, and she'd left my office as fast as she could.

My biggest fear was that I was not helping my patients, not like they needed. And if I couldn't help them . . . what would happen to them? That responsibility weighed heavy. With Ella, we'd come so far, I worried about the backward steps we'd take.

Not being enough. It overwhelmed me. I'd walked the park, journaled my thoughts, meditated to relieve stress, yet the fear was always there, gnawing like a dog with its jaw locked around a bone.

Anytime I attempted to get to the root of that fear, something inside me growled a warning to retreat.

So I did. I retreated.

Was this avoidance? One hundred percent. I was my own worst patient, and I knew I needed to talk to someone about it. Maybe it was time.

The Patient

It took Tami's text message to get my ass off the couch.

She was going to stop by and was craving cake.

There was no comparison when it came to stress loads. She carried more than I did, which had me offering to bake that cake she craved.

By the time she knocked on my side door, I'd made a fresh pot of coffee, and her favorite Bundt cake was cooling on the counter.

"Oh my God, you made it. I could kiss you." She went straight for the cake, dropped the mail she'd gathered from my mailbox on the table, and inhaled the cake's sweet, warm scent.

The smile on her face was real. Genuine. Beautiful.

"And coffee? Seriously, Dee, who do I have to thank for a friend like you?" She took the offered cup I held, closed her eyes, and inhaled.

I'd never met someone who enjoyed coffee more than her.

"You seem jittery," she said. "Please don't tell me this is your first cup today."

"More like my second pot," I confessed. We took our coffee and cake into the living room and settled on the couch.

I watched as Tami inhaled her piece of cake before I managed to take a few bites.

She was exhausted. I could see it on her face. From the black circles beneath her eyes to the double tap of her lashes as she blinked and the effort it took for her to raise the fork to her mouth, open, and chew.

"When was the last time you had a decent night's sleep?" My therapist hat went on.

"I look that bad, huh?" She yawned, covering her mouth with the palm of her hand. "I've caught a few hours here and there, but there's been no time."

"Why don't you try to rest? I want to go over a patient file before this afternoon, and I promise to wake you if anyone calls." She wasn't going to be any good to her partner or her case if she didn't get some sleep.

I thought about the note I'd found yesterday. I wanted to tell her, confess that I felt unsafe, that I was worried about how easy it had been for someone to enter my house without my knowing.

But then I'd have to be honest about the headaches and the sleep-walking, and there was no way I could keep from revealing the words on the note, which meant I'd have to tell her about Ella's past, and I wasn't sure I was ready for that.

"A few of these"—she lifted her coffee—"and I'll be fine. Talk to me, will you? Tell me something interesting."

I wanted to insist she take a nap, even just a power one, but maybe if I talked in a low tone, she'd fall asleep anyway.

I pulled my knees tightly to my chest, my fingers laced around them, and thought about what I could tell her.

I had so many stories, but not all could be told. Not all were mine either.

I thought about what I hadn't told her, the stories about myself, my own life, that I'd kept secret. I could trust Tami; I knew this, just like I knew I could tell her the things I would never have shared with anyone else.

Maybe it was time to start.

"I've never really told you much about my parents, have I?"

Tami leaned her head on the couch and looked toward a photo on the wall across from us.

"There's not much to tell." I stared at the photo as well. Two lovely people, arms wrapped around one another with picture-perfect smiles on their faces. "I generally tell people they were good parents and leave it at that."

What I hadn't told were the stories of the endless fights late at night, the militant schedule Mom kept for cleaning and meals. Or the fact that I barely knew my father because he was never around. I was never honest about my lonely childhood, how I wasn't allowed many friends because my mom didn't trust the neighbors.

I never told the truth. Only what people expected to hear.

"You lived a fairy tale, then?" Tami's disbelief was as clear as the moon on a cloudless night. "I wish I had your life. My father was an alcoholic, and my mother worked two jobs just to keep food on the table. I grew up realizing that if I wanted the world, I'd have to fight like hell every step of the way."

Is this the part where I tell the truth? The real truth?

"It wasn't a fairy tale, but it could have been worse. My parents were middle class and lived below their means. My father worked hard, and my mother knew how to stretch a budget." The meals my mother cooked were simple but filling, the same meals I made now and considered to be comfort food.

"They sacrificed so I wouldn't have to," I continued. "I knew they had their faults, but compared to the stories I've listened to over the years, I had nothing to complain about." The words spilled out, unplanned, but the twisted worm that wound its way up my throat whenever I thought about them and my past, it wasn't there.

That surprised me.

"Tell me about your birthday parties and what Christmas was like for you as a child. Paint me a picture of what that type of life looks like, and don't leave a single detail out."

A smile slid across my face as I thought about her request. I waited a split second for that worm to appear, but nothing.

"Birthdays were family events. Not the big parties kids have nowadays. My parents never rented out the library and requested my favorite princess to read me stories or organized roller-skating events or booked the local park for hours on a weekend. Mom would make my favorite cake from scratch, letting me lick the bowl afterward." I held my coffee between my hands. "Dad would take the day off work, pull me out of school, and we would go on an adventure—a hike in the woods, a drive through the countryside—it didn't really matter where. By the time we made it back home, dinner would be ready and the cake iced.

She always made chicken potpie, my favorite, with fresh buttermilk biscuits on the side."

It was always the perfect day, spending that time with my father. There were nights when I still dreamed of those drives, when we would come to a stop sign, and I would get to choose which direction we headed. A lot of times we'd end up lost. A few times we didn't make it home in time for dinner. And many times I caught the forced smile on Mom's face when we walked through the door and the whispered voices when they thought I couldn't hear.

"I would get one gift for my birthday. Three for Christmas."

The skepticism on Tami's face reminded me of my mom's when I told a giant fib.

"Yes, one gift. When I was younger, it would be a doll, then a bike, then new shoes or a book I couldn't wait to read. For a few years, I'd ask for a baby brother or sister and would get a doll or doll furniture instead."

"Did you mind being an only child?" Tami asked, her voice sleepy.

How could I miss what I didn't have?

"I was one of those kids with an active imagination, so even when I was by myself, I was never alone. I had an imaginary friend until I discovered books."

"I never pegged you for one of those kids." Tami's eyes were closed, the edges of her lips lifted into a smile.

"One of *those* kids?" I smothered the anger that rose from her innocent remark.

"You know, the ones who were always a little weird, didn't have many friends, somewhat shy on the school grounds." She opened one eyelid. "You know the type, right?"

"Those . . . types"—I spat the word as if it were poison on my tongue—"happen to be very creative, gifted, and probably the most productive members of society, I'll—"

Tami sat up, reached for my leg, and squeezed my knee. "Whoa, I didn't mean it as an insult." Her eyes were wide with worry, and when she swallowed, I watched the awareness settle on her face.

"Ah, I'm sorry." I ran my fingers through my hair, knowing I'd overreacted.

I didn't want to look at her, to see the pity or concern on her face.

Why? Why had I lashed out like that? At Tami, the one person who knew me better than anyone else.

That was so unlike me. The headaches were clearly affecting me more than I'd realized.

"Honestly, Dee, I didn't mean to push a button." She rubbed the area on my knee, like a mother would with a young child. "I'm sorry. I'm just . . . exhausted, and there's no filter."

"No, no, it's my fault. It's a sore spot, obviously." I let out a long breath, one that came from deep in my belly. "You're probably right. I was lonely. I just never thought of it that way. I'll be honest—I didn't have very many friends."

Tami sat back, placed her head back on the couch, eyes barely open.

"In that we're alike," she said with a yawn. "I never had many friends either. Funny how that happens, isn't it? Two kids raised on the opposite sides of the tracks, and yet here we are, best of friends with more in common than we probably want to admit."

I often thought about that too, the unlikelihood of us meeting, and yet, here we were. Which meant keeping secrets from her was killing me.

"It's not funny." I infused my voice with warmth. "It's destiny. It doesn't matter how we were raised—we were meant to be in each other's lives."

For the next thirty minutes or so, she slept while I went over Ella's notes once again. It was good to see her rest. I thought maybe I should ask her to stay the night on the pretext that I wanted to make sure she rested and not because I was too scared to be home alone.

I kept my fears to myself when she woke up, filled a coffee mug, and headed back to work.

I was tempted to have another piece of cake, but then the mail Tami had tossed on my table caught my attention. I flipped through some flyers until I noticed a plain envelope with no writing on it.

Curious, I opened the envelope.

Five words written in black ink.

Shock, anxiety, fear, they all collided with the nausea in my stomach—burning, rolling, clashing—and my hand fell to the table for support. A chill wrapped around my spine and wound its way upward, one tendril at a time, as I read those five words.

Why haven't you stopped them?

Chapter Twelve

PATIENT SESSION: ELLA

"Ella." I'd finished reading another section from *Alice's Adventures in Wonderland*, but I couldn't wait any longer. I was exhausted and ready to crawl into bed. Ever since the second note, I hadn't had a moment to relax and really think things through like I needed to.

The killer. The notes. My sleepwalking.

That wasn't fair to Ella. Especially after what had happened at the end of our last session. I needed to be present and on track.

"When you were here on Tuesday, you admitted you had a confession to make, but then our session ended. I'd like to pick up where we left off if that works for you. Do you think you're ready to tell me today?"

Ella's lips trembled, her lashes fluttered against her porcelain skin, and I wasn't sure she'd be able to.

"It's my fault," she said.

"I'm sorry?"

"It's my fault they're dead."

"Your parents?"

"No."

My pen dropped onto my lap.

"Who?" I licked my dry lips. "Who is dead, Ella?"

A million scenarios went through my head at her confession. Who had died? Her fault? What did she mean? How? I knew Ella, and despite her past, she wasn't a killer. Not anymore.

And yet her words planted a seed of doubt.

"Who, Ella?" I asked again.

"I . . ." She cleared her throat and fidgeted in her spot. "The parents."

"Parents? What are you saying, Ella?" Panic rose in my voice as I struggled to understand her words.

"I knew them. The parents. The mother. That's why they're dead."

Her words sucked all the air from the room.

Ella knew the parents?

Questions were glued to my tongue. I lowered my gaze so she couldn't read them in my eyes.

"The library. That's how I knew them . . . or of them." Her broken voice wobbled. "The news right now . . . the mother . . . she . . . she brought her daughter in for our morning programs." She leaned away from me, her fingers tapping like crazy on her knee.

Ella tapped her fingers against her arms, her thighs, her knees—any part of her body—when she was wound up with nervous tension.

I had never felt so confused during a session with Ella as I did now.

"Her daughter is a little butterfly, comes out of her shell the moment she steps into the library, arms open wide as if trying to gather all the books close. The smile on her face each time she finds a new book is contagious. I wanted to scoop her up and bring her home with me, you know?"

For a minuscule moment, Ella was more alive than I'd ever seen her. Vibrant. Glowing. Animated.

I wrote everything down, everything she said.

"The mom, I wasn't too sure about her. She would drop her daughter off, then leave, not even pretend to be interested in any of the books her daughter found." A scowl replaced the earlier smile. "She'd come back thirty minutes later with a cup of coffee in hand and want to leave."

Ella's hands fisted on the tops of her legs now, her tone filled with disdain and disgust.

"I started to keep the little girl with me. I'd call her to my side, ignoring the mom, making her wait longer and longer each time until eventually she was forced to talk to me. At first I thought she was one of those moms who viewed her child as an inconvenience, but the more I talked to her, the more I realized that wasn't the case."

There was an inquisitive tone to Ella's voice, like she really did try to figure the mother out.

"What did you realize?" I asked.

"She didn't know how to parent." Her tone was matter-of-fact. "The last week or so, she would actually stay and sit off to the side, listening in during story time. She'd walk through the aisles and pick out a few books for them to read at home. She was actually quite nice, the more I got to know her."

"You sound surprised." How I managed to keep my voice steady was beyond me.

She shrugged. "I am, I guess. Or I was." The creases of her forehead knitted together in the shape of a W. "I shouldn't have been, though. We were handing out treat bags to kids all last week. It was my job one day to ensure that every child who left the library had one in their hand." She shook her head. "That little girl, you'd think she'd just been handed a treasure when I gave her a bag, but her mom, she gave it back to me. No explanation. No reason. Just *no thank you*, and then she pulled her daughter out of the building."

Ella sucked in her lips and bit hard, leaving dent marks. She had a faraway look in her eyes. Her forehead creased with wrinkle lines, and the frown on her face wobbled. I wasn't sure if she was angry or sad.

"That's bad parenting. I don't care what anyone says."

I thought back to that day outside the library when I'd watched a similar scene play out. I understood the anger, the irritation, the sense of wrongness, but Ella's reaction was almost . . . personal.

"Don't you think you're being a little harsh? Maybe something had happened and this was a consequence," I suggested. "You just said it seemed as if she'd been trying."

Ella's expression didn't change.

"A gift is a gift." A muscle in her cheek pulsed.

"Why are you so upset, Ella?"

I tried to think back through the tidbits of history she'd told me from her childhood. I didn't recall anything having to do with deprivation of gifts, though.

She looked away, unable or unwilling to look me in the eye—I wasn't sure which.

I didn't press. Didn't prod. Didn't push. As much as I wanted to. I remained quiet and waited. Waited for her to open up, to share something new, to reveal why she seemed so provoked by a behavior she'd only witnessed.

"I . . . I didn't have a lot growing up," Ella said. "But when gifts were given, they were never declined. Never. No matter what. No matter who gave it to you." Her voice lowered at least two octaves. "You say thank you. You appreciate the gift. You never appear ungrateful. Never."

I made a note.

"That feels like a trigger, Ella. One we haven't discussed before." It'd been a while since we'd discovered something new.

Ella looked like she'd drunk molasses.

"I guess so."

"How does this make you feel?"

I watched the thought process filter through her head. Ella needed to think things through, to analyze and find a conclusion before she could accept it as fact.

"Right now I feel anger. Toward the mother." She stopped and looked to the side. "Toward you."

She squinted as I caught her glance.

"I see." It was harder to keep the surprise from my voice than I thought. "Why?"

"Why the mother or why toward you?"

"Whichever you'd like to start with."

Ella's chin rested almost on her chest and stayed in that position for three minutes. I would have assumed she'd fallen asleep, except this had happened in the past as well, whenever we touched on a harder subject.

"It's hard to watch a child be mistreated. Accepting that gift would have taken her nothing. It was free and would have made Robin happy. There is a part of me that feels she deserved whatever came her way, you know?" Her voice was low and rumbled as she spoke. Her chin inched higher until she stared me straight in the eye.

"I feel anger toward you for forcing me to do this. We'd gotten to a good point, right? I felt better. But discussing this . . . those old feelings, the memories . . ." She shook her head. "I don't want to talk about my past. You know that."

I needed time to respond, so I wrote this down, but in the back of my mind, all I could think about were the notes. Someone knew about Ella's past—knew what she'd done—and now placed blame on me for the murders.

Why haven't you stopped them?

Those words haunted me.

"By discussing your past, you're proving it doesn't hold power over you. Not anymore."

Ella's shoulders slouched.

"My past will always hold power over me," she said.

"Why?"

"You know why."

We'd discussed this over and over. The past and the power it held over us. Ella believed she could never run from her past, that one day it would hold her accountable.

"You still don't forgive yourself, do you?"

The sound that came from Ella's mouth was something between a snort and a laugh.

"I don't deserve to be forgiven."

"Everyone deserves forgiveness, Ella."

She shook her head. "Not me. Not for what I did. I've accepted that. But maybe . . . maybe I can atone for it? Make it right, even if a little bit."

"You atoned by losing ten years of your life in prison. Wasn't that enough?"

"For what I did? No." She worried her lip. "Should I go to the police?"

"What would you tell the police, Ella?"

I measured my words carefully. I wanted her to know I supported her, but at the same time, I was cautious. It felt like we were talking in circles. There was something we needed to get at, but each time we took a step closer to the truth, she shied away.

"About what I know."

"What do you know?"

She scrunched her face until it resembled a raisin.

Her gaze flitted about the room as if it followed the flight path of a moth. She didn't respond, and I wasn't sure she would.

"Ella." I smothered a sigh. "Let's go back to what you mentioned earlier. You believe it's your fault the parents are dead. Why?"

That was the part I couldn't wrap my head around. Just because she recognized the woman from the library, had interacted with the child, it didn't mean she was at fault.

She'd be at fault if she'd killed them.

Which she hadn't. I knew that like I knew I'd be drinking more coffee by the end of the day.

"I didn't think they would die." Ella covered her face with the palms of her hands. "I didn't like how Robin was treated, but they didn't deserve to die." Her chest heaved as she wiped away the tears that gathered in her eyes.

"How is it your fault?" I asked again.

"I'm going to be there for her, for Robin." It was as if she hadn't heard me. "I don't know how, but I want to be there for her."

Unhealthy relationship. I underlined that twice. That could be dangerous.

"She will have family who will take her in and help her through this." I wanted to dispel any responsibility Ella carried.

She thought about that for a moment. I watched her work through it. The smile that graced her face, however, filled me with dread.

You know a murderer.

Who knew? How had they gotten in? What did I do now?

"I can make it right." Her voice forced my attention back on her.

"What do you mean, Ella?" I leaned forward.

With wide eyes, she inhaled sharply and then let out a slow exhale, her chest deflating like a balloon with the air escaping.

"Robin's life has been changed forever." Ella buried her head between her arms. "Killing them was wrong. *Wrong wrong wrong.* They could change—they could have. They just didn't know." She chanted to herself as she rocked back and forth, back and forth.

"Ella." I called her name a few times. "Ella, it's going to be okay. That little girl will be okay." I wanted to hold her in my arms, to rock her as a mother would a grieving child. I refrained.

I had to.

"Another family destroyed because of me," she said. "Another set of parents killed." Tears flowed down her cheeks, her face streaked black from her mascara.

"Did you kill them?" I asked point-blank.

"Yes," she whispered. A whispered confession with power that destroyed lives.

She was the killer. Something grabbed my heart, squeezed until it resembled a twisted rag. I couldn't breathe. Couldn't speak. Couldn't do anything.

Someone knew. Someone had known Ella was the killer, and what? Warned me? Wanted to see what I would do? What could I do? Doctor-patient confidentiality stated she was protected from crimes of her past if she confessed them to me. Unless she admitted she was about to carry out a crime, her secret was safe with me.

Tami would kill me. She would blame me. I would blame myself.

"It's my fault," Ella said again. I wanted to yell at her. Scream for her to shut up, that I didn't want to hear more, that I couldn't hear more.

"I killed my parents. I killed them. I murdered them just like Robin's parents were killed."

Her head lifted, and I looked into eyes full of something that scared me.

"I'm the reason they're dead." She repeated what she'd said earlier, but it didn't make sense. Especially now. "It's all my fault."

Chapter Thirteen

SATURDAY, AUGUST 10

WE'RE ALL MAD HERE.

The café offered safe haven from the shrill children and crowded streets and sweltering sun, and I escaped as fast as I could. Cheshire was a madhouse this weekend.

I pushed open the door to the Mad Hatter's Tea House to find Sabrina's head half-buried in a large bin. Her messy bun of wiry gray curls, which created a sort of halo, spilled out over her neck. She jerked up, her look similar to a small child caught red-handed in her mother's sewing cabinet.

"Oh God, Danielle." Her hand fluttered over her chest, her smile wobbly. "I'm not a young woman anymore, girl. You could have given me a heart attack." She brushed her hair back and smoothed those wayward pieces of hair.

There was no one else in the café.

"I'm surprised you're not out there." I pointed over my shoulder.

"Are you kidding me? This is the only quiet time I'll have today. I've seen enough parades to last me a lifetime. Come here," she said, her fingers urging me to hurry. "Come see what just came in." By the excitement in her voice, you'd think she'd discovered a rare painting of Alice and the Red Queen.

Instead, she showed me a teacup and saucer.

It was no ordinary cup and saucer.

They were bone china with a sketched black design of Alice, hands folded behind her back, and the words *Curiouser and Curiouser* twisting along the rim. Inside the cup was a key with a tag, and the saucer was full of characters from the story. Where the cup rested was the saying *We're All Mad Here*.

Just like the sign as you entered her store.

Just like the framed saying in my living room at home. I'd once been tempted to place it in my therapy room, but that wouldn't have gone over well.

"I've been waiting forever for these to arrive. I ordered them from the UK."

"Are they for sale, or will you be using them in the café?" I couldn't tear my gaze from the cup in my hand.

"For sale. Want one?" She pointed to the display cabinet off to the right. "I even managed to snag the last cake stands."

Every Saturday afternoon, Sabrina hosted a reservation-only high tea party that was centered around the books with pocket-watch macarons and drinkable potions. Her restaurant was always packed and booked out at least a month in advance.

I left her and headed to the display. I took my time mentally cataloging the new items. My fingers trailed over the cotton dish towels, the white tablecloth, the glazed teapots.

I wanted them all.

Until I saw the one thing I wanted the most.

"That's not for sale." She might as well have said, *I got it, you didn't.*

I ignored her.

I stopped short of touching the worn spine of the book she'd placed up there. It sat alone, not grouped with the other versions she had stacked. This one leaned against a teacup, the spine and cover visible.

It was old. A collectible. Not rare, but old.

I recognized the book.

She gave me one of her you-snooze-you-lose looks.

"That's the last time I mention another online auction to you." Sabrina hadn't been a collector until we'd met and I'd infused her with my addiction.

"I have a gift for you." She squatted down, opened a cupboard drawer, and pulled out a wrapped box.

"You didn't have to do that."

"I know." The smile she gave me was real, genuine, and full of excitement. "But I saw this and just had to get it for you."

I unwrapped the box, opened the lid, and gasped.

"Where did you find this?" My hands trembled as I lifted the item out of the box.

It was an old set of cards, forty-eight pictorial cards for the New and Diverting Game of Alice in Wonderland. The box of cards was rough, worn, torn, and aged but the most beautiful thing I'd ever seen.

"I've seen photos of this but never—" My voice caught. I engulfed her in a hug, so thrilled by what I held in my hand.

"I found them at an estate sale. I knew you'd appreciate them more than anyone else." She hugged me back just as hard. "Plus, I felt bad for bidding against you on the book."

"Okay, you're forgiven." I gave her a wink.

Sabrina showed me a few other items she'd procured. Almost everything was Alice related, and a few were about reading and books, but there wasn't one item that I didn't like and wish to have.

"It's so horrible what's happening," Sabrina said. I knew she was talking about the recent murders. "My heart just breaks for the children left behind." Her hands covered her chest. "I want to do something to help, but I'm not sure what."

"I'm having a hard time wrapping my head around what's going on as well."

Sabrina looked around, then leaned in close. "I've never been in favor of the death penalty, but in this case . . . it hits too close to home. These are our people, part of our community. I've had these kids in my shop. I've served these families. I just—" Her whispered voice broke. "Whoever did this, they're crazy. A psychopath or something."

I leaned away, shocked by her words. *Death penalty?*

"I mean, who in their right mind would even consider killing parents and leaving the child alive? They have to be sick. There's talk that it's someone with unresolved parent issues. I heard that the police are reaching out to local psychiatrists to see if they have any high-risk patients." Sabrina continued to talk in a low voice. "Have they talked to you yet? I'll be honest, Danielle, the idea kind of scares me. That someone in our town with mommy issues is sick enough to murder . . . Just lock them all up. They deserve it." Her body shook as if a tremor full of unfettered anger wound through her.

I shook my head. That was all I could do. If I opened my mouth, something vile and malicious would come out, I was sure of it. I couldn't believe I was hearing garbage like that from Sabrina. In times of crisis, like now, filters tend to get pushed aside in the heat of the moment. Filters that would normally keep our true thoughts and feelings inside.

I backed away, one step at a time, swallowing whatever words were there on the tip of my tongue. She may have felt safe enough with me to let words and emotions slip, but I didn't.

"Danielle? Are you okay?" I heard the worry in her voice and realized my anger must have been showing.

"I'm fine." I snapped the words faster than a crop against a racehorse about to cross the finish line. "I hear what you're saying, but I don't agree with all your thoughts, and I . . . It's probably best I leave before I say something I'll regret." I didn't wait for her reply, didn't bother to see if she'd apologize or have the decency to take back her words.

"I'm just going to go." I left her café and pushed my way through the crowds on the street. I just wanted to head home. I needed to be at home.

The moment I opened my door, a blanket of exhaustion dropped on me. It was all I could do to make it to the couch, my steps heavy, my head pounding. Sabrina's words hung over me like a black cloud. I collapsed on the couch, and the moment I closed my eyes, I welcomed the darkness.

$$\sim$$

A gentle breeze brushed across my skin. I wanted to open my eyes, but the energy was gone. The sun warmed my body, and the sounds of a school band filled the air.

I pried my left eye open.

I was outside.

I bolted up.

I wasn't in my house anymore. Or on my couch. I was outside, on my front porch. My feet were propped on a white wicker stool. There was a glass of iced tea on the table beside me and my journal.

Why was I out here? When had I come out?

I'd never sleepwalked during the day. Never. It had always been at night, in the middle of the night, when I was a child.

Maybe . . . maybe it was too much. Sabrina's words. The murders. The notes. My feelings of failure with my patients . . . maybe they had pushed me too hard, too far.

Maybe it was time to talk to someone. Someone who could help me work through everything and lower my own stress levels.

Someone who could help me figure out everything. Especially who was behind the notes.

Chapter Fourteen

It was Sunday. My one fun day, per se, with the only goal being one hundred percent relaxation, whether that be a movie, a Netflix binge, or baking and, of course, my daily walk through the park. Sundays were *me* days, where I did absolutely nothing but focus on my own mental health and take time to breathe.

Which was why I groaned when I first noticed Sabrina walking up my walkway.

I'd ignored her multiple texts and her four voice messages yesterday. I hadn't been in the right frame of mind then to talk to her, and I certainly wasn't today either.

I had other things on my mind.

Like why I was so exhausted after sleeping ten hours last night.

Like who was sending the notes to me.

Like what I needed to do with Ella and how much to share with Tami and the growing guilt from not telling her anything yet.

I didn't need to deal with someone's guilty conscience for emotions and feelings she'd expressed yesterday.

Normally I wasn't one to get offended easily. We lived in a society that looked for offense, but I preferred to keep the mind-set that everyone was entitled to their own feelings and opinions, just like I was entitled to ignore them when they didn't agree with mine. That didn't give me the right to be offended; it gave me the right to be selective with my friends.

Sabrina stood at the bottom of my stairs with a covered tray in her hands.

"I stress bake. The morning was slow, and I had a lot left over." Sabrina's attention was focused on the tray in her hands, not on me.

She was embarrassed. I got it. Last night she'd said she was horrified by the words that had come out of her mouth and needed to apologize.

"I'm not mad." I sat down on the step, leaving enough room for her to join me.

She handed me the tray, which I placed off to the side.

"You have every right to be if you were."

I nodded.

"I thought long and hard about what I said yesterday. Even my husband agreed I spoke out of turn, which has to say something."

It didn't, since I didn't know her husband other than saying hello a few times when he'd been at the café, but I kept that comment to myself.

"Danielle, I'm overly emotional over the murders, the fears, and the stress every day the killer isn't caught. It's not an excuse—I know that. But I let what other people said taint my own opinions until that's all I could think or see. Like a mob mentality."

"Is that really what people are saying?" If it was, then anyone who sought help for anything had to be worried. No one was safe from public speculation. God forbid therapy actually helped someone with their issues.

All I kept thinking about was Ella.

"People are afraid." Sabrina ran her hands up and down her arms. "Aren't you?"

Fear was a multilayered emotion that many had no idea how to handle. "I'm not fearful for my life. But I am afraid for our town."

Sabrina nodded.

"At the same time, I trust those who are on the hunt for the monsters committing these acts." The conviction in my voice seemed to set her at ease. Her back relaxed as she let out one very long sigh.

"Basically, you're telling me to calm down."

"How about not be as stressed? People are probably looking to you for comfort, Sab, when they come into your shop for tea. Rather than feed into the fear and gossip, do the opposite."

She seemed to ponder that.

"I was thinking about starting a fund for the kids, to help them, you know? Maybe make some special desserts that go toward that fund or have a special tea where all the proceeds go to them? What do you think?"

I stood up from the stairs and turned toward her.

"I think that's a fabulous idea and the perfect way to help turn the attention away from the murderers and toward the children. Please let me know what I can do to help."

Sabrina stood with me and gave me a hug.

"All forgiven?"

I looked her straight in the face and caught the way her smile faltered as I didn't respond right away.

"Ever since I met you, you have been nothing but completely honest with me. You hold me to task when you think I'm retreating, you call me out when I give stupid excuses, and I love that I'm able to call you a friend. Just because we don't always agree on things, or because you buy books you knew I was bidding on, that doesn't diminish our friendship."

Her wobbly smile strengthened.

"I love you too." Sabrina drew her arm through mine. "You know, it's been forever since I've been by this place. It hasn't changed since your grandmother lived here. When I was a kid, I used to come here with the church choir during Christmas to sing carols. Your grandma would always have a plate of cookies ready for us at the door." Her smile was filled with memories, and it made me sad to remember I'd never spent a Christmas here as a child.

"I'm surprised we never met," she continued.

"We never really visited much when I was a child. I remember two different summers, coming for a week, but I grew up on the other side of the country, and my parents couldn't really afford the trip." I felt like I had to explain something that really wasn't any of her business.

She must have caught the note of irritation in my voice, because she turned her attention from me to the house, head tilted, nose scrunched.

I knew the house looked distressed, dilapidated, and derelict. But the roof didn't leak, it wasn't overrun with bugs or vermin, and given a little hard work, it'd be decent. Up until now, I'd just focused on the inside of the house.

"I could give you the name of a handyman, if you wanted," Sabrina offered, as I knew she would. It wasn't the first time she'd hinted I needed to do something with the place.

"I've still got those names you gave me before on my fridge," I said. I wasn't in a hurry, not yet. "Listen, how about if we meet up for dinner this week? I have a friend I've been meaning to introduce you to, and I'll see if she can join us."

Sabrina's face brightened.

"Oh, I know just the place. Have you eaten at the Top Hat yet? They opened a few months ago. They're reservation only, but I know the chef. I might be able to snag us a table."

"Let's try it."

Eventually I was alone again, with Sabrina headed back to her shop, and I thought about our conversation. Did I forgive her for her careless words and feelings? Of course. But I couldn't forget them. Not the judgment or the hatred in her voice for those who sought out help for their mental health issues.

I wasn't in the mood to dive deep into her words today. But eventually we would need to. Not everyone who sought counseling was dangerous, and that was basically what she'd said.

But I had to admit that some were. My thoughts immediately went to my patients. Savannah, Tyler, and Ella. Three very different people with very different issues. Ella had once been dangerous. Tyler could be dangerous. And Savannah was showing signs that worried me.

The notes I'd received so far said someone knew one of my patients was a murderer, and they blamed me for not stopping them. I realized this didn't have anything to do with Ella's parents; it had to do with someone who could be stopped now, in the present. That could only mean one thing.

They believed either Savannah, Tyler, or Ella was responsible for the recent murders in our town.

But which one?

Chapter Fifteen

MONDAY, AUGUST 12

PATIENT SESSION: TYLER

It took a bit of research, but I found a therapist I felt could help me. She was highly recommended and local. I made an appointment for Thursday, the one weekday I had no sessions, and I hoped I wouldn't regret it.

With the increased headaches and stress and the notes, I couldn't do it alone anymore. I would normally share my concerns with Tami, but considering the stress she was under, that wasn't a possibility.

I expected Tyler to show up within the next half hour. I spent some time tidying up the office, cleaning the living room, and doing other mundane things while I waited.

"Dr. Rycroft?" I heard my name called while I was in the kitchen making a fresh pot of coffee. It was supposed to get hot in the afternoon, and iced coffee seemed like the perfect beverage. Hopefully Tami would drop by that night. I was in the mood for a good gab session with her.

"I'll be right there, Tyler." I poured my coffee, added some creamer, and joined him in my office.

He paced the length of the room, from one wall to the other, hands fisted in his pants pockets, the vein in his cheek pulsing as he did so.

"Tyler, why don't you sit down?"

He plopped down on the couch and rested his forearms on his thighs.

"You seem agitated," I said. "What's going on?"

He threaded his fingers through his wild hair.

"I made a mistake."

I reached for my notebook. "What kind of mistake?"

His right leg bounced. "I know you said not to, but I followed her. I had to. She left me no choice." He ran his fingers through his hair again before he patted the mussed hair down. "I knew she'd be furious if she found out, but I decided the risk was worth it."

"When did you do this?"

"Last night." He groaned, and the bounce in his leg sped up to double time.

"What do you mean, she left you no choice?"

He jumped up and walked around my office again.

"She's not happy. When she's not happy, she makes hasty mistakes."

The idea of what kind of mistakes dangled before me. I wanted to ask but decided it might be better if I didn't, that perhaps he'd let more slip.

"Tyler, remember that her happiness isn't dependent on you."

"No." His head shook as he continued to walk back and forth. "It's my responsibility to keep her calm, to help her. If I don't, if I fail . . . it's not good. Trust me. Everyone ends up paying."

That was a line we couldn't seem to cross, his need to keep *her*, whoever *she* was, happy. He wasn't able to process that her happiness wasn't his responsibility, no matter how often we discussed the topic.

I needed to find another way to help him.

"Tyler, how about you sit down, and we will make a list of ways you could help her. Would that work?"

The sigh that escaped his lips deflated the stress he carried. His steps slowed, his breathing eased. The tilt of his shoulders relaxed, no longer pushed back with tension.

"A list, yes. Yes, that will work." He sat down again, this time crossing his legs.

I handed him a sheet of paper and a pen.

"Let's make the list together." That would keep him in one spot and help him feel more in control.

"What's one thing that would make her happy?" I asked.

"A child." There was no hesitation in his voice. "She wants to be a mother. We've tried—God knows we've tried. If I could find her a baby . . . I've done . . . I mean, I'd do anything, anything to make this happen. She will be an amazing mother, I know it." There was a softness to his features, and for a moment, I could see the love he carried for her as more than just a need. It was his everything.

But his word choice was weird. *Find her a baby?* He must have meant *give.*

"Have you talked to a doctor?"

"Not yet. She doesn't want to do that, not yet. She'd rather us find a child—the right child, who needs to be loved—than to have one of our own."

Adoption. That would be something we could focus on in the future.

I watched as he wrote, *Find her a child to love.* The wording was odd, but I wasn't about to micromanage his list.

He tapped the pen on his knee for several moments.

I didn't want to offer suggestions. He needed to find ideas on his own, to realize that there was little he could do to make her happy.

"I'm going to follow her again tonight." He clicked the pen over and over and over again.

"Why is it important for you to follow her?"

He licked his lips, then rubbed his nose. He couldn't seem to remain still.

"I need to know what's going on. I need to be ready, just in case. You don't understand—you can't."

No, I didn't understand. How could I, when he never fully told me the truth?

I set the pad on my lap down. We weren't going to get anywhere today until he was relaxed.

"Why don't you bring her in for your next session?" It wasn't the first time I'd suggested it.

"No, no. That . . . no. She wouldn't agree to that. Not yet."

"Why not?"

He cocked his head to the side, studied me. "She says you're not ready. Not yet, but soon."

I wasn't ready? What was I supposed to be prepared for?

"What does *soon* mean, Tyler? Next week? Next month? Does she expect you to reach a certain place in your sessions before she'll come in? What's the expectation here?" I couldn't contain the frustration from appearing. Whoever this woman was, she was more in control of Tyler's therapy than I was, and it was beginning to piss me off.

He blinked repeatedly, eyes squeezing tight as if in pain.

"You need to be patient. That's all I can say." His monotone voice and blank face had me snapping my fingers together. Not in his face, just to the side, to see if he paid attention.

"This isn't working," he said. He sounded off, and I didn't understand what had happened. He was hot and cold. Needing help one minute and pushing me away the next.

"What isn't working, Tyler?" I asked.

"This." He pointed to himself, then to me. "You're supposed to help me. Why aren't you? I'm supposed to be stronger, steadier, more in control. That's what you promised you'd do. Help me be better. I need to be stronger if she's going to stay with me, but I'm just as weak as I was before."

Blame. I wrote this down, the notepad held at an angle so he couldn't see it.

"I never promised anything, Tyler. Any progress you make is because of the work you complete. I can only offer suggestions. If you don't follow my advice, there's not much I can do."

The frown on his face grew.

"I'm sorry if you believe this isn't helping you." That was never my intention. Knowing he believed that only added to my own personal feeling of failure.

How could I help him? What work could we do, what could I suggest that I hadn't already suggested?

He popped to his feet.

"I need to go. She'll be home soon, and I need to be there. I promised her I would."

He headed to the door, put his hand on the knob, and hesitated.

"You are helping me, Dr. Rycroft. I'm sorry for what I said. I wouldn't have lasted this long with her if you weren't. You're doing a great job. Thank you."

Then he left, leaving me to sit there, confounded by his parting words.

What the hell had just happened?

~

An hour later, Tami dropped by.

"I can only stay for a few minutes. I need to grab a coffee before I head back to the station," she said as she walked in and dropped my mail on the table.

I eyed the stack. *Please, God, don't let there be another note.*

I poured her a glass of iced coffee, added ice and cream, and waited for her to take a sip.

"What have I done to deserve you?"

I smiled, thrilled that it met her standards. I'd followed a video I found online about a different process for making iced coffee.

"Listen, could I ask you a favor?" I hated to do this, but the more I thought about Tyler and his session today, the more uncomfortable I felt.

"Anything."

"Could you do a quick background check on one of my patients? Something seems off about him. I don't know much. He wouldn't give me his address, just a number to reach him and his name. I'm not sure what he does for a job either."

"Name and number should be enough. What kind of information do you need?"

I shrugged. Hell if I knew. I was hoping she'd have an idea.

"Is this Tyler? God yes, I'll check him out," she said at my nod. "I've never understood why you took him on as a client to begin with."

One night over wine, I'd mentioned Tyler to her. I shouldn't have and had always felt guilty for it, but now, not so much.

Chapter Sixteen

After waiting forty-five minutes for Ella to arrive, I gave up.

I'd hoped we could have picked up our conversation, why she felt responsible for the recent murders simply because of her past. I wasn't overly worried. She'd been a no-show in the past, but a phone call or a text would have been appreciated.

I finished my cup of tea, cleaned up the plate of almond biscotti I'd placed on the table for Ella, and looked at my couch with longing.

The idea of a nap tempted me. Last night I'd tossed and turned more than I should have. I'd even tried warm milk to see if that would help but gagged as I struggled to take a sip. Perhaps I'd take a walk to the local pharmacy and see if they had any herbal remedies for sleep. I remembered Sabrina once mentioning a tea she drank at night that helped her.

I didn't want to take anything that would knock me out. Just something to help me fall asleep. I'd finally reached the point of desperation and was willing to do whatever it took to help me sleep.

I grabbed my purse, locked the door behind me, and headed toward the pharmacy.

A figure across the street caught my attention.

A woman, my height, in a long summer dress, hair in a braid, walked opposite me. She looked a lot like Ella from the back.

"Ella," I called out, loudly enough for those around me to stare.

She didn't stop, look around, or even act as if she'd heard me. And yet I knew it was her.

Why would she be so close to my house and not come by for her session?

I called out her name again, louder this time, and jogged across the street when it cleared.

"Ella," I said again once I'd reached her.

She gasped and turned at the sound of my voice.

"Dr. Rycroft, you scared me." Her eyes were wide with fright.

"I called your name a few times. Everything okay?" I was shocked by her appearance as I took in her stained dress, oily hair, and dirt-crusted fingernails. "You missed our appointment this morning."

She blinked rapidly. She reminded me of someone who'd just woken up from a long, hard nap, disoriented and not quite focused.

"I did? But today's . . ." Her voice cracked as she looked around. "Today's Tuesday?"

I placed my hand on the small of her back and led her to a park bench just up ahead.

A couple of teenagers sat there, smacking gum and sharing headphones.

"Sorry, guys, would you mind if we sat here? My friend isn't feeling too well."

"It's okay, Dr. Rycroft, we can find another bench. I'm okay." Ella stared at the pavement, her cheeks bright red.

All the other benches were occupied by older couples or mothers with small children. I honestly didn't think the teens would mind giving up their seat.

Apparently, I was wrong. The looks on their faces were incredulous. They glanced at each other, then to me, and snickered before getting up.

"Yeah, sure. Whatever," one muttered.

"Crazy lady," the other said over her shoulder as they walked away.

"Excuse me?" *What the hell?*

"It's okay," Ella mumbled. "It's okay." She reached for my arm, stopping me from following the teens and asking what their problem was.

"I'm sorry, Ella. That was uncalled for." I was part horrified and part embarrassed that she would be treated that way in public.

"It's not the first. Won't be the last." She glanced down at her dress. "God, I'm a mess. I look like I'm homeless or just came back from an all-night binge."

"Did you?" I'd never seen her look quite like this before.

She shook her head while she attempted to scrub at a stain on her hem.

"Where were you this morning, Ella?"

"I don't know."

"I'm sorry?" I leaned my head closer to her.

"I don't know where I was. I . . ." She wrinkled her nose before she cleared her throat. "Maybe I was gardening or . . ." Her voice trailed off as she looked around, her eyes searching for a visual to spark her memory.

An odd odor drifted my way.

"Oh God, and I smell too." Ella jumped up from the bench and pulled her arms tight across her chest.

"Listen, come with me to the house. I have some spare clothes, and you can wash up. Then together we'll see if we can figure out where you were, okay?"

We took our time as we walked back to the house. I chattered about nothing and everything just to keep her mind off where she'd been, why she looked the way she did, and her memory loss of it all.

I ignored the funny looks pointed our way or how people moved away from us as we walked past. I ignored everything but Ella.

At home, we bypassed the office, and I led her to my bathroom. I loaned her a summer dress I rarely wore and waited while she washed up.

When she asked if we could drink our sweet tea out on the porch, I didn't think anything of it. Today was all about helping Ella in any way possible.

"How are you feeling?" I asked after we'd settled in.

Rather than respond, Ella watched a bumblebee meander its way among my flowerpots.

I didn't press. Instead, I closed my eyes for a brief moment and let the sounds of summer soak in, from the gentle sway of the leaves as a warm breeze blew through to the distant sounds of children's laughter from the playground in the park across the street.

"I think I was dumpster diving," Ella eventually said. Her voice carried a note of surprise and laughter to it. Something I didn't expect at all.

"Dumpster diving, eh? Did you find anything?" I opened my eyes and was going to smile, but she wasn't looking at me. Instead, she looked down at her fingernails.

"I used to do that with my dad," she said. "Except we would drive down old farm roads and see what sort of things people would leave at the ends of their driveways. That's how we got our first couch. Dad noticed an older man lifting it out of his truck to put on the side of the road, so he pulled over and took it. Even gave him money for it, although the man didn't want any."

I could picture it in my mind because I'd done my fair share of picking throughout the years.

"We used to do that when I was a child too," I shared. "But we would drive through towns, and my dad would find busted-up lawn mowers, radios, and lamps and fix them up, give them a new coat of paint or a good cleaning, and then sell them."

The smile on Ella's face was full of nostalgia. "I don't have a lot of good memories from my childhood, but that is one I'll never forget."

"Sometimes all we need are a few good ones."

"I prefer to pretend there aren't any memories at all. It's easier that way." She played with the moisture drops on her glass before she took a sip of her sweet tea.

"Why's that?" I was glad we were talking about her past.

"It's like I can't stop there, you know? I can't just stop at the good memories. I have to push through them and get to the bad ones. Maybe it's to justify what I did. I don't know." Her head dropped so her now-loose hair hung past her face, making it difficult to see her emotions.

But I heard them.

"Ella, it's been a while since we've talked about this, but have you ever forgiven your parents for what they did? Or for what they didn't do?" I wished I had my notebook with me.

She shook her head, her long hair brushing against her legs.

"If I forgive them, then I have to forgive myself, and I can't do that."

"Why not?"

"Because I don't deserve it. Once a killer, always a killer. That sort of forgiveness, it only happens in the Bible or in fairy tales. Not real life."

It made me sad to hear that from her. To know that was her life, with that cloud of reality hanging over her day in and day out. No matter what she did to redeem herself, no matter how much work we did in therapy, she would always be seen as that.

A killer.

I didn't want to think it, but her words lingered. *Once a killer, always a killer.* Was it possible she hadn't changed?

Chapter Seventeen

PATIENT SESSION: SAVANNAH

Tomorrow I'd be the one sitting on the therapy couch, voicing tough thoughts and worries. Today it was Savannah's turn.

The last time Savannah had sat on my couch, she'd admitted she wanted her parents dead.

Her mother had arrived just afterward, stopping me from pursuing the conversation any further.

Nothing Savannah had ever told me shocked me as much as those words.

"Can we talk about what you said before you left?" I stared at the file in my hand, my eyes reading the words over and over and over again. My stomach knotted as I struggled to look beyond what she'd said and see the fear and pain inside the teenager on my couch.

"That I want my parents dead? What about it?" The challenge was clear, and for the first time, I had a feeling I was going to lose whatever battle we were about to have.

It didn't surprise me that she remembered our discussion.

"I don't believe you really want them to die."

"You don't get to tell me what I believe." If her tongue were a knife, she'd have sliced me in half.

"True, I don't. But I do get to call you out when I feel you're not being honest with yourself."

Her facial expression said, *Go to hell.*

"Tell me I'm wrong." I had just sacrificed a pawn in our mental game of chess.

"You're wrong." Her chin lifted as if daring me to betray the mortification I felt.

I blinked once. Twice. Three times before I found my words.

"You're jealous of the kids whose parents are being murdered because they're now orphans. I believe that's what you said to me, wasn't it?" Despite everything in me, I lowered my chin and relaxed my shoulders, the complete opposite of Savannah's body response.

I had her on guard now. She wasn't sure how this would play out, so she did the one thing she loved to do most.

She shrugged.

"I guess I'm a horrible person?"

I yawned.

She frowned.

I would have smiled at her reaction to my forced display if not for how serious the situation was.

Did I really think she wanted her parents dead? No. But when it came to Savannah, I knew to never get comfortable in my assumptions.

"So what if I want my parents dead. Isn't that normal for most teenagers?"

"Normal? Not really. Most teenagers can't wait to move away. But they don't generally wish for death."

She rolled her eyes like the seventeen-year-old she was.

"I'm not normal. Sue me."

Savannah had come to me as a troubled teenager who fantasized about a better life. There had been times her parents were afraid of her.

I admit I'd had those times too. I'd noticed a darkness inside Savannah that could be dangerous.

In the past, her accusations of abuse, neglect, and the hatred she believed was directed toward her were delusions of her own making. After we'd gotten her on medication, those delusions weren't as rampant. Or so I'd thought.

Savannah was smart. She knew how to play those around her. In the beginning, she'd played me to perfection until I'd caught on to her delusions. Now her parents voluntarily took drug tests and had someone enter their home for random checks. A lot of parents I knew wouldn't have gone to these extremes.

"You have less than a year until you're done with school, Savannah. This is only temporary."

"So I should put up with the abuse because it's only temporary? That's kind of a screwed-up way of thinking, isn't it?" She leaned back against the couch, a satisfied grin on her face.

"Savannah." I wasn't going to play this game with her. A war of words was not worth fighting during our sessions.

"Fine. Whatever." She played with a twist of hair, twirling it in her fingers until it was a tight curl. "I've spent a lot of time at the library, in case you're interested. I've read every article I could find online and in the papers about the recent murders. I am probably the only one who knows why they're only killing parents and leaving the children behind." Her words tumbled out, her excitement building the more she spoke. I looked directly into her eyes and didn't like the spark of fire I saw.

Playing with fire was dangerous. All it took was one small flame, one puff of wind against a burning ember, and the flare of heat would take on a life of its own.

Stoking the fire of obsession with someone who lived with delusions was like adding fuel to that flame. If I wasn't careful, I'd be the proverbial moth, getting sucked into the vortex of her delusional obsession.

"You should be happy that I'm focusing on something other than myself," she taunted.

"By researching serial killers?"

Again with the shrug.

"I don't see the connection, sorry."

"Why can't I be happy for once in my life? Nothing I do is good enough for my parents. They don't love me like they should. They *focus*"—she spat the word—"on themselves all the time. So why can't I?"

Focus. I wrote the word down and underlined it a few times.

"There's nothing wrong with placing yourself first or focusing on your happiness." This was something we'd discussed in the past. "I just don't see how you focusing on research is a sign you're placing yourself first. But since you brought it up, I think we could work on healthier options, don't you?"

"As long as they are alive, I will never be healthy." She stared at me while her hands fisted at her sides, daring me to contradict her.

"So they need to be dead for you to be happy?" I clarified.

"And free."

"So only when they are dead will you be happy and free?"

Her eyes rolled. "That's what I said."

"I just wanted to make sure I heard you properly. Do you have a plan on making this happen?" If I believed for one second she would intentionally harm her parents, I would contact the authorities. On a scale from one to one hundred, I placed the chance that she would at twenty-five. Which, considering her history, was pretty good.

She didn't respond.

"Savannah." I placed my notepad facedown on the table. "Do you have a plan? Remember, this is a safe place for you."

Now I started to worry.

She leaned back hard against the couch, her shoulders pushing against the fabric, adding as much distance between us as she could.

"Like I'd tell you." She mocked my words. "You don't even believe me when I tell you how bad the abuse is."

Were her parents abusive? No. She was right about that. What I did believe was her conviction in how bad her life was. So I listened, and I tried to help her create a life she could handle.

"It's easy to focus on the negative and never see the positive. That's what we're trying to do here, to help you see the positive aspects of your life."

"Whatever," she mumbled like a small child as she sipped her tea. "Tell me the truth, though. Don't you find the mind of a serial killer fascinating?"

"Fascinating? I'm not sure that's a word I would use. *Complex* would fit better."

"Complex. You're right. It would be like a puzzle almost. Right? Do you think this is nature versus nurture or . . ." Her voice trailed off, and I wasn't sure if she was egging me on or not.

I decided to give in, to play the game with her.

"The idea of nature versus nurture has always fascinated me," I admitted. Were people born with *bad* genes, or were these characteristics developed? Could a person change their predisposition, or was fate just an ill-treated spouse in this journey called life?

"Life is about choices, Savannah. It's what we do with those choices that define us."

"But those choices, is it destiny that leads us, or is there really free will? Take God, for example." That spark of fire was back. "Daddy dearest says God is all knowing and all powerful. If that were true, then how could there be free will if he knows the choices we're going to make ahead of time?"

How God had come into the discussion I wasn't sure, but I wasn't surprised either. Savannah liked to jump topics just for a reaction.

"What do you think?"

"I think my father is full of shit."

I let that sit between us for a second longer than necessary.

"It's possible," I said. "But why?"

"All he does is spout religious nonsense about the love of God and other crap. Words mean nothing. He doesn't live what he believes, so why should I believe what he says?"

And there, in her voice, was the petulant teenager who only wanted the love of her father but was too afraid to admit it.

"Parents will always disappoint, Savannah. They're not perfect."

"What does that have to do with anything?" She pulled her gaze from mine before standing. "I know they aren't perfect." She pushed the window curtain to the side and looked out. "I tell you that every time I come in." She traced something on the glass, leaving a slight smear from the oil on her fingers. I couldn't make out what she drew. "They sure as hell aren't bloody angels in disguise."

The imagery of her words flashed in my mind. A beautiful, grotesque angel, wings flared out, every feather dipped in blood.

I shuddered. The sight of blood transferred from the angel in my mind to the angel standing at the window. The sun created a halo around her head through the window, the glow casting a red haze along her skin. She flashed me an I-know-I'm-evil type of smile, and I swallowed.

Hard.

That number on the scale, of whether I was worried or not, jumped higher. I'd place her at a forty or forty-five.

"What—" I cleared my throat. "What are your plans for the day?" I picked up my notepad from the table.

"My plans?" She turned around, the questioning look on her face telling me she had no idea where I was going with this.

"Your plans. After you leave here, what will you do? Do you want to discuss methods and strategies to . . ." I dropped my voice, not finishing the words, hoping she would fill in the blanks.

"I'm going to the library." Her chin dipped to her chest. "I'm going to research murderers, to get a look into their mind-set, to figure out what makes them tick. What makes them able to do what they do."

While I was thrilled she was headed to the library for research, her choice in subjects was less than ideal.

"Do you think this would be an area of study you'd like to pursue at college?" I wasn't that naive, but hopefully I was planting a seed and perhaps changing the direction she was headed.

She shrugged.

"Savannah. I allow three shrugs per session. You know this." She'd used up her quota. "Words, please."

Her eyes rolled wider than a Ferris wheel at an amusement park.

"Fine. Maybe. Who knows?" She came to sit back down on the couch. "I thought you'd be happy that I was learning something."

Happy wasn't the word I would have used.

"I would prefer a healthier focus."

Her eyes rolled. Again. "Like what? Self-awareness? Research is good."

Interesting choice of words. *Research*. For what?

"My uncle is coming to town."

Her uncle?

"My parents need a vacation, apparently. A time-out to focus on themselves and get away from the stress called *parenting*."

To say I was surprised wouldn't be accurate. More like shocked. Normally her parents discussed trips with me so we could plan accordingly. While they were away, Savannah came in daily. But they hadn't said a word.

Nor had they told me about an uncle or his arrival.

"Your uncle is staying with you, I take it?"

A smile played with her lips, a smile I knew she struggled to contain.

"I've mentioned him before, right? He tends to come around every couple of years. He's a consultant for some big company. Every time he visits, my parents jump at the opportunity to leave."

I wrote this information down along with a note to follow up with Savannah's mom.

"But anyway. Wouldn't you like to get into the mind of a killer and find out all the questions no one ever asks?"

I wanted to say yes, that I was intrigued, more than I wanted to admit, but that wasn't something this seventeen-year-old needed to know.

"It seems you do, since you continually bring our discussion back to this. Let me ask you, what questions would those be?" I asked instead.

She thought for a minute, her index finger tapping against her bottom lip while her eyes scanned my room, not really seeing anything.

"Savannah," I interrupted her. "You mentioned you had a theory about the recent murders. Did you want to share that?"

She sat up straighter, her chin tilted up, and her lips widened into a smile full of . . . unspoken secrets. It unnerved me.

"The killer is practicing."

"Practicing for what?" That wasn't what I'd expected her to say.

"My hypothesis," she said, her face shining as if she were laughing inside, "is that they hate their own parents and are practicing until they have enough nerve to kill their own. They're targeting other parents who don't deserve to be parents for now."

I didn't mean to sigh as heavily as I did.

"What? What's wrong with my theory?" She sounded wounded, hurt even, that I didn't call her brilliant.

"It's a theory, and like all theories, there's nothing wrong with it. But I wonder if maybe there's more to it than that."

"Why assume there's more to it than there is? They hate their parents and want them dead. Better make sure you can do it on the first try than have it go haywire and you end up in the loony bin or prison."

The way she said this, it was as if she were speaking to herself, reminding herself of something.

I didn't like it.

"Savannah, if you want to study psychology, why don't I recommend some case files you could look up at the library? Those might give you a better sense rather than reading autobiographies of serial killers."

She lifted her arms in a stretch and stood up.

"Why?" she asked as she bent over, her face almost hitting her knees. "This has me interested. Remember those questions I'd want to ask? I've already thought of them. I'd want to know what their first killer-instinct memory was. When did it start? Is it like they say, with torturing cats or mocking those with handicaps? Were they always evil, even as a small child, or were they good, even for a short time? Are babies evil? Can they be? That kind of stuff."

"Hmm." Not a really a word, more like a sound, but she heard what I didn't say.

"Maybe I should take psychology and study the best." Her smile was full of sarcasm, the kind that meant *I'm not as dumb as you think.*

No, she certainly wasn't dumb.

"Have you asked yourself those same questions?" She sat back down on the couch, her legs folded beneath her. "Do you remember what you were like as a small child?" I asked. "Do you remember your first temper tantrum? Were you difficult as a child?" The questions came before I could stop myself. I didn't even think about what I was saying or how she would take it.

The question was meant in general terms; a regular person wouldn't be able to remember what life was like as a baby or toddler. Of course I didn't believe her capable of murder.

Right?

"Why? Do you think I have killer tendencies, Dr. Rycroft?" Her eyes lit up with a black glimmer.

An icy shiver burned a trail down my arms at her expression.

The timer beeped, breaking the spell.

"Time's up, Doc."

And then she was gone.

Chapter Eighteen

MEMORY

I'm cold. Hungry. Scared.

I wrap my arms around myself. I'm shivering, but I continue forward. One step at a time away from them.

All I want is to get away from them.

I'm grounded because Mom came home in a bad mood and Dad's still away.

He left last week for work and will be away for another week.

Running away from home when you live out in the country sucks.

There's nothing for miles other than stinky cows, and the wind rips right through the fields.

I should have worn a thicker sweater, but everything is dirty, and this was the only coat in my closet.

A low rumble comes from behind followed by a long blast of the horn. Seriously?

I don't turn. Don't acknowledge the fact that he's there behind me.

I walk down the middle of the road, one foot in front of the other.

How close will he get? Will I feel the heat of the truck behind me or even a bump against my legs? He won't dare get that close, right?

Nope. He's a chicken. Instead, he pulls up beside me, window down, and flicks his cigarette my way.

"I'm heading into town," he says. "Want to come?"

I keep walking, my face forward and away from him so he won't catch my surprise.

He's taking me into town instead of home?

Does my mom know I left?

"Come on, Firefly, get in the truck. We'll get some ice cream and drive around town with the windows down and music blaring. We'll go all redneck. What do you say?" He bangs the side of his door twice before he stops the truck.

I keep walking but turn around, being careful as I walk backward.

"Why do you call me Firefly?" I've always wanted to know.

"Get in the truck, and I'll tell you." That wink of his brings a smile to my face. No doubt he knew it would.

"Fine." I swipe the smile off the moment he laughs.

"Does Mom know?" I ask once I've climbed up and closed the door.

"You kidding me? Your mother would be flipping her lid if she knew you took off." He goes to put the truck in drive but stops.

"You want to take the wheel?"

"What? I can't drive! I'm not old enough. Besides"—I kick my feet up—"I wouldn't even be able to reach the pedals." I eye the distance between my foot and where his feet are and know I'm not tall enough.

When he pushes his seat back and pats the space between his legs, there's a flutter in my stomach, like a pair of june bugs caught beneath a jar, trying to escape.

"Come on, you know you want to. We'll just go to the stop sign, okay?"

"Mom will kill you and me if she finds out." I scoot across the seat, climb over, and sit between his legs. It feels a little uncomfortable, but when he takes my hands and guides them on the wheel, I forget about everything else and just have fun.

I'm driving! It's slow, and I jerk us all over the road until I realize you don't have to move your hands much on the wheel to steer straight.

He's laughing, I'm laughing, and it's the best thing that's ever happened to me.

Like he promised, I only drive the truck to the stop sign.

"That was awesome." I can't keep the grin off my face. "We can't tell Mom, though."

"Oh God no. You know how much trouble we'd both be in?"

Uncle always knows how to make me laugh, which is good, because Mom only knows how to make me angry.

"This'll be our little secret," he says.

"One of many." I hold up my pinkie, and we swear on it.

I look out the window at the farms we pass and think about the years I still have before I can escape all this. I'm young, but I know I'm meant for more than life on a farm.

"So why Firefly?" Watching the fields and barns and houses makes me dizzy, so I turn from the window and look at him, waiting for his promised answer.

"Ever since you were little, you were the only bright thing in my life. I can't wait till you grow up and fly away because I know you're destined for more than what all this"—he waves his hand—"has to offer. There's a fire burning deep inside you no one can snuff out. All I've ever wanted was to be close to that fire and help keep the flames burning." He looks at me like Dad used to look at Mom, and the june bugs in my stomach go wild.

I don't know what to say.

He reaches over and grabs my hand, holding it tight in his.

When I think about my family, Uncle is the one I know will always be here. He has been since I was five years old when he came to stay with us. Dad only leaves. He took a job with a trucking company to bring in more money so Mom wouldn't have to work so much, but he's never home, and we never have money.

That's what Mom says, anyway, when she thinks I'm not listening.

"What do you think, Firefly? You okay with me helping to fan that flame of yours?" He lets go of my hand and squeezes my thigh.

"You're the only one who seems to care." I pull up my legs onto the seat and cross them. His hand slides from the top of my thigh to the inside and stays there.

"I love you and always will."

I know Dad doesn't like Uncle being around so much.

He says it's unnatural the way Uncle dotes on me, that it's not healthy.

I know Mom doesn't think anything of it.

She says it's perfectly natural to be as close as Uncle and I are.

No one ever asks me what I think. Maybe it's because they don't think I'm mature enough to have my own opinions.

No one understands what's between Uncle and me. He's my real family. Real family loves one another without limits. Real family accepts one another and doesn't abandon them.

Real family puts their children ahead of their own needs.

At school we were asked to write down the one thing we love most about our family. It took me a long time to think about what I loved most until I realized I had Uncle, who made me laugh and made me believe I was important to him. So that's what I put down.

Uncle gave up his life and moved in with us all to watch me while Mom worked. He gave up his job, his friends, and being single to take care of a five-year-old niece.

My dad found a job that kept him away from home for weeks at a time.

My mom works long hours, comes home exhausted, yells or cries all the time, and rarely wants to be with me.

That's not love.

When I grow up and have a family, I will put my children first all the time. I will sacrifice whatever I need to in order for them to know I love them. I will be a better mom to my children than the mom I have.

We make it to town and grab sundaes.

"Want to tell me why you left?" Uncle asks just as I fill my mouth with ice cream.

I don't even have to think about my answer.

"I hate her sometimes, you know? She thinks life is so hard for her, but she never thinks about how her hard life affects me. Do you think it's fun for me to always try to keep her happy?" I stuff another spoonful into my mouth.

Uncle taps his spoon against mine.

"She's not your responsibility, Firefly. You need to stop thinking you have to take care of her."

"Yeah, like that's going to work." I stir my hot fudge into my ice cream. "She grounded me because of exactly that."

I was watching television when she came home after staying at work late to train a new employee. Like that was my fault. Apparently not having dinner for her or having the table set or being selfish and just sitting on the couch was my fault, though. I was ungrateful and only thought of myself and never considered how she felt.

I told her that maybe it was time she started to act like an adult and a mother rather than expecting me to do it for her.

That had earned me a slap across my cheek and then being grounded for a week.

Like what was that going to do? I don't have a life as it is. I live out in the country, for Pete's sake.

"Firefly, I'm here. I'm here for you, and I'm here to help your mom. She's not a strong woman emotionally. Never has been, not even when we were kids. I always had to take care of her. Did you know that? Our parents were . . . busy, just like yours, so it was up to me to make sure your mom was fed and had a bath and was tucked into bed most nights."

That makes me sad. Not for my mom but for him.

"Who takes care of you?"

He shrugs. "Maybe one day I'll find someone who loves me enough to take care of me. Until then . . . "

Now I feel really bad.

I lean my head on his shoulder and put my arm through his.

"Until then," I say, looking up at him with a big smile, "you've got me."

He leans down and kisses my forehead.

He loves me more than my own parents do.

By the time we make it back home, Mom's asleep.

If she noticed I wasn't in my room when she went to bed, she obviously didn't care.

Maybe she didn't even check, though. She had, after all, grounded me.

If it weren't for Uncle noticing I was gone, no one would have missed me until the morning.

At least he loves me enough to miss me.

Chapter Nineteen

At Dr. Brown's office, I wondered if I'd made a mistake in coming.

What if I was wrong? What if I was overreacting? What if everything that had happened wasn't as bad as I'd made it out to be?

I'd never felt more unsure of myself and my instincts as I did then.

I stared at the black-and-white chalkboard sign on the bookshelf opposite of where I sat.

TAKE A DEEP BREATH AND COUNT TO THREE.

Good advice.

But no matter how deeply I breathed or how high I counted, my hands wouldn't stop shaking.

I snuck them both beneath my thighs, wiping them first on my pants, my nose wrinkled in disgust at the damp marks left behind.

Get a grip, Danielle. I shouldn't have been this nervous, but it had been a while since I'd been on this side of the office, so maybe it wasn't a surprise.

Dr. Brown, my new therapist, clutched a notebook tightly to her chest and spoke in a low voice to someone on the other side of the door.

I pretended she was just like me. Warm, caring, encouraging, and nonjudgmental.

"Is everything okay, Danielle?" Her soft-pitched voice didn't match the crusty exterior she presented, and it surprised me. She was an older woman, her hair streaked gray, her outfit polished, heels low and black. My research told me she was one of the most respected therapists in the area, which was exactly what I needed.

"Your office is nice. Have you been here long? You could add some color to the room, maybe add some pictures on the wall or a potted plant or two?" I babbled like a toddler, the words pouring out like a broken gumball machine.

Shit. Shit. Shit.

She wouldn't see me as a strong and steady professional like her if I acted like a newbie.

"This office is new. We used to be over on Palace Lane, across town, but the building is old, and a bunch of water pipes burst last month, so here we are for now. I really haven't had time to decorate." She looked around, as if noticing how utilitarian everything was for the first time. "A few plants and maybe some newer cushions would soften things, now that you mention it."

My shoulders relaxed some, and the tension eased. A little.

There was a knock on the door, and it opened.

She took the two offered cups from the person beyond the door. I appreciated the gesture, took the cup full of tea, and held it tightly between my clammy fingers.

I raised the cup and let the liquid coat my upper lip. The tea wasn't hot, more like tepid, but it would do.

The past week I'd been frozen into a block of ice, a chill seeping through my bones, and nothing I did warmed me.

"Have you tried the Mad Hatter's Tea House?" I asked. I tried to pretend I wasn't as nervous as I looked. "I know the owner, and if you have a favorite blend, she will see if she can order it in for you."

Dr. Brown's eyes lit up. "That's where I got this," she said. "I love that shop, with all the books and home decor, not to mention her homemade scones."

We smiled together, both happy at the connection we'd made. The vise around my chest released, and the trepidation I'd felt when I sat down was mostly gone.

When I looked at her now, there was an instant trust. I could share my fears, my worries, and she'd not only listen, but she'd help. "How are you feeling, Danielle?"

I bit the corner of my lip as I thought about how to reply.

The first few moments were essential—they provided the foundation of our sessions to come. They showcased more than most patients realized.

I wished I were just a regular patient right about now.

"Do you rate emotions by numbers, colors, or . . ." I knew there were more methods used, but for the life of me, I couldn't think of a single one.

She shook her head.

"Stop. This is a safe place. You're flustered and extremely self-conscious—I get it. Try to relax." She rested back in her chair, hands folded in her lap, and smiled like a cat about to pounce. "Let go of all those thoughts and questions clogging your mind. We're just two women having a conversation. Sound good?"

My right brow buried itself beneath my unruly bangs in surprise.

She laughed a little. It was a soft sound, not one full of judgment but rather understanding.

"I know," she said. "Two women having a conversation in a therapy room. Not quite the way most people start their relationships, but . . . you're here because you need someone to trust, someone to share something with, and I'm honored you chose me to talk to."

Honored? I pasted the sweetest smile I could stomach on my face and nodded. I was here because I'd made a mistake, because I was in over my head with a patient and was desperate to be told I wasn't overreacting.

"So, how are you feeling, Danielle?"

I swallowed the stress ball full of sharp rocks in my throat and said the first thing that came to mind.

"I've a bit of a headache, to be honest. Feeling a little unsettled and . . ." I searched the room as if the word were hidden behind an invisible book. "Uncomfortable."

She wrote this down. "I'm sorry about the headache. Do you get them often?"

I shrugged. Daily. Constantly. My head always felt like it was about to explode, but when you said things like that, people tended to produce weird looks.

"Enough. I take Tylenol, which helps dull it."

"Have you tried any alternative methods instead of pain medications? Yoga, massages, meditation, oils?"

I reached for the small gold cross around my neck and rubbed, the slight etching around the sides grounding me.

"I've tried it all, but nothing seems to work. I think it's stress." The corner of my lip lifted as I stared at the ground. "But that's why I'm here."

Normal people might have no issues admitting when they're stressed.

I wasn't normal.

I was a trained therapist who should have been able to handle stress. I knew all the classic signs, I knew all about boundaries and ways to alleviate stress, and yet . . . here I was.

I knew what to do, but for the life of me, I couldn't grasp on to it long enough for anything to work. I was the mouse riding a crocodile crossing a flooded river, and I was about to drown as the creature dragged me beneath the swirling waters.

"Stress is normal, Danielle. Even the best of us"—she paused, swallowing hard—"get bogged down by it. I'm sorry you have a headache today. We'll try to keep our session as light as we can, okay? Is there anything I can do to help before we begin? Would you like the window open? More tea?"

I ran my fingers along the base of my neck, pressing hard into the tissue, hoping for one second of relief from the pressure that continued to build the longer I sat there.

"I'm good, but thank you."

There was a buildup of silence between us. She reached for a file, I assumed mine, and flipped through a few pages.

My heart raced, and beads of sweat formed on my forehead. My nostrils flared as I tried to keep my breathing shallow, but the pit of snakes in my stomach made me queasy.

"Let me start off by saying I know exactly how you're feeling today." Dr. Brown smiled as she closed the file and set it down. "I've had my fair share of time being on a couch, having to trust a complete stranger with information I'm too ashamed to admit. This is a safe place, Danielle." She leaned forward, clasped her hands together, and rested them on her knees. "There's nothing wrong with admitting we need help. You know that, I know that, and yet, as therapists, we seem to believe we're Wonder Woman and can take on the world without needing someone to support us in the background."

"You've . . ."

She nodded.

That caught me off guard. Of course she would have her own therapist, which made sense. Didn't it? Why wouldn't she?

That helped. A little. I could breathe easier now.

"Does it ever get better?" I asked. "I mean, it does, it has to, but how do you get past the feeling of not being enough?"

Dr. Brown looked me straight in the eye.

It was a little uncomfortable.

"Not being enough for your patients, you mean?" Dr. Brown clarified.

I nodded.

"Can I be honest with you, Danielle?" She crossed her legs and tapped her pen against my file sitting on her lap. "You'll never be able to meet all their needs, and if that's your goal, you'll always feel like you're failing." She tented her fingers together. "That's a hard lesson I had to learn, and there are still times I feel like a failure."

"Feeling like a failure and knowing you are one is a big difference," I said as the response of wanting to hide, to curl in a ball and ignore the rest of the world, nudged me, demanding attention.

"You haven't failed." She smiled with a confidence I didn't feel, and I wanted to grasp hold of it and call it mine. But I couldn't.

"I don't just feel like I've failed—I know I have." Memories assailed me, taunted me, forced me to question every step I'd taken, every decision I'd made since all of this began.

"Tell me why. Tell me how I can help." Dr. Brown's voice was like a mother's caress over a child's long and tangled hair.

"Why?" Here was the crux of it all, why I was there. I looked up at her, my eyes smarting with tears I wasn't ready to shed. "I'm the worst therapist ever." The words scraped against my throat, rubbing it raw.

Emotions I didn't want to accept rose so quickly it shook me.

"Why do you feel that way, Danielle?" Her words were a lifeline, granting me freedom and providing a sense of security to admit everything I've tried to ignore.

My shame. My fear. My failure.

"I think . . ." It was hard for me to admit this, even though I had practiced. But it was time to tell someone else. "I think one of my patients is a serial killer. I just don't know which one."

Chapter Twenty

The memory of my first session with Dr. Brown wouldn't leave me.

When I'd told her about the notes and my fear that one of my patients was the serial killer, I'd felt a mixture of both shame and freedom.

It had hurt speaking those words out loud.

I'd betrayed them. Betrayed their trust. Betrayed their secrets. But it was betray them or myself. If I didn't help myself by getting the help I needed to talk things through, I wouldn't be any good to them.

I had the worst sleep last night. It felt like I'd barely slept a wink. By the time one in the morning rolled around, I'd tried everything to quiet my mind—a long walk, listening to an audiobook, drinking a full pot of the chamomile tea I'd picked up, and even a hot bath.

Knowing Ella needed me alert, I'd done everything I could think of to keep myself awake this morning. I went for a run and drank several cups of coffee, hoping to induce a little bit of energy so I wouldn't fall asleep on her when she arrived.

I had a little more than an hour before Ella's session, but I had something I needed to do first.

I opened the door to the Mad Hatter's Tea House and walked into a full café. The room bustled with noise: spoons clinking against teacups, laughter, and the dull slam of the swinging door from the kitchen to the dining area. Sabrina was probably too busy, and now wasn't the time to interrupt.

When I went to leave, my name was called out over the dull roar in the room.

"Danielle, over here."

I found Sabrina over in her gift section.

"I was just thinking about you," she said as she gave me a hug. "You missed our date this morning." She *tsk*ed, her finger wagging in mock anger.

Wide-eyed, I pulled my phone from my purse. How had I forgotten?

"Are you okay?" She pulled me to the side. "I hate to say it, but you look horrid. Those dark circles beneath your eyes tell me you're not sleeping, are you?"

She turned her back and opened one of her loose-tea containers. "Here, I want you to drink this an hour before bed. It'll help calm your mind so you can fall asleep." She filled a bag and handed it to me. "First bag is on the house."

How did she know that was what I was there for?

"I'm sorry about this morning. I totally forgot and didn't set a reminder on my phone."

She waved away my apology. "Don't think twice about it. I had a call-in reservation for a book club, so I spent the time preparing pastries, as you can see." She waved her hand toward the full dining area. "Besides, I figured you probably slept in."

"If that's what you want to call it," I mumbled behind my hand as I covered a yawn. "I had one of those nights where it feels like I didn't sleep a bit, and yet I know I did."

"Those are the worst. That happens to me when I have too much on the go. Your brain must be going a mile a minute. What has you so stressed?"

I placed my hand on her arm and squeezed. "I'm not sure *stressed* is the word for it. There just seems to be a lot going on, you know?" I looked around the dining area. "I've never been part of a book club. Have you?"

"Once, a few years ago. But I hated all the selections, and they never liked mine. I planned to find another one that would be a good fit but never got around to it."

"You should start your own." I was actually surprised she hadn't. Sabrina seemed to have her hand in everything when it came to Cheshire.

Her eyes lit up. "You know, that might be a good idea. Want to join?"

"Unless you're willing to just read the classics or psychology books, I'll have to pass," I said. "But I can help spread the word for you, if you'd like. Make up a flyer and post it in the library and such."

Sabrina laughed. "Like I have time to start a book club right now. I'm up to my eyeballs in reservations and parties and starting that fundraiser for the children we discussed."

With that, we stood there in a somewhat awkward silence, both twiddling our thumbs as we struggled to bring the conversation back to something lighter.

"How about we do coffee tomorrow morning instead? Come by as I open shop. That way we know it'll be quiet. Oh, and I haven't forgotten about getting reservations for dinner so I can meet that friend of yours. Why don't you bring her to coffee tomorrow instead?"

One of her servers came up and pulled her aside. I waved goodbye and headed back toward the house. I grabbed a latte, stopped to talk to a few women about a cute tea display in a home decor shop, and then made it in time for Ella's appointment.

I sent Tami a text, telling her about the coffee date for tomorrow.

Fifteen minutes past Ella's scheduled time, I began to suspect she wasn't going to show.

We still hadn't discussed the confession she'd made last week. I'd meant to bring it up on Tuesday, but she'd missed that appointment, and when I'd found her on the street, it had been clear that discussing the murders was the last thing on her mind.

I worried about her. What I'd seen on Tuesday wasn't normal for Ella. I'd never seen her like that, so lost, so unlike herself.

My fear was that the recent murders were too much for her.

Regardless of what she'd said last week, I refused to believe she was responsible. Yes, she had killed, but that was her past. Not her present.

Thirty minutes passed before I went to sit on my front steps.

Forty-five minutes had gone by when I accepted that she wasn't coming.

I dialed her number, and after three rings, the call went right to voice mail.

"Ella, this is Dr. Rycroft. Please call me back to reschedule your missed session today. I think with everything that is going on, it's important that we meet."

All I could think of was her fear of the repercussions when people found out about her past. Was she upset? Scared? She had to be.

It was time she stopped running, and I could help her with that if she'd just let me.

Why was I left with the feeling I was already too late for that?

Chapter Twenty-One

FRIDAY, AUGUST 16

KILLER

There's silence in this room full of old tomes and contemporary fiction. The silence is heavy as a thunderstorm yet lighter than a breath. It carries more peace than a single-word prayer.

This is my resting place. My cornerstone. My haven.

Of all the libraries I've been in, this one is my favorite. The children's center is right in the middle of the massive room with majestic bookshelves and tall pillars that rise above two floors. The bookshelves on the floor above me are stained dark, the old covers blending in with the wood until they look like one solid piece.

No children are allowed up there. The winding staircase is meant only for the more serious, for the researchers and students whose minds are filled with more information than most can handle.

I like to go up there and lose myself, trail my fingers along the spines, dream of a different life.

Some days I sit up there and watch the children below me, listen to their hushed whispers and excited pleas for more story time. I rest my elbows on my knees and strain to hear the storyteller's voice, which fills the cavern with her childish tale.

Today I'm sitting on the main level.

Today I'm watching a little boy who's caught my attention.

It's the middle of summer, a hot, sweltering day, and he's wearing pants and a long-sleeve top.

I've been here for the past hour. I have a book on my lap, opened to a random page, but I'm not reading the words.

Since my last visit to this library, Cheshire has learned how to be scared. As they should be.

But not everyone has learned their lesson.

Especially the father below.

I first took notice outside when I saw the finger-size bruises on the little boy's arm when he'd had his sleeves pushed up. The way he looks at his dad, wary, fearful, scared.

That's not right.

I don't like to see children mistreated.

Child abuse comes in many forms, but if you know what to look for, you'll see it.

Bruises and broken bones can heal.

Scars and shattered spirits can't.

That little boy is splintered into a million different pieces, and nothing will ever heal him. No amount of apologies or toys or treats will undo the damage.

I wish parents would learn. And care.

It's clear the father wishes he could be anywhere but here. He keeps checking his phone every few minutes and shows his impatience with his son as they walk along the aisles.

At one point, the father stands at the end of an aisle and motions to the doors. His son isn't paying attention. He's looking at a book, flipping the pages, staring at the drawings, and the father's gruff voice rumbles through the library.

A librarian looks up from her position at a computer and frowns his way.

The man lifts his arms and drops them in a what's-your-problem type of gesture. The little boy still isn't paying attention, so his father marches down and picks him up by the collar of his shirt.

I lean forward in my chair, sitting on the edge. I don't like what I'm seeing.

The boy scrambles to his feet, dropping the book in the process. He tries to bend down to pick it up, but his father's hold is too strong. He pulls the boy down the aisle, his other hand fisting at his side the more the boy struggles to keep up.

I shoot to my feet and fly down the stairs. My goal is to pick up the book, to hand it to the child, to shame the father for his impatience.

The boy has a basket of books that he's pulling behind him. A librarian stops in front of the father and bends to her knees to speak directly to the child.

I pause. I'm close to the children's section, where the boy was reading his book, but I want to see what happens. I hope the librarian has caught the repressed anger in the man, that she sees the signs of abuse on the boy.

One minute they're stopped, the next the man is pushing the woman away, almost knocking her down as he grabs his son's arm and pushes him forward. I hear a small cry. I listen to the librarian tell the man to stop, but the man doesn't pause, he doesn't stop, he only stomps toward the front door, pushing his son forward with each step, his intent obvious.

To leave the library.

The basket the boy carries is yanked out of his hand as the doors to the library open. The father throws it to the side, the books cascading out onto the floor. His voice can now be heard throughout the whole library.

"Don't ever ignore me again!"

The door closes behind him, and the librarian rushes to the front desk, where she picks up a phone.

I hope she's calling the police.

If she doesn't, if the police aren't sent to investigate, to see to the child's safety, then I will have to.

I rush after them, opening the door and squinting against the midday sun. I search everywhere, but I can't see them. Not the man or the child.

Until I hear a sound that sends shivers of rage throughout my body.

A sharp slap.

Skin against skin.

It's off to my left. To the side of the steps, where they can't be seen, the *son of a bitch*.

I run to the edge and look down.

I'm trembling with anger. I want to jump down and pummel the man to pieces. I want him to feel the pain he's giving his son a hundredfold. No, a thousandfold.

He slaps his son's face. Then he does it again.

The boy just stands there. Trembling but not uttering a sound.

There's something in his gaze, however. A look I understand. A look that shatters my heart.

Sadness, confusion, and hatred.

Children shouldn't learn to hate their parents.

When they do, it destroys their soul. It forces them to become someone they were never intended to be.

The father smacks his son hard, with enough force to make him crumple to the ground. He's yelling foul words, words that should never be said to a child.

I run down the rest of the steps, and I'm about to turn the corner to confront the man when a police cruiser shows up, its sirens blaring, lights whirling.

The man yells at his son to stand up. The boy slowly climbs to his feet, his hand covering his red cheek, and winces.

An officer comes out of the car and looks at me. I point to behind the stairs and grin with satisfaction when the officer follows my direction.

I stay to listen. I find out the man's name, his son's name, and their address. I walk to the side, sit on a bench, and wait to see what happens.

I wasn't on the hunt. That last kill was satisfying and purged the rage in my soul until it simmered with barely a puff of smoke.

Until now. Now that blaze is lit, on fire, with a need to ensure that boy is never hurt again. I'll be paying them a visit. Soon.

Chapter Twenty-Two

Ella never called about her missed appointment. I waited, a small part of me hoping she would, a larger part of me knowing she wouldn't. After spending the afternoon doing some cleaning, I managed to nap. It felt good to get some sleep, even for a few hours.

Curled up on the couch with the last bit of wine from the bottle I'd opened a few hours earlier, I caught the glare from a vehicle's headlights streaking through my windows and the familiar sound as Tami's car door slammed. I knew it was her because it was the only door that squeaked when it opened.

I waited for her in the kitchen, poured her a glass of wine, and hoped she had some news for me as she entered the house.

"I shouldn't," she said, but took the glass regardless and collapsed on a kitchen chair. "You wouldn't believe it, Dee. We've connected more murders to this case. That's six cases now, and God knows there could be more." Her head dropped, and her hair covered her face.

"Six?" The air squeezed out of my chest like a deflated balloon. "Six cases? Twelve murders in total?" I was going to throw up.

Tami didn't respond.

With both sorrow and exhaustion etched all over her and the sharp claws of intense anger burrowed into her shoulders, my concern for her doubled.

"What can I do to help?" I barely spoke the words, and I wasn't even sure she heard me.

I saw the moment she reached deep for that inner strength of hers. It was when she brought the wineglass to her lips and drank half of it.

"Can you help me understand the mind-set of someone who would kill parents and leave a child untouched? What kind of person would do that?"

Person. Not persons. One man or woman committing despicable acts—tearing families apart—for what? There had to be a reason, something that happened to them, a significant event that had brought them to this point.

"Don't you have a profiler to help you?"

"I do. The FBI sent down a team to help us, but . . . just let me bounce things off you, okay?"

I leaned back and yawned. Despite the long afternoon nap I'd had, I was still exhausted. I could sleep for a week and still not feel rested. "I'm not a profiler, Tami. This isn't my area of expertise. I'm just a therapist."

A therapist who didn't know much about serial killers. I was more familiar with mental health issues, teenage drama, and other complexities.

"But you understand the mind and how it works."

My fears, suspicions, and secrets about my patients hovered in the back of my mind.

"I'm not a serial killer expert. Just remember that, okay?" I needed that to be clear. She would have to lean on the profilers made available to her. But I could be a sounding board, someone to confirm what she already knew.

"Most serial killers can appear quite normal," I continued. "They live in plain sight, can have families, serve as a board member at a church, or even coach Little League." What little I knew was from what I'd read.

I had shelves lined with books on various subjects that dealt with mental health and psychology. I'd always wanted to know more, be more, do more . . . and I had a few books dealing with murderers, but . . .

"Right. So it's likely each victim knew their killer," Tami said.

I shook my head at first, but after a moment I nodded. "Yes and no. It could be a crime of passion or premeditated. You said the children were all unharmed?"

"Just the parents killed. The children slept through it all."

Children.

There was a brick wall inside me, built to protect my heart. That one word held the power to crack the foundation of that wall, and it scared me.

Why?

I worked with people who dealt with childhood issues.

I grew up in a life full of complications but emerged unscathed. Relatively so.

"Do you still believe it's one person, or could this be a team?" Rather than dig deeper into my issues, I preferred to focus on Tami's case. "Either way, the person in charge would have been triggered by an event in their childhood. Most serial murderers are the products of their environments, I believe, so that includes how they grew up and choices they would have made into their teenage years."

Tami pulled out a small notebook from her purse and jotted down some notes.

"So they were probably abused," she said. "Neglected, had access to drugs—"

"Tami"—I placed my hand down, covering her writing—"there's no boilerplate characterization for serial killers. No one-size-fits-all jargon. There might be certain traits that are common to some killers, but they might not be in others."

The pen dropped from her hand.

"I was hoping you'd say otherwise, but . . . I know." She grabbed the back of her neck and dug her fingers into her muscles. "There has to be something or someone linking these murders together. I just wish I knew what it was."

I pulled my right leg up onto my chair and hugged it tightly to my chest, my fingers linked around my shin. Pressure in my temple beat like a faraway drum, the rhythm soft but steady. I'd give it a few minutes, see if it would build into a real headache or if it was just from tension.

There was something I'd wanted to mention to Tami, but for the life of me, I couldn't remember. It was there, on the tip of my tongue, ready to blurt out, except when I tried to hold on to the idea, even by the tips of my mental fingers, it slid away like fine sand particles. I had to be more exhausted than I realized. Either that, or it was the wine. Or the exhaustion and wine combined.

"We're canvassing the neighborhoods and trying to find more connections. Any little detail will help." She scrubbed her face, the exhaustion in her eyes enhanced. "I can't believe there's been so many murders."

Six attacks. It was unfathomable.

"How did you link them?"

From the way she hesitated, I realized I'd stepped toward a line, and she was contemplating how close I'd come. "Same methods, different towns throughout the course of almost three years."

Three years? "And no one put them together till now?" How was that possible?

Tami took another swig of her wine. "It's not like in the movies or television shows, Dee. The first three were in a different county, with different investigators, and it's been over two years since the last

murders there. It's a miracle we were able to find the connection at all."
She rubbed her face, a tell for when she was both tired and frustrated.
"I need to figure out a common thread between the victims. Tomorrow
I'm headed to places where kids would hang out—daycares, schools,
gyms—"

"Parks, libraries—" I started to contribute, but then it felt like a
bomb went off in my head, and the earlier drumming turned into a
boxing ring where my brain was the practice bag.

"What's wrong?"

Her words were garbled, like they were being said beneath water.

"Dee." She reached out, her grip so hard I knew it'd leave a bruise.
"What's wrong?"

The pain intensified, like a rocket going off, without missing a beat.
Every nerve in my body fizzled like an electric current, and I swear to
God, the tears that streaked down my face were hot lava.

I tried to form the words to say that it was my head, but the words
wouldn't come.

It felt like there was a fist thrust down my throat, blocking any
airflow.

My chest was tighter than a noose.

I couldn't swallow.

I couldn't breathe.

I couldn't do anything.

I looked to Tami, implored her for help. One second she was beside
me, the next she knelt at my side. I pushed my leg off the chair and
shoved my head between my knees.

I screamed in pain. My cry echoed in every crevice of my mind
from the pressure of her hand on the back of my skull.

I needed her to stop, to let go. It hurt too much, but the words . . .
I couldn't say them.

I was immobile. Frozen.

The pressure from her hand, the pain in my head—it was too much.

My silent scream swallowed me whole until there was nothing but darkness.

~

The next thing I knew, I was on my couch, my soft white blanket tucked in around me, and Tami sat at my feet.

"I think you need some potted plants in here. I've been trying to think about what's wrong with your living room, and other than it being cluttered, there's no greenery."

She watched me as I blinked, the fog over my eyes disappearing as I came to.

I looked around the room, sure that I had plants, but she was right. There were none.

What kind of person didn't have plants in their house?

Why had I never thought about having plants in my house?

"Before you ask, I helped you over to the couch. You were pretty out of it. You fainted twice on our way here, and you've been asleep for over an hour now. I had some migraine tablets in my purse and gave you one. I hope you don't mind. I know how you feel about taking anything stronger than a Tylenol."

I licked my dry, chapped lips, and she handed me a glass of water with a straw. I drained the glass before I laid my head back on the pillow.

I passed out?

"You told me that it was okay, that this happens quite often." The tips of her lips turned downward in displeasure. "How come I didn't know that until now?"

What was she talking about?

"What happens quite often? The headaches or passing out?" None of this made sense.

Tami's jaw clenched before she pushed herself up off the couch.

"You tell me," she said before she took my empty glass back to the kitchen.

I listened to the tap turn on as I shuffled myself up to a sitting position. My head still hurt but not like before.

Before was . . . horrific. Like a dozen gongs had gone off in my brain simultaneously. I'd never felt anything like it and never wanted to again.

Was it possible for a head to feel bruised inside and out?

"Thanks for staying with me," I said once she returned.

"Where else would I be? Now answer my question." She sat on the opposite chair and crossed her legs.

"Headaches, yes. But you know that. Fainting? No."

"You should go see a doctor."

"Why?"

She gave me *that* look.

"One fainting spell doesn't warrant a doctor's visit."

"Danielle."

There were benefits to having a cop as a friend. If anything went bump in the night, I called her for help, and considering I lived across from a public park, things often went bump in the night.

One of the downfalls, however, to having a detective as a friend was she saw more than I liked and never stopped until her questions were answered to her satisfaction.

"I'm fine, Tami. Honestly. I haven't eaten much today, and that wine was probably the last straw. I've been fighting off a headache all day, so I should have known better. Stupid migraine."

I could see her skepticism until she processed my words. I knew the moment she believed me because she relaxed her posture in the chair, sat back against the cushion, and tucked her legs beneath her.

"You should know better." She gave me a softer smile. "You need to take care of yourself. I worry about you."

I didn't want her to worry about me. "Well, you can stop. I am seeing a therapist now."

She didn't say anything, but I noted the happiness in her eyes.

I thought about the role reversal between us. Earlier, when she'd arrived, she'd been the one exhausted and needing to be taken care of.

"I'm not the one running on empty trying to stop another murder from happening."

"The FBI have brought in psychologists and have made them available for us, but . . ."

"But nothing." I knew where she was going with this. "You make sure you go, along with everyone else on your team." I would hound her if I had to. "If I can see a therapist to help me figure out why I'm so stressed, then you for damn sure can see one too."

"I know. I know." She rubbed her eyes. "It's one thing to read through reports and look at crime scene photos, but to be there in person, to see . . ." This time she scrubbed her entire face. "I'm going to have nightmares for years."

An image of what she must have seen flashed through my head.

A bed drenched in blood. Splashes of red across the headboard. Droplets on the carpet.

"I can't even imagine."

Tami slapped her thighs. "It's going to be a long day tomorrow, so I need to go to bed, but not until I know you're safely tucked in your own."

She helped me up off the couch, watched me with a steady gaze.

"I'm fine," I said despite my tight grip on her arm. The room spun as I stood, but she didn't need to know that.

"Of course you are." Her sarcasm was loud and clear. "Let me help you to your room."

I rolled my eyes but let her help me.

"Are you able to join me in the morning? I'd like you to meet Sabrina."

For a moment, she didn't reply.

"I can't, Dee. I'm sorry. I know you want us to connect, but . . . tomorrow is going to be a long day, and this case has to be my priority."

Of course. That made sense.

Alone again and ready for the sleep of the oblivious and one not filled with nightmares, I turned my night sounds on. I should have done that last night. It might have helped me sleep better.

When the lights were off, my brain woke up. All the thoughts, feelings, and emotions I had pushed away during the day returned on full blast when my defenses were down.

I used to recite the Lord's Prayer until I fell asleep.

That didn't work anymore.

So I listened to the waves.

The thoughts continued, but the crashing of the water drowned them out until only a dull roar remained.

When my patients complained about this, I told them it was okay, normal, that your mind finally had a chance to relax and catch up on all those things you subconsciously pushed to the side throughout the day. I'd tell them to keep a journal close at hand, to write down all their concerns, fears, worries, ideas, and then look them over in the morning.

Would it always work? No.

Sometimes I wondered if that was why some people went crazy. Why there was more crime at night than during the day. If it was because everyone was trying to find a way to shut the craziness off, and some people just . . . couldn't.

But then again, maybe some people were just plain crazy.

Chapter Twenty-Three

SATURDAY, AUGUST 17

I shook my numb hands as I raised myself from my curled position on the couch. The drapes were drawn, and I didn't have my watch or phone close by, so I had no idea of the time.

It was a struggle to orient myself. The last thing I remembered, Tami had tucked me into bed before she left. The bed, not the couch.

I wrapped the blanket around myself due to the slight chill in the air, and pushed aside the curtains.

Soft light greeted me, the warmth of the sun a welcome heat on my face as I gazed out.

It was early. Dew lingered on the grass, and one of the boys from down the street rode past on his bike as he threw his bundle of flyers on lawns. That was one of the things about Cheshire I loved, the small-town vibe. In the city, you collected your mail from neighborhood boxes, but here, the mailman still walked the streets, leaving the mail in the box by your door, and the newspapers and flyers never ended up on your front porch but rather in bushes or front yards.

I headed toward the shower, passing my bed, and stopped in the doorway.

I turned and looked.

My bed was made.

The clothes I'd worn the night before hung over the arm of the chair by the bed.

My room had been cleaned. The basket of clothes I'd needed to fold had been put away, and a bag I'd thrown in the corner was gone. The stack of books on my bedside table had disappeared, and in its place was a book I'd been wanting to read.

Tami, the angel, must have stayed and cleaned up.

My phone was on my china cabinet charging. I scrolled through to see if Tami had left me a message.

Hope you don't mind. I slept on your couch till about two in the morning. Got called in early. Sorry I left such a mess! I'll make it up to you and buy take-out tonight.

Tami hadn't cleaned?

The blanket around my shoulders had dropped to the floor when I picked up my phone. When I bent down to gather it in my arms, I noticed what I wore.

Navy-blue jogging pants and a white T-shirt.

I hadn't worn these pants since the winter. In fact, I'd packed them away in my closet when summer had started. Why would I have them on now?

Tami had apologized for the mess, but there was none to be seen.

I had to have cleaned the house after she'd left. Maybe the sound of her car pulling out of my driveway had woken me. Maybe I couldn't get back to sleep, but because I was so exhausted, I couldn't remember. Maybe my sleepwalking was getting worse.

I hated not knowing.

I hated that I couldn't remember.

I hated that more than anything else.

I pulled out a chair from the table and plunked down.

My hands shook. My chest felt like someone with Hulk-size hands pushed against it, threatening to crush every rib. But it wasn't until I saw it, another damn note propped up against a vase of wildflowers, that the overwhelming sound of blood rushed to my ears, that high-pitched squeal of decibels, that narrow-focus black hole of anxiety, announced a panic attack.

I bit the inside of my cheek, welcoming the rush of pain even as I tasted blood, and I reached for the paper.

Please God please God please God not another one.

I was going to cry. I didn't want to, but the tears were there, gathering until they pooled and my vision swam. I tried to shake off the fear that slowly wound its way through my veins, freezing everything in its path. I tried, but I failed.

I opened the note.

I can't keep cleaning up your messes. Time is running out. Stop them before it's too late.

Chapter Twenty-Four

MONDAY, AUGUST 19

PATIENT SESSION: TYLER

Five long minutes had passed since Tyler first entered the room.

Five excruciating minutes when I'd watched him walk the length and width of my small office.

The first minute he'd muttered incessantly.

The second minute he'd stared at his feet while he wiped his hands down his pant legs over and over.

By the fifth minute, he was casting furtive glances my way before he hugged himself tightly.

"Tyler, why don't you sit down?" I suggested. Again. After the third minute, I'd stopped watching him walk around me and picked up a book, pretending to read.

"You . . . you can see me, right?" he asked, pointing to himself. "I mean, I'm real to you, not a figment of your imagination, right?"

Increased delusions, I scribbled.

"Yes, I can see you. You're not invisible." I contemplated suggesting a walk to grab a cup of coffee down the street to prove my point.

"I'm real." He pounded his chest with a closed fist. "I'm real." He held out his hands, turned them over, as if seeing his skin for the first time.

"Tyler?" I leaned forward. "How are you feeling? Do you have a headache? Feel light-headed? Have you eaten?" I counted off a number of things that might have contributed to this.

He waved his hands. "No, no, I'm fine. I'm fine."

"Then"—I softened my tone—"why do you feel you're a figment of my imagination?"

"Because *she* says I am nothing." His whole face scrunched together.

"Did she say why? What brought this on? Did you have an argument?" Maybe, just maybe, he'd tell me more about this woman and offer stronger clarity about her hold over him.

He shook his head, his shaggy hair flopping over his eyes before he lifted his shoulder in a shrug.

"Not so much a fight but . . ." He swallowed hard and fidgeted, crisscrossing his legs, then planting both feet on the ground.

Reading his body language didn't take a professional.

"I followed her again."

"Why?"

"Because she needs to be stopped." The look on his face dumbfounded me. It was like he expected me to know this already.

Have patience, have patience, don't be in such a hurry . . . The children's song my mother used to sing when I'd sit at the oven door waiting for the muffins to finish baking popped into my head.

"Explain to me what happened." I set my notepad down and picked up my glass of water.

Today I'd infused the water with frozen strawberries and kiwi.

Tyler had yet to take a sip.

"I just want to help her, you know? Be her partner. Be a strength for her. But she doesn't see me that way. It doesn't matter what I've done for her—it will never be enough."

There wasn't much about this woman I liked, not from the way he described her to me.

"Moving here has been good for us. Things have been good. We came here to get a fresh start, a new beginning, to reimagine our life together. We were happy and partners in life. I've been trying really hard to find her a child to raise so we can start our family. But then . . ." He swallowed, his Adam's apple bobbing, before he coughed.

The coughing wouldn't stop. He pitched forward, his body racked with tremors, his hands covering his throat and chest.

I held out his glass of water, urging him to take a sip, but he couldn't. His cough turned into a choking sound as he struggled for air.

One moment he was choking; the next his body was straighter than a ruler. He inhaled, his chest ballooning with air.

His gaze, frozen with fear, locked on mine, screaming words I didn't understand, until the tension in his body receded and the air in his chest cavity released.

He sucked in air, desperation on his face.

"Tyler, it's going to be okay." My pitiful platitudes were pointless.

"I'm sorry," he said, the terror in his voice sending chills racing over my bare skin. "I'm sorry. I'm sorry. I'm sorry."

"Don't apologize. I think you were having a panic attack."

"I just . . ." He swallowed, the struggle on his face real. "You don't understand. She likes you. She's protecting you. But you're not allowed to know. I'm not allowed to tell you." He dropped his head into his hands, his body shaking as he rocked himself on my couch.

I had so many questions. For starters, who the hell was *she*? Who was I being protected from? What was I not allowed to know? And how, how could she like me if I didn't even know who she was? And then I had a thought—did I know who she was?

Tyler had a wild look in his eyes.

"I'm sorry," he repeated. "I won't say any more." His lips tightened, and his gaze felt off, like he was looking over my shoulder to someone there, and that's when I felt a hint of warm breath on the back of my neck.

I shivered but refused to look behind me. I'd let him lull me into a false reality, and my imagination was on full alert. A breeze must have come in through the open window, but the fear in Tyler's voice was enough to fill my heart with ice.

"You don't have to apologize to me, Tyler."

His head shook back and forth, his lips tighter than Fort Knox.

"Why don't you tell me how the past few days have been." I tried a different approach, hoping to get him to start talking once again.

He looked at the water, then at me, and I saw the question he wouldn't ask.

"It's just strawberry and kiwi water. See?" I reached for my glass. "You saw me pour them both from the same jug of water, and I'm fine." If I could help him with anything, it would be with this fear of poison.

I didn't even try to mask my smile when he picked up his cup and held it between his hands.

"You mentioned earlier that you followed her. Where did she go?"

"It was late at night, and she was just walking the streets." He didn't look up.

"The downtown area or residential?"

"Where all the nice houses are."

"What do you mean?"

Tyler stood and headed to his favorite area in my office, in front of my window, and looked out toward the park.

"Our . . . home . . . is small. We don't own a lot of things, but we're happy, you know? Or"—his shoulders dropped—"we were happy. But she's out a lot now. She barely comes home at night, and I'm afraid of what she's doing."

"Like?"

Despair was etched on his face when he looked at me over his shoulder. He stared into my eyes before he focused his attention back out the window.

"Do you fear she's met someone?"

"No. Nothing like that."

"Then what is it you're afraid she's doing?"

I thought back to our last session, when he'd shown me a glimpse of his anger when we'd ventured onto this same subject. He'd said then that I didn't understand, and he'd repeated it again today.

"Tyler," I said, venturing a guess. "Tyler, what steps do you think you can take, starting today, to bring back that feeling of partnership with her?"

"There is no partnership, Dr. Rycroft. Don't you get it?" His eyebrows became one straight, angry line, and I clutched my pen tighter.

"I get," I said, my voice soft, "that you don't feel there is one. But I'm wondering if there is a way to bring that back. Sometimes all it takes is an open dialogue. Maybe she could join you here for your session next week?" I'd asked this before, and he'd always said no. One day, the answer could change.

I was prepared for the anger, prepared for the outburst, prepared to not show my reaction.

But nothing could have prepared me for his response.

"Not yet." The conviction in his voice was unrecognizable. "She says you're not ready to meet her. Not yet. But soon you will be."

A snake that had been coiled tightly in my belly attacked, and venom spread throughout my veins. Icy-cold streams of fear slid through my body until I was numb from head to toe.

"What do you mean, Tyler?" How my voice remained steady when I was the complete opposite was beyond me.

"You're just not ready yet. But you will be." He cocked his head. "I'm not allowed to say more." He turned to me with begging eyes. "Please don't ask."

"Can we discuss why you asked if you were real to me when you first arrived?" I wasn't sure where to go with our session. There were so many paths we could take, but they all led to the same destination. To his relationship with her. Whoever *she* was.

I wondered if he realized that.

He studied me for a moment.

"My life is wrapped up in her." He sat, hands fisted together between his knees. "I never minded it before. She's all I need. She was . . . is, is my life. My breath. My heart. Without her, I'm nothing, and to have her in my life . . . it gives me meaning. Without her . . . I don't know who I am. Without her, I don't exist. I can't lose her. One day I'll find the perfect child for her. She won't need to keep searching, and she'll realize she needs me too."

That last part he mumbled to himself, and I almost missed it.

Almost.

"How long have you been trying to adopt, Tyler?" A thought buried itself in my head that the children being orphaned might be tied into this, but I pushed it away as quickly as I could. He had to mean something else.

Please, God, let him mean something else.

"I just want her to be happy again, you know? The old me could do that. I always did that. Kept her happy. I knew how to. But now . . . now I . . ." He shook his head. "Now I'm no one."

No one? Invisible? His words bothered me. Alarm bells rang in my head that this loss of self, of his individuality, required a type of treatment that was beyond my purview.

His needs had to come first.

"Tyler, you've never told me her name."

He didn't respond.

"Let's talk about who you were before you two met." Not knowing her name frustrated me, left me more determined than ever to figure out who she was. Especially now.

"That's just it. I wasn't anyone before I met her." His voice rang with a note of truth, similar to a church bell's clang at the stroke of noon.

I needed him to see that he was someone, that his identity wasn't wrapped completely in this woman. I needed to find a way for him to not just see it but understand and grasp it.

"What kind of music did you like? Where did you live? What about the friends you hung out with and your family? You were someone, Tyler." My lips rose into a you-can-trust-me type of smile I hope he believed.

It didn't work.

"None of that matters because I didn't matter until she came into my life. It was like . . ." He raked his hands through his hair and puffed out a breath. "It was like I suddenly mattered when she decided I was needed. Wanted. I don't know how else to describe it."

"But you no longer feel that way?"

His mouth opened, and his lips moved as if to say something, but no words, no sound, came out. Instead, he gave me this look, first of exasperation and then of realization.

"She doesn't need me anymore," he whispered. "She . . . doesn't . . . oh God, oh God, I'm too late, it's . . . it's too late."

Watching the reality of a situation hit someone was always difficult. Being a spectator to a life-changing thought could be heartbreaking. There were no words to say, no platitudes to give, no actions to take to make things easier.

Tyler crumbled. His head bowed until his chin hit his chest, his shoulders heaved with tremors, and he rocked himself while mumbling something unintelligible.

Up until now, he'd been afraid she didn't need him, that she didn't want him, that she was moving on from him. But now, now he realized that all his fears had come true.

What happened within these next few minutes would determine his reaction. Would he dissolve altogether and become suicidal? Would he grieve and lose himself in that grief until eventually he found a way to crawl out and live? Would he allow anger to consume him?

Most times I knew how my patients would react.

Most times I could predict how they would respond.

But with Tyler and his emotional and mental instability, I was blind.

"If I"—he reached for a tissue—"if I can't be her partner, then I have to stop her."

"What do you mean, stop her?" I was on the edge of my seat, literally, my pen leaving scratch marks on the paper I held on my lap. "Tyler?" I asked again.

"I . . . I have to do this on my own. Just . . ." He stood with a look I couldn't read. "Just be careful, okay?"

"Tyler, what do you mean?"

The signs of abuse were there. In the words he said, in the fear in his eyes, the way he responded to certain questions. I wasn't sure if it was Stockholm syndrome or something else.

He placed his hand on my shoulder.

My body stiffened from his unwanted touch.

His hand dropped, and his gaze was full of sadness.

"I'll do my best to protect you, Danielle. But I need you to promise me something."

The use of my first name shocked me and stole away any thought, any words I attempted to utter.

"Don't go searching too hard, all right? You're safe right now, but you won't stay that way if she thinks you're overstepping. Just leave things be, and we'll all be okay."

I tried to process his words, but before I could say anything, he walked out of my office, taking with him all my personal sense of safety.

Either I moved too late, or he was too fast. He was gone by the time I made it to the door.

Chapter Twenty-Five

The clock on my phone said it was a few minutes before midnight.

My kitchen was a disaster zone, my apron covered with splattered cream cheese, and I'd already drunk half a bottle of French wine.

I couldn't sleep. Too many thoughts were rushing in my head—concern for Ella, the notes—so I figured I might as well stay true to my earlier promise about baking a cheesecake. Tami wouldn't be able to find an excuse this time to not meet Sabrina.

I knew this recipe as well as the back of my hand. At least I used to. But this was my third attempt at the cheesecake mixture, and it still didn't look right.

I'd added three eggs in one at a time. I'd creamed in the sugar. Didn't use too much vanilla. Used sour cream. But the mixture was lumpy instead of creamy and tasted like shit.

I sat at the table, sipped the wine, and thought about where I'd gone wrong. It didn't escape my notice that the way this cheesecake was going was similar to my life.

I should have known better than to bake at night when I had brain fog.

I looked through all the ingredients strewn about the counter.

I was down to my last cream cheese blocks. For some reason, I'd bought a bulk pack the last time I'd shopped. Then I looked inside the sugar container to see if I needed a refill and noticed something was off about the granules. It took one taste test to realize it wasn't sugar, it was salt. *For the love of . . .* And the container I'd grabbed from the fridge wasn't sour cream. It was cottage cheese.

I poured the rest of the wine into my glass and downed it in one gulp.

I spent the next hour cleaning my kitchen. I threw everything into the already overflowing garbage, wiped down the counters, and eyed the clock.

The wine, along with my lack of sleep, had my eyes darting to and fro of their own accord. My head felt woozy and my steps sluggish.

I thought maybe I could actually sleep.

I hefted the garbage bag out of the bin and went to place it in the garbage can outside.

"Dee? What are you doing up?"

I screamed. The bag dropped from my hand as I stumbled, backing away from whomever was out there.

"Dee? It's just me." Tami stepped toward me, her hands held outward.

"For the love of all things holy, what the hell are you doing out here, scaring me like that?" The words rushed out of my mouth, my heart thumped so hard my chest ached, and every muscle in my body was ready to run as far as I could.

"Sorry," Tami said, her lips moving into a grin. "But you should see yourself right now. I swear you jumped two feet."

"Not even funny, Tami. Not in the slightest." My lips pursed but not from anger. I was trying not to laugh along with her. "What are you doing here?"

"I come by most nights when I'm on duty, Dee. Just to make sure everything is okay. That the doors are locked, you know . . ."

I lunged forward and enveloped her in the biggest hug I could give her.

"You have no idea how much that means to me." It was as if I'd been drowning in quicksand and someone had just thrown me a rope. The fear that had plagued me lifted.

"What's going on?" She gripped my shoulders with her hands and peered close. "What haven't you told me?"

I thought of telling her about the notes, explaining exactly why it meant so much that she was making sure I was safe, but it was the look in her eyes—not quite fear but more alarm and concern—that stopped me.

She carried so much already. I couldn't add one more thing.

"Nothing," I said. I hugged her again so she couldn't see the lie on my face. "It just means a lot that you would do this for me."

She measured me then. Measured my words, my voice, the look on my face.

I must have passed, because she looked at her watch and frowned.

"Why are you up? I thought maybe you'd fallen asleep on the couch again and that's why your kitchen light was on."

"I couldn't sleep. Rather than toss and turn, I tried to make that cheesecake I promised."

Her eyes lit up.

"Don't get too excited. I should have tossed and turned." I told her about the salt replacing the sugar and cottage cheese instead of sour cream, which had her laughing.

"Laugh all you want. But my kitchen was a mess, and I'm done making cheesecake."

"You seriously need to go to bed. Didn't you take anything to help you sleep?" She led me to the door and opened it.

"You know I don't like pills." I stifled a yawn behind my hand as I walked in.

"So you prefer to not sleep? Come on, Dee. Suck it up. Your body needs rest—you know that. The bags under your eyes are ridiculous, and you'll be no good to your patients soon."

She rummaged around in her purse and pulled out a small box.

"Listen, I bought these. It's an over-the-counter sleeping pill, full of melatonin." She tossed me the box before she pulled out a cup and filled it with water.

"You're supposed to open it," she said.

I tore the box open, pulled out the bottle, and looked it over. She was probably right, and one wouldn't hurt. Savannah wasn't due to come in until the afternoon, so if I went to sleep right away, maybe I'd be able to sleep in.

"I'm not leaving until you're in bed." She watched me swallow the pill and then marched me into my bedroom.

She waited until I was in bed, covers tucked around me, before she sat down.

"Can you reschedule your session tomorrow?"

I shook my head. "It's Savannah. Her uncle is supposed to join us tomorrow, so I'd rather not. But she's not in until two in the afternoon, so I promise I'll get a lot of sleep."

"Turn your phone off." She reminded me of my mom when she'd catch me reading late into the night.

"Why don't I text you when I'm awake, okay?" I suggested, the smile in my voice contagious.

"I'm just worried about you, Dee. Someone needs to take care of the caretaker, you know." She rubbed my leg.

"Thank you for taking care of me. I really appreciate it." I stifled another yawn and closed my eyes as she turned off the light and shut my bedroom door.

It felt good to be looked after, to be taken care of.

For the first time in days, I actually felt safe enough to fall asleep.

Chapter Twenty-Six

PATIENT SESSION: SAVANNAH

Tick. Tick. Tick.

Savannah had been in my office for fifteen minutes, and we'd hardly said two words to each other.

Her uncle was supposed to show up, and he was late.

She'd called, texted, left messages, but gotten no response.

We both looked at the clock at the same time.

"He's going to be here."

I looked down at the notes I'd written after Savannah arrived.

She was full goth today. Black ripped jeans. Black tank top. Wide black cuff on her left wrist. Black lipstick, thick eyeliner, mascara, and nail polish.

Such a dramatic change in just one week.

"Have you heard from your parents?"

The scowl on her face deepened as she leaned against the couch, her feet up on the coffee table. She knew I hated her boots on my furniture.

She picked at the threads of the holes in her jeans and didn't answer.

"Savannah?" I asked, my tone sharp as barbed wire. I wasn't in the mood for nonsense today. Despite sleeping until around one in the afternoon, I had woken up groggy and irritable.

"They've called. Talked to my uncle. Not me." Sullen. Hostile. Brooding. Everything I didn't want to deal with today.

"Your choice? Your uncle's or your parents'?"

"Mine."

Avoiding her parents, I wrote.

"I didn't want to talk to them, okay? I don't care if they're having the best vacation ever or that they saw dolphins and had sex in the sand."

I smothered a laugh as best I could. "I doubt they said they'd had sex in the sand."

"I have no idea. I didn't talk to them."

"It sounds like you might be a little upset they didn't take you on their trip."

"I wouldn't want to go on a shitty trip to some shitty beach where there's nothing to do but snorkel with the shitty fish." She slouched even more on my couch.

I raised one brow at her choice of words.

"Sure sounds like a shitty trip to me," I said, tongue in cheek.

I caught the slight turn of her lips before she noticed I was looking.

"I wish my uncle would hurry up." She continued to play with the threads on her knee, picking away at them little by little until the hole grew in size.

"How are things going with him? Has it been as awesome as you expected?" By her attire, I would say no.

She shrugged.

"Have you done any exciting things yet?" They must have had their pizza party and movie night at least.

She shrugged again.

"Savannah? How about we use our words. I'm not that great at shrug reading."

"We've done stuff." Her voice was soft. "We've watched a few movies."

"Anything planned coming up?"

She shook her head. "He said we would go camping, but it seems like he just wants to stay home and play house."

I perked up at that, not liking what I heard.

Play house? That was an odd choice of words to use.

"How do you feel about that?" I kept my words steady, slow, but my tone light.

"Whatever. It's fine. Like I said, we watch a lot of movies, and he doesn't bug me about sleeping in like my mom does."

I pushed away my initial concerns for the time being and snickered. I couldn't help it. "It must be a mom thing, because mine used to do the same thing. She used to get up at the crack of dawn, and sleeping in was eight a.m. to her."

Her eyes lit up in surprise.

"Having a hard time thinking of me as a teenager?" I moved my pen on the paper as if I were writing something down.

"It's hard to think of any grown-up as a teenager, you know?" Savannah planted her feet on the floor and sat up a little straighter. "My uncle, he treats me like an adult. Like you do, but different."

"Different, how?"

She played with her bangs, twirling a piece in her fingers until it was a tight coil. "Like I'm a grown-up, can handle things that grown-ups do. Doesn't treat me like a kid who doesn't understand things. He asks for my opinion and talks to me like I'm not a little kid."

"That must feel nice." I tried to remain positive, to not allow my thoughts to twist to the darker side of what her words suggested.

"It is. He . . . he says he loves me and sees me for who I am inside, that he isn't trying to mold me into someone I'm not, because he sees the real me."

My body stilled, like a rabbit caught in the glare of headlights. My heart raced, but I only nodded. I didn't like what I heard.

"Is he respecting you?" I had to ask. It was my duty as her therapist, as a friend.

"Isn't respect the same as showing love?" She sounded like a little girl, a small child, her voice quiet, soft, and uncertain.

This was a pivotal moment between us, and I had only one chance at saying what she needed to hear before her defenses rose higher than the Berlin Wall.

"Savannah, I'll be as plain as I can. If he is touching you in a way that is inappropriate, that is not love or respect. That's abuse because, for one, he's your uncle—let alone the fact that you are underage, and he knows better." I gripped the pen in my hand tighter.

Sexual abuse by uncle? The tip of my pen left indents in the paper. If she'd been hurt . . .

"Underage? I'm seventeen."

"You're still a minor. And he is your uncle." I tried to place every single emotion in how I gripped my pen.

"He's the only one who truly loves me. He wouldn't hurt me or disrespect me like that. I thought . . . I thought you meant something else." She rubbed her hands down her legs before replacing them in her lap.

Something else? She was a smart girl. She knew exactly what I meant.

"Savannah. I'm worried about you."

"Why?"

I motioned to her clothes. "On the scale, your clothing tells me something's wrong. You're distant, evasive, and everything you're saying via your body and your words tells me that something's off. I've got a soft spot in my heart for you, and I just want to make sure you're okay."

The obvious tension in her eyes eased, her shoulders relaxed, and it took a moment or two, but a gentle smile appeared on her face.

"Thank you," she said, her voice a sweet whisper. "I'm okay, though. I promise."

If she expected me to believe her, she was going to be disappointed. I wasn't about to be played.

"I think you're as far from okay as you've been in a long time."

I was trying to figure out what was going on with her.

Was she disappointed about not speaking to her parents?

Was life with her uncle not as amazing as she'd thought it would be?

Was he hurting her?

Was it something else?

"I wish he'd hurry up." She looked at her phone. "He promised he would. He just had to run an errand first. Then we were going to go to the library."

It was now half past the hour.

"You are still spending a lot of time at the library?"

She blinked—once, twice, three times. A mask settled over her face each time she lowered her lashes. It was fascinating to watch. Disturbing at the same time. Why the need to hide?

"Did you know there are books detailing how to kill people? Not just about the mind-set of serial killers, but step-by-step instructions on how to re-create their murders. It's fascinating. I've made a list even."

"I'm s-sorry," I sputtered. "You've made a list of ways to kill people?"

"Yeah? It's just research. It's not as easy as you'd think it would be."

"I'm sorry?" *Research?*

Her face was a clean whiteboard, every emotional tick gone.

"Savannah."

"What?" The venom wrapped in that one word settled into the open sore of worry that grew larger each minute we sat there. "God, you're so dense. Fine. Would it make you feel better if I said it's research for a horror novel I'm thinking of writing?"

I rubbed at the wrinkle lines on my forehead. "It would make me feel better if it was the truth."

"Fine. It's the truth."

I wanted to believe her. I really did. But this was the first I'd ever heard her speak about what she'd like to do in the future and the first she'd spoken of the future without adding her parents to the discussion.

If it was true, it was a good sign. And being a writer, well, who wouldn't want to be able to write books?

"If that's your reason for all this research, I think that's great."

"Oh, that's not the only reason. But you know that already." She held the sly look of a teenager who carried secrets she thought adults too stupid to understand. "My uncle is interested in all this too. He thinks the recent murders in Cheshire are fascinating."

Fascinating? More like deranged and despicable. Foul. Not fascinating.

"I can't wait to meet this uncle of yours."

Her eyes shifted from me to the door, then to the floor.

"Is he even coming, Savannah?"

She refused to look me in the eyes, which basically answered my question.

Mentally I counted to five. Measuring each number with a slow breath. *One.* My chest expanded. *Two.* My fingers relaxed. *Three.* My muscles unwound. *Four.* I slowly let out the breath, releasing the frustration along with it. *Five.* I felt a little . . . calmer.

"I'm sure he's coming." She cleared her throat. "He said he just had an errand to run and would be back in time . . ." Her cheeks bloomed with a pink blush.

"In time to pick you up after our session—is that what you were going to say?" I didn't hide my disappointment. "If he didn't want to come, being up-front about it would have been appreciated."

I was keener now on meeting this man than before. If he loved Savannah so much, if he was concerned about her well-being, why wouldn't he be here?

The thought of her being hurt in any way had my toes flexing and my nostrils flaring.

"You're upset." Savannah sounded surprised.

I decided to be honest about it and nodded.

"Why?"

"Why?" She really didn't understand, did she? "Savannah, I could say it's about disrespect, I could say that I don't see the love you speak of coming from him, especially if he wasn't willing to come, something both your parents have done time and time again." I wanted to point out that difference. Her parents were here every time I requested their presence, no questions asked.

"But if I were to be honest, I'm upset because him not showing up tells me something is going on, that something is off, and like I said before, I'm worried about you."

That wall I knew she'd throw up rose higher and higher. Nothing I said or did mattered now.

I leaned forward and took her hand in mine.

"I care about you, and I just want you to be okay." It didn't matter how many times I had to say this. I'd continue to repeat it until she believed me.

"Not happy?" Sarcasm seemed to be her second language.

No. Not happy. That wasn't something I could help her be.

"Happiness is a choice, Savannah. Whether you are happy or not depends on you. As much as I would wish you were happy, I'd rather you be safe, strong, secure. You alone are responsible for your own happiness, no one else."

I could see that surprised her. What had she expected me to say?

"No one says they want me to be okay. Just that they want me to be happy. They'll do anything to make me happy." Her eyes shone bright with defiance. "What the fuck do they know about happy?"

"Who says they want you to be happy?"

"Everyone. My parents. My uncle. Every fucking person who says they love me."

This whole conversation reminded me of being on a crazy roller coaster with no end in sight.

I needed to bring us back around to the different things that had been said and revealed today.

"How does that make you feel?" Yes, this was a cop-out on my part, but I needed time to put it all together without there being any awkwardness.

"God, you and your *feeling* crap." The words burst out of Savannah with the same speed that had her jumping up from her seat and heading to the window.

Why did my patients always go to that window?

"Can I just leave now? I don't even know why I came. I should have just called and said, *Screw it, see you next week.*" Her long and lean figure rested against the window ledge.

"I'm not keeping you here, Savannah. You're free to leave whenever you'd like." I wasn't surprised by her reaction. In previous sessions when we'd started to encroach upon subjects she wasn't comfortable with, she'd had the same reaction.

I'd offered the same response.

She'd never left. She'd remained sullen and broody, but in the end, she'd returned to the couch, and we'd picked up our conversation.

I wasn't worried.

"Whatever." Her eyelids shuttered, her focus turned downward, and she headed toward the couch.

Then she walked straight past it to the door.

"I don't need this shit. I'll wait for my uncle outside."

Before I could get a word out, she left.

I wanted to shout for her to come back.

I wanted to follow her and force her to stop.

I wanted to make her stay and talk to me. Really talk to me.

To make sure she was okay.

To make sure her parents were okay. That her uncle was okay. That *okay* meant not being sexually abused or encouraged to murder family members.

But everything I wanted to do cemented me to my seat, and in the end, I did nothing.

All because when she opened the door, I noticed another note on the floor.

A note with bright-red words.

More people are going to die.

Chapter Twenty-Seven

MEMORY

The silence in the kitchen kills me. It's full of every hurtful, hateful, harmful emotion that's circled our family for years. I want to throw my glass on the floor or, better yet, across the table at my father just so he will look at me, pay me some attention.

God, I'm pitiful.

But it would serve him right if it hit him in the eye.

I twist the cup in my hand, then tip it, first one way, then the other, seeing how far I can go before the water spills out onto the table.

"Oh for God's sake, child, stop playing with your cup. You'll make a mess." Mom, her voice laced with exhaustion and frustration, grabs the cup from my hand. The glass tumbles to the floor, spilling water every which way.

"Clean it up," my father dictates from his seat. He's the benevolent head of the table, imparting his orders with a cold voice.

Where has the warmth gone? What about the love? I can't remember the last time he kissed me hello or good night. Tucked me into bed or even opened my door to make sure I was in bed. Before Uncle moved in, probably.

I ignore him.

"*Clean it up.*" *His voice doesn't raise or lower. He is lord of this castle, and dealing with shit like this is beneath him.*

"*I didn't make the mess,*" *I say, challenging him to look me in the eye, but it's a waste of time. He shovels another forkful of mashed potatoes into his mouth while looking over my report card.*

"*You're an ungrateful child, you realize that, right?*" *Mom shakes her head before getting up to grab a towel.*

She's limping, and I know it's from being tossed across her bed last night and onto the floor.

Father dearest finally decided to come home after two weeks away.

I wish he hadn't.

Why can't he just leave already? Leave and never come back. Or better yet, drink himself into a ditch.

"*So help me, if you don't get off your ass and clean your mess, I'll make it so you'll never be able to sit down again, do you hear?*" *This time his voice does rise, but only slightly.*

Oh my God, he does have feelings. Wonder what it would take for him to yell at me.

But then he probably wouldn't yell. Not at me. He'd take it out on Mom instead, and I'd end up feeling guilty for the bruises etched in my name.

I push my chair back hard enough it scratches a mark into our cheap vinyl floor.

He growls.

I ignore him.

"*Here, let me do it.*" *I take the cloth from Mom as she limps back over. I toss the towel on the floor and use my foot to wipe it through the water.*

Mom sits down. I catch a faint whiff of vodka when I kneel down to grab the towel. I'm about to take it back to the kitchen, but another bearlike growl has me turning back.

"*Laundry.*"

"*Fine.*"

He grabs my wrist as I march past him, his grip tighter than a stuck jam lid.

"Disrespect your mother like that again and it'll be the last thing you do."

I stand as still as a broken grandfather clock. My hand goes numb. His fingers are crushing the veins, and I know my wrist will be black and blue come morning. I'll have to wear a long-sleeve shirt to cover it. Again.

I try to wiggle my fingers to keep the blood flowing, but even that proves impossible.

"Hurts, don't it? Keep it up and next it'll be broken."

I yank it from his grip the second I feel his hand let go.

I don't say a word as I head to the laundry room. Or when I return to the table.

"You want to explain to me what this shit is?" He waves my report card in the air before dropping it.

"Not really."

Mom gasps. "Don't be stupid." She says it quietly enough for me and only me to hear.

"You want to try that again?"

I want to push him like he pushes us, but not only will he take it out on me, Mom will feel the brunt of it too. As much as I hate her, I don't want to see him hurt her.

I wish Uncle were here. There's no way Father would be like this if he were. I think he's afraid of Uncle.

He should be.

My father is a fat old trucker. Uncle works out and has muscles. He threw my father across the room once after seeing a bruise on Mom's face.

My father wouldn't get away with this crap if Uncle were here, and he knows it.

I called Uncle last night, told him what's happening to Mom, and he promised he'd come as soon as he could, but he was doing a job for a buddy.

I know he wants to be here, that he feels bad for leaving. But no one knew my father would come home this weekend.

"Are you proud of your grades? Have you suddenly turned stupid? Is your mother babying you too much? Well? Answer me."

"It's boring." I speak no lie. It is boring. Uncle says I'm the smartest person he knows. We work on my homework together, and I never get anything wrong. But the moment I'm in class, it's like there's a wall, and I can't jump high enough to reach the top to climb over. Nothing makes sense then. The words won't come, the numbers all jumble together, and no matter how hard I try, no matter how well I do at home when we practice and study, I can't answer a single question on any of my tests.

"She's not stupid. My brother works with her every night."

My father scoffs. "There's the problem right there."

"Then maybe you should be home and help me yourself." The words blow out of me like an unjammed hose.

He rises, his bulky frame filling the space and sucking all the breathable air from the room. Mom visibly shrinks in her chair.

I straighten in my chair and lift my chin, expecting the worst.

"You think you're so tough, don't you? You're a goddamned teenager. Life's been too easy on you, I see. I slave away for weeks on end, am a bloody stranger in my own home, and you have the nerve to treat me with disrespect?" He hovers over me, his towering form monstrous as spit flies from his mouth and onto the table.

I refuse to back down, to let the terror churning in my stomach reflect in my eyes.

Uncle says the only way to beat a bully is show him he means nothing to you.

My father means less than nothing, if that's possible. I hate him.

I wish he were dead.

I used to love him. I used to look up at him and believe I'd always be safe. I used to think nothing would ever take his love from me. He was my hero.

Some hero. His arm rises, and I know he's going to hit me.

I imagine the strike, the power behind it, the way my flimsy chair will fall and I'll be on the ground.

I imagine my mom sobbing in her seat, not having the guts to intervene.

I imagine my father looking at me with disgust.

"What's going on?"

The sound of Uncle's voice stops my father's arm from propelling toward me.

The sound of Uncle's voice saves me.

"I said what's going on?" Uncle comes into the room and stands beside me, his one hand resting on my shoulder, the other fisted at his side.

My father looks at Uncle, at me, notices his hand on my shoulder, and takes a step back.

"You're . . . you're home early." Mom's timid voice holds a note of relief.

"Not early enough, I see."

"I showed them my report card," I say, trying to explain what's going on. Uncle nods.

"They don't really mean anything, you know that, right?" he says. "Those lazy teachers assume everyone learns one way and then judge you based on their incorrect assumptions. You're smarter than they give you credit for, and no tests will tell me otherwise." The love and acceptance radiating from his eyes as he looks at me send tingles over my body.

All my friends moon over him. They call him Uncle Abs because of his six-pack. They get jealous whenever they see us together, because they want the attention he gives me.

The attention he gives only to me. They can be jealous all they want. He'll never love them, never want them the way he does me.

I've heard Mom and Uncle whisper at night when they think I'm asleep. I've heard her ask him to be careful with me, not to hurt me like he hurt her, to promise her he's different. He tells her I'm different, that I'm special in a way no one could ever understand. He gets me when no one else does. He loves me in a way no one else will. He would never harm me.

She believes him.

"So now you're her parent?" My father roars like a baby lion who believes his roar is ferocious, but in reality it's only a pitiful meow.

"Firefly, why don't you go on up to your room?" Uncle picks up his bag and hands it to me. "Can you take that up with you? Don't look inside, though, because there's a gift for you." The wink he gives me tells me he wants me to do the exact opposite.

I grin like a girl about to lick the cake bowl and head up the stairs, ignoring everyone else in the room.

I want to pause at the top of the stairs and listen in, but Uncle watches me as I climb, and he won't say a word until I'm out of range and in my room.

What he doesn't know, though, is I can hear every word through a hole in my closet wall. The vent in there, when uncovered, makes it sound like I'm in the next room.

"I thought we'd come to an agreement," Uncle says as I listen in. "This wasn't your weekend to come home."

"I can bloody well come home whenever I damn well please," my father blusters.

I imagine him puffing out his fat, ugly chest before sitting back down.

"Can we not do this, please? It's late, and we're all exhausted," Mom begs, pleads.

I wonder if she knows how weak she sounds.

I will never be like her when I move out of the house. I will be strong. Capable of anything. I'll never let a man hurt me the way my father hurts her.

"Why don't you head up to bed, sis. I've got this. Your husband and I need to have a chat." The authority in his voice sends a chill down my arms. When Uncle gets angry, he's scary.

He gets a look in his eyes that I swear can stop a man dead.

I've always wondered if he's ever killed someone. I think he has.

"Sit back down in that chair, woman. He doesn't get to tell you what to do." My father almost chokes on his words.

I imagine my mother trying to decide which side to step to. If she were smart, it'd be Uncle's side. He's the only one who's protected her from my father, even though she doesn't deserve it.

Uncle says he's getting tired of her, that one day soon he'll have to do something about her.

I don't know what that means. I asked him once, but he said he'd share when he was ready. When I was ready.

I think I'm ready.

"I still need to tidy up the kitchen—"

From the way she stops, I have no doubt Uncle gives her a look. I count how long it will take her to climb the stairs and head to bed. One second, two seconds, three seconds, four . . . and then the squeak of that second step happens.

I scamper out of the closet, re-cover the vent, and sit on the bed.

Will she come in? She rarely does anymore.

There's a soft knock, then the twist of the knob before she takes a step into my room, a sad smile on her face.

"You called him, didn't you?"

I nod.

"Thank you."

We share a look. A look that far surpasses the age and familial distance between us. A look that I know I'll always remember.

She views me as an adult in that moment. Someone with more courage, more strength than she'll ever have.

Before I blink, she's gone.

I creep to my door and open it an inch. I listen to hear if she locks her door, if she feels safe enough to now that Uncle is home.

When Father comes home on weekends, he either sleeps on the couch or in his truck. Never in bed with Mom. Not anymore.

Last night he did.

Last night he forced his way in before she could lock the door.
Last night I'd had to hear things no child should ever have to hear.
I've never hated them more than I did last night.
Him for being . . . him. Her for letting him be . . . him.
I think about going back into my closet to listen in, but I know Uncle will ask, and I want to give him an honest answer.
Instead, I open his bag and find a small gift inside.
I pull it out, excited to see what he bought me.
It's the most beautiful nightgown I've ever seen. It's a brown color with a pink ribbon on the hem and at the waist. It feels like satin. It's wrapped around a book.
A used copy of Alice's Adventures in Wonderland.
The cover is tattered, the pages bent, and it has that musty smell.
It is the most beautiful thing I've ever been given.
I look at myself in the mirror, amazed at the tears in my eyes.
Another person looks back at me.
Someone with a sparkle in her eye, defiance in her face. Someone who wears the body of a young teen but has an old soul.
Someone I don't recognize but welcome all the same.

Chapter Twenty-Eight

KILLER

Fear is a wonder drug.

The chain reaction it creates within our bodies is amazing. Prepare and protect. The adrenaline released into our bloodstream tells us to prepare. The goal of our inner reaction is to protect us from perceived threats.

Even if we have no idea where that threat is coming from or when.

I've been a student of fear. I grew up with its ever-hovering presence in my life until I was strong enough to fight back.

Fear doesn't control me. I control it.

I can't have anyone discovering my secret. I'm playing the role I was meant to play with perfection. No one suspects a thing, and I mean to keep it that way.

During the day, I play the role of someone else. It's not until I'm here, back at home, that I can relax and be whoever I want to be.

Tonight I'm a hunter. A watcher.

I've been watching a family for the past little bit.

I'm watching a few families.

My judgment has been delayed, but tonight will tip the scales toward either life or death.

~

Drip. Drip-drip. Three drops form a small puddle. The elixir of life soaks into the carpet, the stain growing with every drip from the knife in my hand.

The parents. Dead. Blood pools beneath them, soaking the covers, sheets, mattress.

I watched them earlier from their backyard, hidden behind the walnut tree, as the father slapped his son for a dropped glass of milk. I cringed as he was spanked. I broke as his tears fell, cries rang, and sobs carried over the wind from his open window.

It was hard to sit and wait. Harder still to not rush into the home and stop the father.

I could have called the police. I could have rung their doorbell. I could have done any number of things to stop the breaking of that little boy's heart, but I didn't.

That's on me.

This . . . this is on them. I was willing to walk away tonight, to leave them be, keep my promise that I would stop. Willing until the milk dropped.

They didn't have to die.

I want to spit on the bed. I want to turn back time and be slower, savor the kill. I acted too fast, too hastily. They deserved slow deaths. Painful deaths.

I focus on the scene, memorize every last detail. It's time to stop. I've killed too many too soon. I've been impatient.

I hit the talk button on the kitchen's cordless phone and dial.

"Nine-one-one, what is your emergency?"

"This is the Cheshire Mad Queen." The name the press gave me is fitting. "Your presence is requested at 342 Hatter Lane. Front door is open. Keep your voices down. There's a little boy fast asleep. His room is the first right at the top of the stairs. I suggest taking him from the house before he notices all the blood, and yes, there is quite a bit." I place the phone back down on the counter and take a photo off the fridge.

He really is a sweet thing. Big blue eyes, wide forehead, even wider smile. It's not his fault he's different and a little clumsy. He deserves a family who will accept him for who he is, not punish him for it.

I slide through the back door, cross the yard, and pause on the other side of the fence. With careful precision, I undress and roll the clothes along with the hat, gloves on both my hands, and shoes into the waiting backpack. With a gentle swipe of a makeup wipe, I clean my face, and then I make my way down the back alley and enter the west side of Wonderland Park before the faint scream of sirens fills the air.

They are too late.

They are always too late.

~

The wheat field dances in the glow of the moonlight, and the husky song of nature is my dance partner as I trail through the rows in search of something no longer there.

Control is a beast that can never be tamed, and yet I've tried over and over and over. I've failed more times than I prefer to count. Each of those times, the repercussions have almost destroyed me.

I thought my time here would be different.

I hoped it would be. I had high expectations and planned things to ensure past practices wouldn't be repeated.

Fuck.

I'm my own worst enemy.

What am I supposed to do now?

Hell if I know.

I received a warning last night. A warning from *him*. *He* scares me. We have an arrangement—I follow his orders and he lets me do what I want. Unless I go too far.

His warning is that I had better fix this mess I created before he has to. A warning I'd better heed.

Fuck.

There has to be another way to handle this fuck-fest.

In the distance, a light in the window at home beckons me. That call, it holds a promise of what could be, of what was.

That window represents all the good in my life. The small illumination that breaks through the darkness, that casts a glow and offers a welcoming path. It is my heart. It's who I am.

I am that light breaking through the darkness. I am that path leading those I love away from the abyss of darkness, of annihilation.

I'm the Protector. I can't forget that.

Chapter Twenty-Nine

THURSDAY, AUGUST 22

I didn't recognize the face of the woman who stared back at me. She was pale. Exhausted. Haggard. I turned away from the mirror in Dr. Brown's office and sat down on the couch.

I still wasn't sleeping. What if someone broke in again and left another note? I didn't feel safe in my own home. I pulled the light knit wrap tighter around my chest, my fingertips frozen because my body was running on fumes.

Dr. Brown didn't say much as she held a glass of water and looked over my file. What was she reading? I wanted to lean forward to read it, to peek at her notes, but I didn't.

"There's a few things I'm concerned about," she said after what felt like an hour of silence. "The first being your sleeping patterns. I'm not sure that you should be seeing your patients as often as you are if you're not sleeping. It affects your cognitive ability, and you won't be of any help to them." She waited for my response.

She was right. Of course she was right.

"The other thing is your safety. You need some checks and balances if you're sleepwalking. Since you live alone, you need to set up some sort of system that will wake you up or keep you in the house instead of leaving. Could your friend Tami possibly stay with you?"

"I've asked. She'll stay when she can, but she gets called in at all hours."

She scrunched her nose. I took it that was her main plan.

"I'm not tying myself to the bed, if that's what you're thinking." I softened my sarcasm with a grin.

She chuckled. "No, I was thinking more along the lines of placing a bell on your bedroom door. What if you set up your alarm system so Tami got a text if you left in the middle of the night?"

I gave that some thought.

"Have you thought about taking sleeping pills?"

I recoiled at her suggestion. I hated taking pills. It was bad enough I took something for my migraines.

"I'd rather not."

She leaned her head to the side, tapped her pen against her cheek. "Is there something about the idea of taking the pills that bothers you?"

"I don't like how they make me feel." That wasn't a cop-out. It was the truth. I'd taken them in the past and hated the grogginess that followed the morning after. Not to mention the brain fog.

"Someone has come into my home and left me notes. My doors are locked all the time. I don't feel safe, and if I take those . . ." I didn't finish my sentence because I didn't need to.

She nodded. "That makes sense. Which is why I suggested Tami staying with you. I hate to say it, Danielle, but considering you have no recollection of what you're doing while you're asleep, I'm not seeing any minus signs, you know? You're right, someone has come into your home, and it doesn't seem safe."

My eyes narrowed somewhat as I realized what she was really saying.

"You're saying there's no difference between taking the pills or not taking the pills."

"Right. But"—she paused and looked down at her file—"I'm not about to ask you to do something you're really uncomfortable with.

There are more natural sleeping options if you'd prefer to go that route. You'll have to play with them, see what works and what doesn't. But you can find them in any drugstore."

I let that thought play around in my head. "Natural as in herbal?"

A grin bloomed on her face. I think she heard the hope in my voice, the acceptance.

"I would prefer you taking a prescription, but I'll be happy if you do this too. Just ask the pharmacist to assist you. There are a lot of options, and they'll be able to help find the right one. I really think it would help." She leaned forward. "I even take them," she admitted.

Knowing that, it helped.

I'd ask Tami to stay, but I'd make it casual and have it appear as if I wanted to look after her while she worked these murder cases, not because I was scared. But . . . what if I had a bout of sleepwalking when she was there? I hadn't yet, not any time she'd stayed in the past, but there was always a first time for everything.

I didn't want her to worry about me, and she would if she knew the truth.

"Let's talk about the notes you've received. Have you told Tami?"

She wanted me to say yes. I wished I could.

"No."

"Why not?" Tiny lines of disappointment crinkled along her eyes and forehead.

It was a simple question, although the answer was anything but simple.

"I know what the notes say, but I don't want to believe them. I don't want to believe one of my patients is the killer." There was a level of certainty in my voice as sure, as solid, as stable as concrete. Would she believe it? I doubted it. I wasn't sure if I did.

"But what if it is true? What if one of them is the killer?" Dr. Brown asked, her hands folded on top of her lap with a look on her face I didn't want to read.

It's not that I couldn't read it—I just didn't want to.

"Danielle." Her voice had that it's-time-to-face-reality tone to it. "You're here not just because you need help handling your stress but also because you need help in reading your clients. You're not sure if you're helping them, which tells me you're not sure if you know them enough."

I sat there, stone cold, a blank statue without facial features she could read.

"If you don't know them the way you feel you should by now," she continued, "then how can you be so sure that the notes aren't warnings about them?"

I didn't know what to say. She was right, to a point.

"I understand what you're saying, but—"

"But you don't want to accept it." She stood and headed to her desk. She pulled something from a drawer.

"You can't be expected to know everything about your patients, Danielle. This might sound harsh, but the reality is you're never going to be everything your patients need. That's Psychology 101, something your professors would have said year one. It's definitely something you learn within a few patients into your practice."

The way she watched me, careful, with considerate caution, unsure of my reaction, bothered me. I was wary now of what she would say.

"Just after I started my own practice, I had a client who touched my heart. She was a twenty-one-year-old college student, came from a family who sacrificed everything so she could succeed. She was bright, intelligent, and had so many friends who loved her." She was holding a photograph in her hands, and the smile she gave me was full of sadness and guilt.

She turned the photo so I saw the student in front of a building, a bag full of books across her body. She wasn't smiling.

"I thought I knew her. Our sessions were focused on strategies to handle the stress of her parents' expectations, of her own, and I really thought we'd made progress. Sometimes we would meet in my office. Other times, I'd join her for coffee while she worked on assignments.

This photo," she said as her sad smile wobbled, "was taken one day
before she died by suicide."

Like a gut punch, I flinched. She'd told me this story to share a
message. One I heard loud and clear.

"I had no idea," she continued, "no idea she was that close. I knew
she was depressed. It was something we'd discussed and had some strategies to help with, but if you would have told me she'd be dead the day
after our coffee meeting, I would have called you a liar."

She set the photo down on the coffee table faceup so it was there,
a subtle reminder.

"If it's true," I said, "if it's true that Savannah, Tyler, or Ella is the
killer, why tell me?"

"Good question. Why do you think?"

I shrugged. Hell if I knew. "Why not just go to the police? If they
know something I don't, why play this game with me? It doesn't make
sense."

"Why are you so sure it's not them?" Her voice was strong but soft
and missing everything I'd expected to hear.

"I . . ." The words disappeared. The things I wanted to say, the
things I needed to admit—they were glued to my tongue. I couldn't say
them because, deep down, I wasn't one hundred percent sure, was I? It
was hard to face that truth.

"Are you a mind reader?" she asked.

I sighed.

A small ball of stress appeared beneath my fingers when I placed
them at the base of my neck. Despite the pain relievers and the neck
warmers, no matter how much I massaged it myself, that ball wouldn't
go away.

"Okay. Let's discuss the notes." She paused, looked around as if
collecting her thoughts. "If you're scared, then you need to share them
with the authorities. Especially Tami. Someone has come into your
home. That would scare me."

"No, I can't."

"Can't what?" she asked. "Share them with the authorities or tell Tami?"

"They're one and the same, and I don't want her to know yet."

"Why?"

"She doesn't need the stress. Not right now. Her focus needs to be on catching the killer."

"What if your notes hold a clue?"

What if. I didn't want to play this game. "There's no clue because it can't be real."

Did she hear the doubt too?

I was my own worst enemy right now, going back and forth.

"What you're telling me is that you're not ready to tell Tami. Which is okay. For now." That last part she added with a smile.

I smiled back, wobbly and uncertain. I bit my lips and stared at the potted fern she'd added since I had last seen her.

"How about we focus on trusting yourself?" she asks. "Trusting your instincts, especially when it comes to your clients."

I wanted to snicker, to scoff at the idea that I could trust my instincts. Not being able to read those instincts was why I was there. Which, given our conversation about my certainty that none of my patients could be the killer, was hilarious.

I saw what she did there.

"I think my instincts have taken a vacation." Sure, let's add some humor to the discussion. You didn't need to take Psych 101 to know humor was used as a deflection mechanism.

"Let me rephrase that," I said. "How do you know if your instincts are right or not? I mean, I've been working with my patients long enough now to know that they should be getting better. Right? Or am I just being too hard on myself?"

"Therapy is just a means to healing. It's not the cure."

I wanted straight talk, not psychobabble.

"Okay," said Dr. Brown. "Let me put it this way, then. Just because someone comes to you for help doesn't always mean they are ready for it. There's only so much you can do as their therapist. You know that."

"I know." Air puffed out from my compressed lips. "But that doesn't negate the fact I feel like a failure."

"I think you asked the perfect question before. Do you think you're being too hard on yourself?"

"Wouldn't you be?" The challenge in my voice was loud. She looked at me like she was waiting for me to say something, to maybe retract my words. I wasn't going to.

My question was real. I wanted to know. I needed to know.

"Yes, yes, I probably would be if I truly wasn't helping my patients," she admitted. "But I wouldn't let it linger, and I would remember that I was doing the absolute best I could, and that includes seeking help. You're here, and that's a huge step. You're doing everything you can, Danielle."

I was ready to argue that point, because we both knew it wasn't true.

"You mentioned self-love." Dr. Brown tapped the notepad on her lap. "Did you ever focus on this with your patients?"

Self-love? As a focus?

"Of course." It came out more like a question than an answer. "Especially with Ella." I added some strength to my words so I seemed more in control, like I knew what I was talking about.

She wrote Ella's name down on her pad of paper.

"I know you believe you failed all your patients, but why don't we focus on how you helped them. Sometimes all it takes is a different outlook to counteract the negative voices in your head."

I flinched. I didn't mean to, but she'd hit the nail on the head.

Before now I would have said I was a positive person, that I looked for the good in people, for the bright side, for the rainbow, so to speak.

But now I was all doom and gloom. I saw only the damaging, never the positive.

When had that changed?

"Danielle." Dr. Brown twisted in her seat. "Why don't you list for me five positive things that happened today." Her voice was upbeat and as sugary as a lollipop.

I hated lollipops.

"Fresh coffee, hot shower, blue sky." I counted off the first three things that came to mind. She waited with a mixture of exasperation and encouragement. "I'm alive, and . . ." Listing five things off the top of my head wasn't easy. I wanted to go for a run, clear my head, focus on only my breathing and the sound of my feet as they smacked the pavement.

"And I'm here with you." I said this last one with a feeling of triumph, like a little kid who finally got the answer he'd been searching for all day. "I suppose you want me to find five ways I've helped my patients too, right? Is this where we're headed?"

I didn't wait for the good doctor to agree with me.

"Let's start with Ella. When she first introduced herself to me, she was a shell of a person. No eye contact, jumpy, and when she spoke, I could barely hear her."

Looking back, I realized just how far Ella had come since we'd first been introduced, and a little bit of hope bloomed inside me.

"It's been a process, but she's better." I let that sit with me for a moment.

"Better how?" Dr. Brown asked.

"She looks me in the eye more than before, she can handle sudden noises, and we can have a conversation without me having to ask her to speak up." I touched that bump again at the back of my neck. Pushed on it. Pushed through the pain my touch brought.

"Did you notice any other changes with her?"

"Ella . . ." I paused to find the right words. "Ella is a strong and amazing woman, full of surprises. But she doesn't see herself like that. I'm not sure she ever will. She's had to remold herself into a new person more than anyone else I've ever known. That's . . . not healthy, and damaging to one's true identity."

"What's her true identity, then? Did you ever see it? Did she ever reveal it to you?" Dr. Brown's shoulders were hunched over her chest as she leaned forward, her arms straight out, resting on her knees.

My answer was important to her.

Why?

Chapter Thirty

Ella and her missed sessions had to stop.

No word, no warning, no response to my multiple messages to make sure she showed up tomorrow. Something didn't add up, and my gut told me that whatever was going on with her, it wasn't good.

In the past, I wouldn't have stressed so much. In the past, I would have assumed she was busy working. But after her admission about the murders, I wasn't just worried.

I was scared.

Her last words to me had been a confession that it was her fault those parents were dead, and then she'd bolted from my office.

She said it was her fault. She said she was responsible. She never explained how.

I appreciated how Dr. Brown had walked me through my thought process regarding the notes. No matter how convenient it looked, I knew it couldn't be Ella. I refused to allow her past to tarnish her future. "Once a killer always a killer" didn't apply to Ella. She'd been a child under extreme stress.

She'd changed. She was no longer that young girl she'd been.

And yet doubt clouded my mind like mist drifting off a mountain.

Since Ella wouldn't come to me, I would go to her.

From my home to the library was about a thirty-minute walk. I grabbed a coffee from one of the many coffee shops lining Wonderland Street and took my time.

I loved the town of Cheshire. Loved everything about it, from how quaint the stores were to the little boutiques and bed-and-breakfast locations. I adored all the secondhand shops and the bakeries. The town reminded me of what you'd find in Europe, minus the cobblestone walks.

When I first moved here, I wasn't sure if I would fit into such a small town, where secrets were never kept, where life moved more slowly than normal, where things appeared to be too good to be true.

When things appeared to be too good, most of the time they weren't.

Serial murders happened in big cities, not towns far from the bright lights and busy streets. Sleeper towns were just that . . . sleepy. People moved here to get away from the busyness, because they needed to feel safe, to raise their growing families in a community they believed they could trust.

On my way to the library, where normally I'd see smiles and laughing children flocking the sidewalks, there was almost no one out.

"Danielle." I heard my name being called.

Sabrina had stepped out of her store and waved. She wore a flowing blue dress and held a pale-yellow scarf around her arms. Her hair was in a loose braid that fell over her shoulder, and if I didn't know better, I'd have thought she knew the secret to remaining young despite the gray in her hair.

"I just wanted to check that you were feeling okay," she said, her voice soft and full of concern as I backtracked to see her.

By the puzzlement on my face, she must have noted my confusion.

"Last night, remember? You were sitting there on that bench when I closed up the café." She pointed to the one in front of her store. "You said you were feeling a little dizzy, that you'd been so busy you'd forgotten to eat, so I gave you a trail bar I'd baked that morning. I didn't realize you were hypoglycemic."

"I'm not." I looked to the bench and then back to Sabrina. "Last night?"

"You don't remember? You were supposed to call or send me a text once you got home."

Last night I had been at home.

"I stopped by a little while later, after running to the store, but you were fast asleep on the couch." She lightly rubbed my arm with her hand. "You really do need to close your curtains, especially at night. Don't worry, I couldn't see anything since you were under a bundle of blankets, but with you being so close to the park and all, you don't want any Peeping Toms looking in, especially since you're single."

My curtains were always closed at night. I was fastidious when it came to privacy.

"What time did you stop by?" I knew for a fact I hadn't slept. The mound of blankets had been just that. A mound.

"Oh, I don't know." Sabrina glanced at her watch. "I saw you here around eight o'clock, then I ran to the store, chatted with Gloria, the one who works the night shift and bakes all those cakes. It's been a while since I've seen her, so . . . I was probably there almost two hours. My husband texted, wondering if I was coming home or not."

"You stopped by when?"

"Probably around ten or ten thirty. I—"

"I wasn't sleeping." I cut her off. "You should have knocked."

"You looked like you were asleep. Honestly, Danielle, I don't mean to be rude, but you need new furniture. Don't you think it's time to claim the house as your own?"

"What? No, that'd be . . ." I shivered, cold fingers trailing along my skin. "Maybe I just like the seventies style of decor," I said, realizing I sounded defensive. Sure, most of the house looked like it was just waiting for my grandmother to reappear, but buying new furniture really wasn't at the top of the priority chain right now.

Her brow arched as she measured my words. "Are you feeling better?" She repeated her question, dropping the subject of my interior decorating decisions, thankfully.

My memory was as blank as a brand-new chalkboard. Sabrina was worried about me, but maybe I should be concerned about her. I had been at home all night. Other than when I took a walk around the park, but I didn't recall seeing Sabrina. Whoever she saw, it wasn't me.

"You should get some blood work done, Danielle. I swear you told me you were hypoglycemic, which is weird because I am too. Or maybe I just noticed the symptoms and assumed." She pursed her lips. "You look exhausted. Are you sleeping enough?"

"Not really. I've tried that tea you gave me, but it seems to have no effect."

"I don't think anyone is sleeping lately. Isn't it horrible? Everything that's been happening?" She stared out at the park. "To think that something like this could happen in our small community. I heard"—she leaned forward to whisper—"that the FBI is now involved." She punctuated the FBI letters in a way that made me imagine her poking someone in the chest as she said each one.

The change in topic was sudden. "Tami needs all the help she can get on this one. She's the one I'm worried about, to be honest." I knew I was feeding into the local gossip, but if I could take the focus off me, that was all that mattered.

"Tami?"

"Yeah. My friend I've been trying to introduce to you. She's one of the detectives on the case."

"I didn't realize you knew anyone on the case." Like a blind mouse sniffing cheese, her curiosity was about to get the better of her.

"Well, now you do," I said.

"So the elusive Tami is involved in solving the murders." Sabrina's lips quirked with surprise at the news. "I can't believe I haven't met her yet. Has she never come into the shop?"

She almost sounded hurt.

"I was trying to make a cheesecake two nights ago. I've been wanting to get the two of you together so you can meet. She's so busy, so I thought a cheesecake would entice her to at least stop by if she was free. But I kept mixing up ingredients and finally accepted defeat after midnight."

"Why didn't you say something? I've been wanting to make a cheesecake for a while now. Why don't you let me do that, and the two of you could come by for tea?" Sabrina offered.

I smiled in agreement. Tami wouldn't be able to stand up cheesecake, especially if she knew it was made with her in mind.

We said goodbye, and I continued on my walk, but her words bothered me more than I'd let on. Why had she said she'd seen me? I would have remembered, right? I'd tried to sleep last night on the couch, but other than a few fitful naps while a movie played in the background, I'd been wide awake.

And yet she was so sure it had been me.

Chapter Thirty-One

Inside the library, it was deathly silent.

A few children sat around the bookshelves and quiet corners, but their heads were buried in books.

Tables were full of college-age students, their ears covered with headphones, books and notebooks spread out in front of them.

The book aisles were abandoned.

The upper floor was forlorn. The seats along the railing were empty, and the only real sound was the slap-slap-slap of the librarian's shoes as she walked down the length of the room, her arms full of books, glasses perched on the end of her nose.

We nodded at one another before I made my way toward the children's section. If anywhere, this was where I'd find Ella.

Except I didn't. She wasn't stocking shelves. She wasn't reading quietly to a group of children. She wasn't curled up in a corner chair reading a book on her own.

I thought maybe I'd find her stacking books in another section or maybe helping someone discover a new author.

No matter where I thought she'd be, she wasn't there.

I waited to speak to the librarian, but every time I stepped close, she became busy.

I headed out into the playground area, where children were surrounded by their parents and other staff members of the library.

Gone were the ease and friendliness.

Gone were the smiles and playfulness.

Gone were the hope and laughter.

Caution, whispered fears, and anxious glances were all I found as I walked down the steps of the library and looked out onto the field.

I pasted a welcoming look on my face and lifted my hand in a slight wave to those who huddled together. A few waved back, but most turned their backs to me and continued to watch their children.

Ella wasn't down there, not playing with the children, not talking to the parents.

But she was sitting on a park bench off to the side, beneath a tree, with a book on her lap. Her legs were curled beneath her, and her head was bent so that her hair partially covered her face.

She didn't notice my arrival.

I didn't think I'd ever seen her so relaxed, so at peace. So much the opposite of everyone around her.

"Ella." I called out her name a few times before she looked up.

"Dr. Rycroft, what are you doing here?" She closed the book in her lap with a gentleness I'd come to expect from her.

"Hmm, let's see. You've missed appointments, haven't returned any of my calls, and I was worried about you." I should have picked up coffee for the two of us; having my hands empty felt weird.

She looked out over the park.

"Sorry," she said. "I . . ." She fidgeted with the book on her lap. "I had some days off and just . . . closed myself away at home."

I noticed she wouldn't look at me now.

"Are you okay?"

She nodded.

"Everyone needs time away—I get that." I crossed my legs and relaxed my arm over the back of the bench. "Did you get some reading done?"

She patted the book on her lap and looked up at me with a faraway expression.

Escapism didn't bode well for Ella. She escaped when she felt threatened, scared, unsettled.

"Remember, you promised you would come see me if things became too much, too stressful?" I wanted her to be able to trust me, to come to me for help in those crucial moments.

I thought we were getting there.

"It just . . . happened." She played with a strand of hair that hung over her shoulder.

"Was there a reason you felt the need to escape?" My voice remained gentle, as if I were speaking to a child or wanted to coax out a kitten from beneath the couch.

It was wrong, but my thoughts immediately ran to the notes I'd received. What had Ella been doing the past week to miss our sessions?

Was she alone? Where did she live? She once told me that when she escaped, she had no memory of the hours lost or how she handled the basic needs like food.

"Have you ever left one place and arrived at another without being aware of the drive?" She smoothed her skirt. "Or found yourself in a place you didn't recognize? Or maybe woke up in your room, but you were still so lost in your dreams that nothing was recognizable?"

Yes, yes, and yes.

"That's what it's like. One minute I'm enjoying the warm sun, and the next thing I know, days have passed. I've fed myself, bathed myself, even put myself to bed, but I don't recall any of it. I live in a dream within my head."

An innocent look of wonder filled her face.

"Or maybe the dream is my reality, and this"—she spread her arms out—"is the dream world. Maybe you're not real. Maybe I'm not real. Hell." She tilted her head back and greeted the sun. "Maybe my whole past isn't real, and I'm just living in a nightmare."

"I certainly feel real." I added a little laughter to my voice.

"Are you?"

My nose wrinkled. I didn't like where this was going.

"Please call me, Ella, the next time it happens, okay?"

She shrugged. "It's not like there's a warning, you know. I don't plan it."

I nodded, giving her that.

"Can I ask you a question?" I felt weird asking, but I needed to know. "It's been a bit since we've seen each other. You . . . you haven't been by the house and left me a note or two, have you?"

The blank look on her face told me no.

Now I felt uncomfortable.

Nothing. Nothing on her face.

"Okay, forget I asked." *Shit.* I didn't know why I asked, why I thought she would be the one if the notes were about her. So where had they come from?

"Was it a helpful note? My roommate often leaves me notes. Reminders to eat or appointments she thinks I'll forget."

This surprising tidbit of news caught me off guard.

"You have a roommate?" I had been under the impression that she lived alone. "Is this new?"

She turned to me with a peculiar look on her face. "I've always had a roommate, Dr. Rycroft. I thought you knew that."

I racked my brain for this information. I don't ever recall her mentioning a roommate. Ever.

"She's . . . well, you might not like her. She's someone from my past life."

My brows shot up faster than a firecracker.

"Ella, do you think that's wise?"

"Ava took care of me in prison. She was the only one I could count on. She's . . . good for me."

There were so many thoughts going through my head, and none of them told me this Ava person was anything close to being good for Ella.

"They usually advise you not to have contact with anyone you befriend in prison," I said cautiously. "The goal is to start new, to start fresh with nothing from your past holding you back."

Ella nodded, and for a moment I thought she was actually considering my words.

"Ava is different. I'm the way I am because of Ava. It's . . . it's hard to understand, harder to explain. But she takes care of me, Dr. Rycroft."

"Will you tell me about her?" If she was that important to Ella, I wanted to know about her. I needed to know about her.

A semisweet smile lingered on Ella's face. She glanced up at me a few times, her head still slightly bowed as her fingers drew circles on the cover of her book.

I finally noticed the book.

Alice's Adventures in Wonderland. Of course.

It almost looked familiar. Like the one I'd tried to buy.

Like the one from Sabrina's shop.

It couldn't be, though. I thought that one had faded gold-stamped letters on the cover, whereas the book on Ella's lap just looked worn.

"I knew who I was this morning, but I've changed several times since then," Ella whispered softly.

I recognized it as a quote from the book in her hands.

"What do you mean, Ella?"

"Ava says that's my life motto. She encourages me to grow, to change, to be someone better than I was back then. Without her, I'd be lost in a darkness of my own making with no way to get out."

There was a tone of reverence as she spoke of Ava.

"I think you've always had that strength inside you," I reminded her.

She shrugged. "It might have been there, but without her, I would never have found it."

She then turned her body toward me, angled so her knees almost touched my thigh.

"You like me, don't you, Dr. Rycroft?" she asked. "You like the person I am, the one I present to you in our sessions and even now, right?"

She didn't give me a chance to respond.

"You wouldn't have liked me then. When I was lost in hatred and anger. When all I could think about was how to destroy my parents' lives like they'd destroyed mine. I burned with a hatred so bright everything around me ignited too. When they died, I . . ." She shuddered. "I liked it. It filled me with a high I'd never felt before. I was in control of my destiny in that moment. I became someone new that night."

"But you didn't allow that to consume you," I reminded her.

"You don't understand. I found the taste of death to be addictive. Addictive and compelling. Intoxicating to the point I wanted more. Like a drug. If it hadn't been for Ava . . . I'd be an addict."

I worked hard to not react. A brush of wind touched the back of my neck, and I shivered.

"When I was sent to prison, I'd already been judged. I was guilty, and I didn't try to hide it. No one cared *why* I killed my parents, only that I did. But Ava . . . she cared. She saw past the label others had placed on me and saw a broken soul."

She reached down and pulled out a water bottle from a bag I hadn't noticed at her feet.

"Ava recognized how damaged I was, and she looked beyond my actions to find the reason. She understood my monsters. She wept at my stories, about how my mother would turn the other way when my stepfather tucked me into bed. She didn't care that he sexually abused me. She knew and didn't care."

Ella gripped the water bottle in her hands, her fingertips white from the pressure.

"I'm so sorry, Ella." I wanted to wrap her in my arms and hold her, tell her it would be okay, that she was okay, but I knew she wouldn't appreciate it, not in public.

This was the first time she'd been so open with me about her past. I knew all the details, of course, from her police records and articles I'd found online. I also had access to her previous medical reports and psychological tests. But I'd never pushed her to open up.

The facts weren't always as important as the feelings behind them.

"Ava was the one who helped me navigate the ugly path I was on. She made me a promise once, one I've never been able to forget. It's why we live together."

She slowly unwrapped her fingers from the bottle, setting it down beside her on the bench. She patted the book on her lap, and the briefest semblance of love passed across her face.

"She promised we would make it right. Make sure no other child is ever hurt like I was. We can't save all of them, but we can watch out for the ones in our path." Ella nodded her head numerous times as she spoke, as if she was reminding herself of this truth.

I wanted to smile. I wanted to say how happy I was for her, that she'd found such a friend to support her, but all I could focus on were the words she'd spoken.

Make sure no other child is ever hurt . . .

Then I recalled the words she'd said to me previously. How she was the one responsible for the deaths, that they were her fault.

"Ella." I cleared my throat. How did I even ask this?

She watched me with a slight wariness, unsure of what I was going to say.

I wasn't even sure.

I didn't know Ava. I had no idea of her past, her present, who she was, what she looked like, or what she even did. For all I knew, she could have been sent to prison with Ella for petty theft.

The note I'd received claimed I knew the killer. Maybe they just assumed I did. Maybe they were wrong. Maybe the note had nothing to do with Ella and her past and everything to do with her roommate and the present. I cleared my throat again.

"Does Ava ever come here, to the library?"

A fear bubbled inside me.

"Ava doesn't really like crowds," Ella said with a hesitation that didn't settle my sense of foreboding. "She tends to stay home during the day. She's more of a night owl anyway."

That didn't really answer my question, but a commotion in the playground caught our attention.

Several police cruisers with their lights on had pulled into the library parking lot.

The parents on the field all called their children to them, their voices filling the air with panic.

I watched the scene and the officers who got out of their vehicles. There were five in total, all armed and all advancing toward the library steps.

When I turned back to Ella, she'd disappeared.

Chapter Thirty-Two

FRIDAY, AUGUST 23

The coffee shop where I waited for Tami was empty.

Other than the barista, I was the only customer, which was odd.

I watched the steam from my coffee rise and swirl with the cool breeze from the open window.

I zipped up the light jacket I wore and wrapped my hands around the mug.

By the time Tami arrived, I'd received a refill, ordered a coffee for her, and eaten halfway through a fruit bowl.

"Sorry," she said as she shrugged off her raincoat and draped it across a chair. "I got caught up with a phone call." She snagged a grape from my bowl and popped it in her mouth before she noticed the coffee in front of her.

"Thank you," she said before she took her first sip and shuddered.

"Oops, forgot to add sugar," I said. "I wasn't sure when you'd get here, so hopefully it's warm enough."

I couldn't even imagine how busy she was.

Today had been her idea. She'd called me with a plea to join her for coffee. I'd offered to bring one to her, but she claimed the need to escape for an hour or so. We had planned to meet at Sabrina's café, but when I'd arrived, the place had been jam-packed with the bridge club meet-up. For someone who needed to escape, drinking coffee in a busy café wouldn't do the trick.

Escape. There had been something behind her voice when she'd said the word, a tinge of pain laced with fear.

I hid a yawn behind my hand.

"Didn't get enough sleep last night?" She poured copious amounts of sugar into her mug before stirring. "Why aren't you taking those pills I gave you?"

I yawned again. My eyes smarted this time. "You know I don't like self-medicating."

She peeked over the rim of her cup as she took a sip. "I don't like this."

"I'm fine."

"No, you're not. Are you watching television too late? Reading? On your phone? You know, they say screen time at night disturbs your sleep patterns."

I didn't even bother to hide my eye roll.

"Hey, someone needs to look after you. Who else is going to do it if I don't?"

I almost snapped back but caught the twinkle in her eye, so I smiled instead before I bit into a piece of strawberry.

"What would I do without you?" I let a tiny bit of sarcasm leak into my voice.

Honestly, though, what *would* I do without her? I wasn't too sure.

"How are you?" I asked after pushing my bowl of fruit toward her. She'd been eyeing it ever since she'd sat down. "You look about as exhausted as I feel."

The rings beneath her eyes were more pronounced, darker, fuller, deeper.

"Bone tired is more like it. I could sleep for a week, and I'd still feel the same way." She leaned back in her chair. "I'm not doing enough."

Her voice was full of anger, agony, and anxiety, raw emotions she rarely revealed, let alone admitted to.

I reached out to grasp her hand. "You've got this, Tami. I know you. You won't fail those children. You'll find the killer."

The emptiness in her gaze reminded me of a moonless sky in the dead of night.

"I've already failed them, Dani. I'm going to fail even more families before this ends if we don't catch the killer soon. I know you want to encourage me, but you don't have to. I'm more than aware of my shortcomings," she confessed. "My own supervisor is starting to doubt my skills."

She rubbed her face before closing her eyes and dropping her head.

I wasn't sure if she had fallen asleep or was about to whisper a prayer.

"It's media madness outside the station. No matter how tight of a lid I keep on all of this, things are getting out." She rolled her head then, slowly, until she'd completed a full circle.

"Why don't you go home and have a nap? Surely you can get away for a few hours?" She was going to fall apart if she didn't start taking better care of herself.

Her answer formed on her lips, then disappeared. "That actually might be a good idea," she said. "I basically pulled a double."

Her fingers flew over her phone before she turned it facedown on the table.

"I'll head back in later this afternoon." She drank more of her coffee and then picked at the last bits of fruit in the bowl. "Mind me popping in tonight?"

"Not if you bring some ice cream with you and stay the night. I could use the company, to be honest. Any news about Tyler?" I drank the last bit of my coffee and considered asking for another refill.

"Yeah, about him. I did a background check." Her nose wrinkled. "Can you refer him to someone else?" Tami asked.

"Should I be worried?"

"I didn't like what I found—or, rather, what I didn't. He gave you a false name, so I couldn't pull anything up. I'll dig deeper, but until I get more info, I want you to be careful. Okay?" Her brow rose as she gave me a stern look.

It had been a long time since I'd felt such protection.

I needed to tell her about Ava. I wanted to, but whenever I held her name on the tip of my tongue, I hesitated. I was worried for Ella, worried that she was being influenced by someone who would hurt her in the end, and that was the last thing she needed. But before I placed a spotlight on Ella and her past, I needed to make sure I was right.

Above all, my goal was to protect Ella. I knew she wasn't the murderer.

"Hey, I have a question I've been meaning to ask."

Tami's smile dropped.

"Yesterday I happened to be at the library when several police cars pulled up."

She nodded.

"Was everything okay?"

"You were there?" I seemed to have caught her off guard. "You weren't on the list."

Now it was my turn to be surprised.

I leaned forward and whispered, "There's a list?"

"Why are you whispering?" she asked, copying my body movement and tone of voice. "You realize we are alone in here, right?" she said a little louder.

I glanced around. Not even the barista was in the room.

"Of course there is a list. We had to make note of everyone who was in the library. Where were you?"

"Not in the library."

"You just told me you were." Her words were laced with confusion.

"I was with Ella on a park bench." I hid another yawn behind my hand. "She's missed too many sessions, and I'd hoped to catch her on a break. We sat outside for a bit talking, and that's when I saw the cars."

Tami's face scrunched up into one of those I'm-thinking-too-hard-and-my-brain-hurts looks. "Ella? She wasn't on the list either." Tami's eyes tightened, the wrinkles more pronounced. "Danielle." She leaned forward and rested her crossed arms on the table. "We talked to everyone who was on the park grounds as well. Neither you nor Ella were on that list." There was a mixture of disbelief laced with worry in her voice.

I leaned back, away from her. "Well, I was there. I was outside, on the far side of the park. You know the slight hill? That's where I was sitting with Ella. We both saw the cars."

"Shit." Gone was the worry, and in its place was tension.

"What's the problem?" I asked. "Why are you getting upset with me?"

Tami's whole demeanor changed. Gone were the tired lines, the exhausted haze in her eyes, the wilted shoulders and look of ease.

Gone was Tami, my friend, and in her place was Detective Tami Sloan, the sharp-eyed, tough detective who'd fought her way to where she was because she was smart and didn't let anything pass her by.

What had I done? I didn't understand. All I'd done was ask a simple question.

"I'm not upset. I'm just trying to piece everything together. I don't have either you or your patient on my list, and that makes me wonder who made a mistake. I don't like mistakes being made, not on my watch. You know that."

"Right." I let out a hesitant breath. "It's really not that big of a deal, Tami. I must have left before your officers were out in the park, because I only recall seeing them walk into the library. They were in there awhile. I eventually left and went home."

"What about Ella?"

"Ella? What about her?" I became alert. The mama-bear roar rumbled deep within me, and I was resolved to do anything to protect her.

"You said you were there to talk with her during her break," Tami said. "Was it her lunch break or after her shift?" She pulled out her slim notebook and opened it, ready to write down whatever answer I provided.

"I'm not sure."

Her right brow rose in disbelief.

"Honestly, I have no idea. I found her there, sitting on the bench."

She scratched notes down. "Did she go back into the library or leave with you?"

I was about to admit she'd left once the police had arrived, but I knew how that would sound.

I couldn't lie either.

"We both left at the same time." It wasn't a lie. The moment I'd realized she was gone, I hadn't stuck around. I'd headed back home, stopping at the grocery store for some fresh vegetables.

A mask swept over her face. "You know, I've actually never seen Ella. I remember there were times I'd just missed seeing her. Can you describe her to me?"

Describe Ella? The more Tami spoke, the more anxious I became. Ella was the sweetest soul around, but she'd be crucified if her past were ever discovered.

Knowing Tami, it would be.

"She's not a suspect, is she?" I straightened in my chair, my grip around my empty mug tight.

I released the mug and hid my hands in my lap, fisting them together until my nails dug into my skin.

"Right now, everyone is a suspect until I rule them out."

The mother bear in me came out.

"She didn't do this, Tami." I would fight tooth and nail for Ella if I had to. I loved Tami and trusted her, but I wouldn't allow Ella to be destroyed.

"I need a description, Dani. Please? Don't make this harder than it needs to be, okay?" The weariness I'd noticed before settled back on my friend like wet cement.

Ella wasn't the only one who needed my protection. Tami was just as important to me, and I didn't want her to get destroyed by this case either.

"She's about my height with light-brown hair. She wears skirts or long dresses with flats. Size wise, we could probably trade clothes. Wears glasses." I counted off a description of what I could see in my head. "Actually, she's what you'd assume a typical librarian to look like."

Tami's head bobbed as she wrote down the description I'd given.

"Funny." Tami closed her book and set the pen down on the table. "That's the description that was called in, and yet she seemed to vanish by the time we arrived."

"What do you mean, called in?" The muscles between my shoulders snapped tight.

"The head librarian." She paused and looked up. The barista approached with a pot of coffee in hand. Tami covered her cup with the palm of her hand while I held mine out. I needed all the coffee I could get.

"She noticed someone in the library who caught her attention," Tami continued once we were alone again. "We've been looking for a connection between the killer and victims and have narrowed it down to family programs."

"You think the killer was in the library?" My skin iced over in a deep freeze from the blast of wind through the open window, its chilled fingertips dancing up my arm and settling deep into my shoulders.

Tami nodded.

My gasp came out more like a hiccup as I realized I'd been there, walking through the bookshelves in search of Ella, at the same time as the killer.

"It's not Ella." A piece of my heart tore out of me with my words.

I was torn. Torn between my love for Tami and my protective feelings for Ella. I knew it wasn't Ella, but unless I managed to convince Tami of the same, my patient would be judged and convicted by everyone in this town. I wouldn't do that to her based on my own fears. Not unless I knew for sure Ava was involved.

"You don't know that, Dani." She watched me, eyes narrowed, deep in thought.

"You don't know it is either." I needed her to forget about Ella, to get her off her radar.

"Let me meet her, and then I will."

"I can't do that."

"You're saying no?"

I hated saying no, but I had to.

"Are you going to make me get a warrant?" A hard glint appeared in Tami's gaze.

"It's not Ella," I repeated, desperate to have her believe me.

Tami pushed her cup forward and stood. The disappointment on her face cut deep.

"It would be better for her if she came to the station willingly. If you talk to her before I do, warn her I'm looking for her, please." She grabbed her purse and pushed in her chair.

"Tami, please."

"Please what? I have a duty, Danielle. You do realize that, don't you? There's a killer on the loose, and if your patient isn't guilty, then there's nothing to worry about. Unless you know something you don't want to tell me."

So many thoughts rolled through my head. Ella's past, the similarities to the murders, her roommate . . .

"Can you give me some time? Time to check into something first? Please?" I would do anything, even beg, for Ella. I believed in her, I knew she couldn't have done this, but I didn't know her roommate.

Guilt by association would destroy Ella, however, and I wasn't about to do that to her if I didn't have to.

"Fine, but you need to answer something for me first." She was solid, like dried concrete. "Tell me where Ella went when you left the library park. Did she leave with you or return to the building?"

That should have been a simple question, one that I could answer with ease, without hesitation.

Except I couldn't, for one simple reason that would eat away at me for a very long time.

"I can't." I cleared my throat. "I wish I could, but I can't."

"Oh for Pete's sake, Danielle. It's a simple question!" Frustration laced her tone. Failure filled her gaze. "I can't believe you, of all people, would—"

"Tami," I interrupted her, not wanting to hear the rest, afraid of what she'd say and the damage it would inflict. "I can't tell you because I don't know." Regret ate away at me. Regret because I knew what my next words would mean and the impact they would have on Ella.

"I've no idea where she went. While I was so focused on the action taking place outside the library, she slipped away without a word."

"Dani . . ." Disappointment lined the way she said my name.

"I know how that looks, I really do, but I need you to trust me," I begged. "Please trust me. I know it wasn't Ella. I'd bet my life on that."

For the longest second, Tami closed her eyes.

"Unfortunately," she said, her voice as calm as the morning after an ice storm, "there are too many lives at stake for me to trust that."

Chapter Thirty-Three

SATURDAY, AUGUST 24

The sky was washed in a beautiful blanket of summer colors. Red and orange blended together to create a gorgeous canvas for the setting sun. It was a nice break from the rain we'd had all day.

I left the house to shake the cobwebs from my mind. A good walk might help me sleep later. Fingers crossed.

The park was quiet, too quiet. Almost eerie. A single note whistled through the branches, rustling the leaves heavy with dew. A light fog covered the ground, hovering just over the blades of grass, reminding me of that movie where the mist was inhabited by dangerous creatures. I waited for withering blades of grass to greet me as I walked the paths, sure that death either followed or led the way.

The guilt of not telling Tami about the notes, about Ava, hounded me like a shadow. I'd never kept anything from my best friend before. I could validate my hesitation and blame it on the stress Tami was under, my own doubts, lack of sleep, or anything else, but no matter how I spun it, it all came out to the same thing—I was afraid. Plain and simple.

A sense of restlessness grew as I walked. Normally I'd take my time, meander through the winding pathways, stop and lightly touch each of the statues, and take a look at the gardens. Not tonight. Tonight, all

I focused on was the mist, the way it swirled around me, similar to the thoughts in my brain.

It didn't take long until I hit the edge of the park. If I turned left, I'd head toward the tea party section designed as a children's play area. Right would take me to the White Rabbit's house section.

Straight led me to a farmer's field full of corn.

A sudden touch of lethargy hit me, and I slowed my pace. Maybe that was all I needed. To be so tired my brain was free to recall those things I tried to control. Maybe. Maybe I should have stopped psycho-analyzing myself too.

I remained silent as a scene played out in my mind where I sat in the library, a heavy book on my lap, as Ella read to a group of children circled around her. She could have read all day. I loved the sound of her voice, the hitches, whispers, grumblings, and silliness that came out of her tiny frame. I was so proud of her, amazed at how far she'd come since her years in prison.

I couldn't let Tami destroy her. She wouldn't mean to, I knew that, but it would happen all the same. Word would spread no matter how careful or cautious Tami was.

I didn't realize where I was until I stood on a hill in the farmer's field, looking at a derelict building in the distance.

It was the type of old wooden structure you knew had once been a home but now looked as if a strong gust of wind could blow it away. The wood had darkened with age, boards were missing, and half the roof had caved in, but there was a car to the side that looked fairly new.

I couldn't even begin to guess the age of the building, but something about it unsettled me.

That feeling when you turn down an unmarked road and get shivers all over your body? When you walk down a long, dark hallway and swear you feel the breath of someone behind you? That was the feeling that raged through me like a waterfall, gushing over the edge, racing to meet the bottom.

I turned from the home as fast as I could, walked an alternate pathway that led me toward safety. Toward my home. My steps were heavy, my mind weary.

I stood in my bathroom and stared at myself in the mirror. I didn't like what I saw—too many tired lines beneath my eyes, heaviness on my shoulders, the way my eyes weren't clear, bright, or focused.

I needed to sleep, and yet I knew that the minute I lay down on the bed, I'd be wide awake, my brain playing a game with me, unable to shut off.

The pills Tami had bought me sat beside my bed. I held two in my hand. Taking them would bring the sleep my body desperately needed.

Taking them would also mean waking up groggy, disoriented, with a feeling of heaviness that wouldn't leave for hours.

I hated taking pills. Any kind of pills. But I hated how I felt at that moment even more.

Tami was right.

Dr. Brown was right.

I needed sleep. I needed rest. I needed to be at my best so I could help my patients, and those pills might hold the key.

Without another thought, I placed the pills in my mouth, gulped half the water in my glass, and closed my eyes.

How long would it take for them to start working, for me to fade away into a restful sleep? Would it be restful or the sleep of the dead, when anything and everything could happen and I wouldn't hear it?

My throat tightened, and my stomach heaved at the idea. What if someone came into the house again while I slept and left another note? What if they didn't just leave the note but watched me? Hurt me? A shiver ran over my body, and I found myself bent over the toilet, fingers down my throat until there was nothing left in my stomach, including the pills I'd just swallowed.

I wanted to sleep, but on my own terms and in control. Just in case.

Chapter Thirty-Four

A soft glow broke through the darkness around me, and the deep pounding in my ears softened as my head lifted.

I was freezing.

I rubbed the bare skin on my arms and looked around.

I didn't recognize the street.

The houses—with quaint, white-painted porches, wicker chairs, overflowing baskets of flowers, and small bikes and toy trucks—were all foreign, unrecognizable.

I was on a bench—at the corner of Fourth Avenue and Trillium Street, according to the street signs—on the outer edge of town, nowhere near my own home. It was the middle of the night.

The street was silent. Fog rolled in with tendrils that reached out to engulf the houses, consuming both them and me.

Why am I here? How did I get here?

Why here, of all places?

My watch, my wallet, and my phone weren't with me.

Not again. Not again. *Not again not again not again.*

I struggled to catch my breath, but the pain was too intense.

I wasn't sure how long I'd been there, but I needed to move. I shivered, and chills rolled up and down my skin like the waves following the glide of a passing boat on a still lake.

In the driveway of the house across from where I sat, a light turned on, a violent blast through the dark.

There was a low click, like a door being closed, somewhere in the distance.

I tried to remember how I'd gotten there. Trillium was across town but close to the outer edges of Wonderland Park. Maybe a twenty-minute walk, if that, through the park. But why would I go there?

It was all a blank. I couldn't recall anything from the moment I'd lain down in bed after throwing up. I should have just taken the damn sleeping pills rather than let the sleepwalking keep getting worse.

Lights flashed behind me as I walked down the street. I turned, shielded my eyes from the glare, and waited.

Tami pulled up beside me, her window down, her face fierce.

"Danielle Rycroft, get your ass in this car before I arrest you."

I wished I could say she teased, but that frown was still there.

She grilled me the moment I closed the door behind me and put my seat belt on. "What the hell are you doing out at this time? Do you have any idea what time it is? It's two in the morning!"

I didn't say anything.

"Don't you realize how serious things are right now? Why would you be outside in the middle of the night so far from your house?"

I wished I had an answer. I wished I knew what to say, how to reply, what would fix the way she looked at me.

Was it time to tell her? To be honest about my sleeping patterns of late?

I noticed the way her fingers tightened around the steering wheel, how tight her body was, locked in position almost. She was upset with me. Upset and bothered.

A feeling we had in common.

"When I was a child, I'd sleepwalk when things became too stressful for me. It's been a while since I've had an episode, but . . ."

"You're sleepwalking? Seriously? Do you get how dangerous it is out here?"

"I can't take the sleeping pills. What if someone came into my home again?" I leaned against the headrest and stared out the window as she drove through town.

"What do you mean? Someone came in your home?" she demanded.

I swallowed something in my throat, something that tasted like regret. I hadn't wanted to tell her. I wasn't ready. But now that she knew, I could admit I felt a sense of relief.

In between yawns, I told her about the notes. She didn't say anything, but I knew she was angry.

"You should have told me. Damn it, Danielle." Her fist pounded the steering wheel. "Do you not trust me? Do you not think I could protect you? There's a killer on the loose, and those notes could be tied to it."

I sat upright. "No, they're not. Trust me."

She pulled up to the curb outside my house.

"Trust you? You can't be serious. You've held back evidence, you . . . you . . ." She turned toward me, and despite the anger in her voice, I saw the true emotion behind her words. She was afraid.

Afraid for me.

"I'm sorry. I don't think—"

She cut me off with a swipe of her hand. "Don't. Don't try to explain it." Her lips tightened. "I just want you to be safe. I wish you'd trusted me enough to share this with me, that you're under too much stress, that you're sleepwalking, that you've gotten these notes, that you're scared to be alone in your house. Let me help you now, okay?"

I wanted her to help.

But I wasn't ready to add more to her list of things to worry about.

"Where are the notes? Please tell me you still have them."

I shook my head.

"I gave them to my therapist."

Beneath the streetlight, I caught the instant relief on her face.

Was it because I'd told my therapist or because the notes hadn't been destroyed?

She shut off the car and opened her door. "Come on," she said.

"You don't need to walk me into the house. I'll be fine."

She unlocked my door and held it open for me.

"You're not fine. I want you to crawl back into bed. I'm staying here now, with you. You need someone to look after you, to make sure you're okay. I will not have you walking out and about in the middle of the night again."

I wanted to kiss her. I wanted to give her an extra-long hug and tell her just how much I appreciated everything she did for me, but my body didn't want to cooperate. I couldn't lift my arms; I couldn't even open my mouth. It all felt like too much.

She took me by the hand as if she sensed how tired I was and led me to my room. She tucked me into bed and stood there, hovering over me as I snuggled in.

"Tomorrow morning we're going to have a chat," she said. "You're going to tell me more about Ella and your other patients. If one of them is a murderer, I need to know about it."

I started to shake my head, but she turned her back.

"Don't even argue. It's either you tell me or I get a warrant. Time has run out, and I refuse to have another person die on my watch. Not if I could have stopped it. Do you understand?" She half turned then to look at me over her shoulder. "I'm serious, Danielle."

I could see she was. From the rigidness of her shoulders to the tightness of her hands. Nothing about her was soft tonight. I'd pushed the boundaries of our friendship, and if I wanted to make it right, I needed to work with her.

"I understand." The words were barely a whisper, but she must have heard me. She gave me one more look before she walked out of my room and closed the door behind her.

Chapter Thirty-Five

SUNDAY, AUGUST 25

I woke to an empty house and a note from Tami saying that she'd be by later for our talk.

Since she didn't say when, I figured it'd be best to not be home most of the day. Our talk really wasn't something I looked forward to.

While everyone else remained indoors, not wanting to get their feet wet as they walked through the rain-kissed grass of Wonderland Park, I was outside, soaking it up.

I loved the atmosphere out there, the stillness, the peace.

If there was something I needed more than anything, it was peace. The one thing I craved seemed to be missing from my life.

In its place there was fear. Fear, unease, and doubt. That wasn't how I wanted to live my life. I wanted—no, I needed—to feel safe, especially in my own home, and I didn't.

Every day I stressed about whether another note would be left or not. First they warned that I knew the murderer. Then they said I had to stop them. And then they blamed me for the deaths. But never once did they tell me whom they spoke of and what I had to stop or even how.

They, whoever *they* were, held all the power, which had left me more than a little uncomfortable. Why me? Why steal into my house and leave notes, violating my security, taunting me, challenging me like they were?

I had this nauseous feeling in my gut that something more was coming my way, something I couldn't control, something that would destroy me, but I didn't know what it could be.

What else could happen that I couldn't handle?

"Danielle."

I heard my name called behind me. I turned to find Sabrina rushing up the path, winding her way around the various puddles to keep her feet from getting wet.

She carried two cups in her hands.

I hoped those held coffee. *Please, God, let that be coffee.*

"Hey!" I raised my hand in greeting. I gave her a side hug when she approached and took her offered coffee with pleasure.

That first sip was exactly what I needed.

"I saw you walking by. I called out, but you must not have heard me. So I thought I'd come out and find you."

She joined me on my walk, our footsteps slow. By the time I'd sipped half my coffee, we'd walked around the Rabbit Hole pathway. I could tell something was off with Sabrina, the way she kept her body angled from me, how she kept her head down or she'd look off into the distance, but never at me, never meeting my gaze or returning my smile.

"Listen, there's something I wanted to talk to you about. Do you mind if we sit?" Sabrina led me to the bench, a pensive look on her face.

Her lips opened, but nothing came out. No words. No sounds.

"Sabrina, what's wrong?"

She played with her hands as indecision crossed her face.

"My . . . my book is missing."

Immediately I pictured the *Alice's Adventures in Wonderland* book. The book I'd wanted, the one she'd outbid me on.

"You . . . you haven't seen it, have you?"

The way she wouldn't look at me, the way her tone accused more than questioned . . . she blamed me.

Not just blamed me. She believed I'd stolen her book. It wasn't in her words, but her tone, her posture—it shouted accusation.

I swallowed the bile of anger that rose through my throat and sat on the tip of my tongue. My nostrils flared. My hands clenched. I fake smiled.

"Other than the last time I was in your shop . . . no."

She sneaked a look through her lashes. "When . . . when was that, exactly?"

She was kidding, right?

"I do not have your book, Sabrina."

The words came out harder than she'd obviously expected, if the widening of her eyes was any indication.

"I just . . . well, I thought . . ."

I stared at her full in the face. "That I stole it?" I finished for her.

I'm not one prone to anger. I'm more of a slow burn type of person, but being accused like that, the slow boil bubbled over until I was ready to scorch everything in my path.

"No, I just, well . . ." She couldn't backpedal fast enough.

"Just what? It's missing, and you assumed I stole it because you knew I'd tried to buy it myself? Yes, I'm a collector, but I purchase my items. I don't take what's not mine." I pushed myself to my feet, furious she'd have the gall to accuse me like that.

Furious. Frustrated. Flustered. And sad.

Sad that someone I'd considered a friend would believe that of me.

"Danielle, I'm sorry." Her cheeks blazed red with regret. It was written all over her face. "I thought . . . I only ask because you left my shop in such a hurry yesterday, before I could say hi."

I swiveled in surprise.

"I was in the back when you stopped by," she kept on, "and by the time I made it out front, the door was already closing behind you. I figured you were in a rush or hadn't heard me call for you. And then I saw a few things on the merchandise shelf had been knocked over, and when I went to put them back, that's when I noticed the book was missing, and . . . well . . ."

I waited. Well, what? The book had gone missing, and she'd immediately assumed it was me?

I couldn't look at her. I wouldn't. If I did, I knew she'd catch the sheen of tears I was desperate to hide.

I had only two real friends in town. Two. Sabrina and Tami.

I would do anything for my friends.

What I wouldn't have done was accuse them of something I knew wasn't in their nature.

"I thought you knew me better than that." My voice cracked under the weight of my heartache.

Sabrina's accusation tore my heart to pieces, ripped and shredded. Stripped and slashed. Our friendship, once solid, now lay in shattered fragments. I couldn't handle being suspected of something I would never do.

I walked away from her, unable to stay. There were so many emotions that bashed around in me, so many feelings I had a hard time dealing with.

All the emotions of a lost friendship rolled through my brain on fast track. Betrayal. Anger. Sadness. Fury. Hurt.

And guilt. Guilt because the thought of taking the book had crossed my mind, and it shouldn't have. I might have been tempted for one crazy moment, but I was better than that. I would never stoop that low.

I never would have actually stolen from a friend. From anyone. Never.

Sabrina should have known that about me.

Chapter Thirty-Six

PATIENT SESSION: TYLER

Soft jazz played over the Bluetooth speakers in my living room as I waited for Tyler to arrive. I kept an eye on my watch, noting his lateness.

Tyler was never late.

Ever.

I stood at the window and looked out around the edge of the curtain, open just enough to see the sidewalk outside my house. The park across the street was crowded as people walked the pathways toward the evening summer concert, some with blankets tucked under their arms and others carrying foldable chairs.

It wasn't like Tyler to be late and not send me word.

I readjusted the curtain so it was closed all the way and thought about Tami.

We'd never had that talk. She'd arrived late last night, fallen fast asleep, and left before I could make a nice breakfast for her. Eventually, she told me, she would slow down, once the killer was caught and not a moment before.

Something weighed heavily on her mind, and I wished she'd confide in me.

I understood why she couldn't, but I didn't like her being stressed.

It wasn't until I heard my side door open that I let out a lengthy sigh of relief.

"I'm sorry I'm so late." Tyler poked his head around the corner. "I wasn't paying attention to the time, and I misplaced my phone. Otherwise I would have called." He beamed a smile at me, one that caught me unaware. It wasn't a nice-to-see-you smile but more of a I-have-a-secret smile.

I don't like secrets.

"How has your week been?"

Once he'd taken his seat, his lips crept wider as he placed both arms across the top of the couch and stretched his legs beneath the coffee table.

He looked like a satisfied lion with a full belly.

"Good. Great, actually." The laughter in his voice edged on hysterical.

I waited for him to say more.

"Why is that?" I finally said when he kept silent.

"No particular reason." He shrugged, which only added to his carefree attitude.

I hated these complacent answers that told me absolutely nothing. It was all a game, one I often refused to play. The person was desperate to tell you their news—in fact, they practically crawled out of their skin with the need to tell you—but they craved the satisfaction of leading you on first.

"That's great, Tyler, really great." I leaned forward to place my paper and pen on the table and stood. "Sounds like you don't really need me tonight, so how about I walk you out? I won't charge you for this session."

His satisfied grin disappeared as he dropped his arms and gripped his thighs.

"No, I need you." His voice changed as well. The laughter was gone. "Sorry, I didn't mean to come across as rude." His hands rubbed over his jeans as I sat back down.

I put the paper in my lap, pen in hand, and waited for him to begin.

"How clearly do you remember your childhood?" he asked.

I wasn't sure where he was going with that, but okay . . .

"Well enough. Why do you ask?"

The corner of his lips lifted in a half grin. "I don't remember anything. Nothing personal, at least. All my memories are from someone else."

"From someone else? Like stories they told you growing up?"

He shook his head. "No, well . . . maybe." He hemmed and hawed for a moment. "I mean, I don't have any memories as a small child. Isn't that odd? These are things we all should remember, right?"

"Not necessarily. There's research that says very few people can remember anything from before the age of three. So that first birthday cake or being taken to the park wouldn't be something you'd remember. It's called childhood amnesia and something all adults experience. Our clearest memories usually start once we begin school. For instance, I can remember the stations set up in my kindergarten class, painting and reading and even playing house with friends. But my memories from before then are foggy and come more from seeing baby photos or being told stories. Does that help?"

Tyler leaned forward, his interest in what I described clear on his face.

A sharp, needlelike prick hit my temple on the right side, and I winced.

"Are you okay, Dr. Rycroft?" Tyler asked.

"Just a headache. I'll be fine." I massaged the area with my finger before I went to the counter and took two Tylenol pills.

I turned and jumped. He stood there, right behind me, with barely any room between us.

"Are you sure you're okay?"

"I'm fine." I sidestepped him, thankful for the added distance between us as I returned to my seat.

He ran his fingers through his hair, then went to sit back down on the couch.

"Someday soon I'm going to be a father, and I want to be a good one, you know? What if I can't do it? What if I let our child down?"

From the line of questioning, I took it to mean they were a step closer toward adoption.

"Then you'll be like all the other parents out there." I wanted to encourage him. "No one knows what they're doing in the beginning. You'll learn as you go, and I'm sure you'll be a great father. What brought on this concern?"

The narrow ridge between his eyes was pronounced as a frown appeared.

"She's getting restless."

She. Would we ever get past her invading our sessions?

"What does that mean?"

"The need for a child is all she can focus on. It's unhealthy."

"Have you told her that?"

"I want her to know I support her. If I admit I'm worried, she'll take it the wrong way. I don't want her to think I'm not ready."

"Are you?"

"Honestly, I don't know. I'm not sure I'm made out of father material, you know? I didn't have the best role model, nor do I really remember much from being a kid."

"Tell me what you remember about your childhood, Tyler," I urged him.

"I remember living in a small town," Tyler said. "I think we were on the outskirts because we had a big backyard. Not like the houses you find in town now, with barely a yard to play catch in. There was a shed and a tractor my dad jimmied up to work as a snowplow in the winter. Sometimes a friend of my dad's would show up. There was a ton of drinking when he came around. He always offered me a sip." A hint of a smile played on Tyler's face at the memory. "My mom would lose her shit every time she found out too. But Dad . . . didn't care. Said a real man learned how to hold his own early in life, and there was no time like the present to learn."

He rubbed his hands over his face, then through his hair.

"Did you like this family friend?"

He groaned, wiping his mouth in a downward motion. "At the time I did. I thought he was cool. Sometimes he'd come around and watch me if my parents were out. Gave me more attention than my own father, that's for sure."

There was something in his voice that said more than he probably intended.

The words he used, how he said it, told me that the relationship between him and this man hadn't been a healthy one.

There seemed to be a recurring theme with my patients. Sexual abuse. I didn't seek out patients who needed help to process those memories, but . . .

"Did he abuse you, Tyler?" I had to ask.

I wouldn't be surprised if he said yes. It would explain a lot about how Tyler viewed himself, how he felt ignored and unseen.

"I don't know," he whispered. "If he did, I sure as hell don't want to know." He looked at me, his pupils dark and small. "Got it?"

My stomach clenched and twisted into a plethora of knots at the threat in those two words. Now it made sense why he didn't have many memories of his past—he'd chosen to forget the painful ones.

"Sometimes we don't need to know." I spoke with a calmness I sure as hell didn't feel. "Sometimes our brains hide events from us in order to protect us."

His eyes, once dark and small, were now wide and alight with interest.

"Funny you should say that." He cocked his head to the right and tapped his chin. "She says the same thing too."

I wanted to prod, poke, and point out that it would be beneficial to know who *she* was.

"She says that my past is hidden from me because it's too painful."

That seemed to be one thing she got right. So the question, then, was whether it was more helpful to Tyler's therapy to dive into that past and allow memories to resurface for healing to occur. Or would it only be more harmful to him?

"But don't you think I would remember something? Even a small detail?" he asked.

I tried to think about my first memory. I had this picture in my head of sitting in front of my mother's sewing cabinet. It was full of needles and pincushions and other things a child shouldn't have access to. I remembered laughter and the click of a camera.

But then I also remembered seeing a photo of this exact scenario in a photo album.

So was the memory real or one that had been told to me? Was the laughter from that moment or from when my mother recounted it?

Another image played out in my head. Of a field full of dandelions, a tattered doll, a handmade blanket, and small pieces of wrapped candy.

A sudden sour taste filled my tongue.

I gulped my water, trying to get rid of the disgusting taste. I had no idea where that memory came from. I tore my focus from that image and turned it back to Tyler.

"Do you want to remember?" I asked.

Tyler rolled his thumbs around each other as he held his fists in his lap.

"A part of me does. But what if the memories destroy me? What if I'm not strong enough to handle them? She tells me I don't need to remember, that the only memories I need are the ones with her, but . . ." His voice trailed off, and I found myself glad to hear the uncertainty in his voice.

"Whenever we make the decision to face our fears, we've already become stronger," I said. "It may be hard, but you aren't alone, Tyler."

There were more words on the tip of my tongue that I wasn't sure I wanted to say. Words I knew he needed to hear.

"I'll make sure you're not alone." I said them anyway. It was the right thing to do.

"I know." The way he looked at me, the amazement along with relief, confirmed it. "I know I'm not alone, but she says—"

I let a small groan escape my lips. "I don't mean to be rude, but I'm getting a little tired of hearing about what she says. Could it be possible she's not always right? That she might have an ulterior motive for the verbal and emotional abuse?"

Tyler bolted from the seat the moment I said the word *abuse*.

"Don't you dare." His voice rose like a kite caught in a violent wind, the inflections unsteady, his pitch similar to that of a teenage boy. "Don't you ever say that again," he shouted.

I sat back, unprepared for his anger.

"She's not abusive. She loves me and is only trying to protect me." He headed to the window and looked out into the night, his body stiff, his hands fisted. "It's no different than you. You have no idea . . ." He looked back at me with tightened lips.

"No different? No idea? Of what, Tyler? What is it you've been wanting to say to me but haven't?"

For the longest time he was silent. Just staring at me with a look I couldn't understand.

"Tyler?"

"Have you thought about who is behind the murders?" he asked.

Why was he bringing up the murders? Why now?

"I mean, have you thought about who the killer is? How it could be someone you know?" He leaned toward me, invading my personal space.

Was Tyler the one who'd left me the notes?

"What are you trying to tell me, Tyler?" I didn't want to show how his words affected me, but I clutched the pen in my hand tighter.

"You don't know?" He stood and towered over me. "You'll find out soon enough."

Without another look at me, he turned and walked out of my office.

I'd find out soon enough?

Find what out? What the hell was he talking about? Tami wanted me to stop seeing him, and to be honest, I was starting to feel the same way.

He knew something he wasn't telling me. Something about the killer. Which was why I followed him.

The sky was dark, but the streetlights cast enough of a glow that I watched Tyler cross the street and head into the park. I rushed after him, not wanting to lose him through the darkened pathways and the crowds.

He zigzagged through groups of people who walked along the main pathway that headed into the park. Not once did he look over his shoulder as I rushed to catch up.

Where was he going? Normally he walked down the street and around the corner whenever I'd noticed him from the window, never into the park.

Why had he left as suddenly as he did? And what did he mean when he said I'd find out soon enough?

My mind was a whirlwind of thoughts until I became too preoccupied and I lost him.

One minute he was there, ahead of me, and the next minute he was gone.

My pace quickened as I searched for him. We were past the music venue, past the crowded areas, past other pathways he could have taken. The one we were on was straight with no curves. I should have been able to see him up ahead.

But there was no one. Not one single person.

How could I have lost him?

Where had he gone?

I stopped and pulled out my phone. Tami had wanted me to call her the next time Tyler said anything remotely threatening. While I had thought she might be overreacting, I couldn't shake off the fear I'd felt earlier.

"How did your session go?" she asked the moment she answered my call.

"Not as well as I'd hoped."

"Did he say anything more?"

I thought about his words, that I'd soon find out. Was that worth mentioning to her? Especially since I had no idea what he was talking about?

"Danielle, listen. I really don't like the looks of him. There's nothing in the system about him. Nothing. You need to be careful."

A chill settled over me.

"What do you mean, be careful?"

"I can't find anything about him. He could be anyone or no one. He could be dangerous or . . . Has he ever given you any indication he's not who you think he is?"

I headed back to my house, pushing my way through the crowded pathway.

"He thought he was invisible, once."

"Invisible? Is he mentally unstable? Danielle." Her voice was more demanding. "Do you feel threatened in any way? Where are you? Has he left? Are you sure he's gone?"

Unstable? Check.

Threatened? Double check.

Did I know what to do about this? Not a clue.

"I'm in the park, surrounded by people, and he's gone. I followed him—"

"You what?" she yelled. "Are you crazy? Have I not taught you anything? That's it. I'm on my way over."

"He's gone, Tami. I'm fine." I wasn't sure I wanted to go home. But I wasn't going to admit that. I was tempted to sit on the grass, become one with the crowd, and lose myself in the music being played.

"I'm coming over."

I smiled into the phone, thankful for such a friend.

I decided not to tell her about his warning.

"Don't worry about me if you're busy," I said instead.

She hemmed and hawed. "Just waiting for the latest crime scene reports. They think they found some viable fingerprints from the last murders."

That could only mean one thing.

"You're close to catching the killer, aren't you?"

"Close," she admitted. "I just hope it's in time."

"In time for what?"

"Before they move on." She paused. "We connected a few more murders, and there's a pattern."

My shoulder muscles tensed as I found an empty bench off the path and sat. I was near enough I could still hear the music but far enough away that I didn't have to yell into the phone.

"Can I ask what kind of pattern?" I knew Tami had told me more than she should have, that this went beyond the line of consulting, especially since my role wasn't official.

By the silence, I knew she'd thought the same thing.

"You have a copy of *Alice in Wonderland* at your house, don't you?" she asked.

"I have several copies, actually. Even a few rare editions."

"Rare?"

"I'll show you tonight if you'd like. I even managed to find leaflets that were inserted into the books for young readers. Those were hard to find, let me tell you." I'd never thought to show Tami all my copies. Everyone had their own idiosyncrasies, and this was mine.

A crowd of teenagers passed by me as Tami mumbled something into the phone.

"I'm sorry, what did you say?" I asked, but there was no response. Just a dial tone.

Chapter Thirty-Seven

TUESDAY, AUGUST 27

PATIENT SESSION: ELLA

Ella sat on my couch, hands clenched tightly in her lap, and for the past fifteen minutes, she hadn't said a word.

I'd read two chapters from *Alice's Adventures in Wonderland*. I'd fixed tea. I'd waited. And waited. Waited until the silence stretched too long and too wide.

I was on edge. The fact that Ella had actually shown up today was the only good spot in my day.

Tami hadn't come to the house last night like she'd said she would. I'd called and called and called, and she'd never picked up. I worried that meant there'd been another murder.

I'd hoped she'd come over this morning. I'd even made muffins for her, but she was a no-show.

"Ella, would you like a fresh cup?" I realized we'd sat in silence for way too long. She gave a small shake of her head but didn't say anything. She didn't even look up at me.

I refilled my cup and thought about waiting her out or pushing the subject.

Pushing never worked with Ella, but I didn't want to just sit there either.

Nor did I want to read another chapter.

What I wanted were answers.

"Ella, where did you go the other day? When I came to see you at the library?"

Various scenarios played over in my head of why she'd disappeared.

She was late getting back to work.

She didn't want to be seen with me.

I'd said something she didn't want to face.

Or maybe, just maybe, she was the serial killer and didn't want to get caught.

That one was foolish, I knew it. Yet I attempted to connect the dots, minute as they were.

Earlier this morning, as I'd grabbed coffee from a local shop, there had been whispered rumors about the serial killer being in the library, how the librarian had recognized someone she'd deemed suspicious and called the police.

"Do you remember?" I prodded. "We were sitting on the bench together when the police showed up? One minute you were there beside me, and the next you were gone."

She mumbled something under her breath.

"I'm sorry?" I leaned forward, hoping she'd raise her voice enough that I could hear her.

"I don't like the police," she said and coughed, her voice rough like a broken boulder.

I sat back, annoyed at myself. Not once had I thought of that being the reason she'd disappeared on me.

Of course she wouldn't have liked the police presence.

Of course she'd felt uncomfortable.

Of course she'd rushed away. I would have too, in her shoes.

"No, obviously. I should have realized that. I'm sorry," I apologized, shamefaced.

I was incredibly uncomfortable as we sat there in silence.

"Where did you go?" I could have kicked myself for asking. Why couldn't I just leave it alone? Why couldn't I just wait for her to speak?

"Home."

I played with the cross at my neck. That made sense. More sense than going back to work or just disappearing into thin air.

I wanted to smack myself for letting my imagination run wild with scenarios that couldn't possibly be true.

I knew better.

"I shouldn't have run—I know that. Ava reminded me that I'm stronger than I used to be, and they can't hurt me anymore, but . . . it's still there. That fear. I knew what would happen if I ran into the police, and I couldn't . . ." She didn't finish, just played with a loose thread on her skirt.

"You couldn't . . ." I prodded. "It's always better to finish the sentence, to put the words out there so we can work on facing them together, Ella. You're safe here."

She nodded, her chin bobbing like apples in a water barrel.

"What do you think will happen if people find out about your past?" I asked her.

She looked up at me then. She let go of the thread she'd been pulling at and flexed her fingers, the knuckles cracking as she did so.

"We both know what will happen, Dr. Rycroft. They'll assume that I'm the killer. I'm automatically guilty because of my past. There's no forgiveness once the truth comes out. People are hypocritical that way, you know? They talk about God and Jesus and salvation as if it were simple. Their grace only works for little white lies, not the real black ones. As soon as they know the truth, it doesn't matter anymore what they once thought of you. They'll turn their backs faster than a bee will sting." Her voice filled with cynicism and bitterness.

"This has happened before, I take it."

She snarled, a sound I'd never heard from her before.

"Every single time. Every town. Every job. Every place I attempt to create a life."

I sipped my tea, gave myself time to think about where to take this discussion. The fact that she felt free to let down her walls and express her anger was good, healthy, and a step in the right direction.

"What if it happens here again?" I asked. It would be good to have a plan in place on how to deal with the inevitable.

She'd be judged. She'd be condemned. And one day it would be too much.

"I'd move. It's what we've always done. It's what we'll continue to do." She hugged herself hard, and the anger on her face slowly dripped away until she was an ugly mess of self-hatred and loathing.

"When you say *we*, you mean you and Ava, right?"

Tears welled in her eyes, and she nodded.

"How does that make you feel, Ella? Having to always be ready to leave town because you are afraid the truth will come out?"

Tears trickled down her face, and pieces of my heart tumbled into her stream of tears.

"I can never let my guard down. Never get comfortable. Never have a place I can truly call home." She looked so broken, as if sharing her truth fractured the cracked walls she'd pieced together around her heart and soul.

I wanted to fix her, to fumble forward with her until our footing was solid and we found peace, together.

In that moment, we were a unit of like-minded hearts, with shared fears and dreams, and it blew me away.

"You're crying," she said. "You've never cried for me before." There was wonder in her voice, as if she couldn't believe the empathy, which broke my heart even more.

"I'm crying with you." I reached for a tissue and wiped away my tears. "The loneliness you live with . . ." The words I wanted to express were like a hot rock lodged in my esophagus.

"But why? You feel it too, don't you? You know what it's like to be alone, to feel this way. Why cry for me? You should be crying for yourself."

The hatred and self-loathing I'd caught on her face earlier were back.

"There's nothing wrong with allowing yourself to feel, Ella," I said.

It made sense she had walls around her heart, that she blocked off emotion when it came to anything personal and instead projected all her hopes and dreams and the love she'd held in her heart onto the children she worked with.

It all made sense. It wasn't particularly healthy, but it was her reality. I got it.

"It makes me uncomfortable, that's all." She crossed her legs and rubbed her calves absentmindedly.

I fingered the chain at my throat.

"Does it make you uncomfortable to feel emotion or when others feel it for you?" I asked to clarify.

She shrugged.

"What about the children you work with? They must like you, right?" I waited for her to think about that. "I've seen you hug them and hold hands with them. I've seen how you interact with them on multiple occasions, Ella. You're very much full of emotion then." I smiled at the memory.

She smiled as well.

"That's different," she said. "They're innocent and kindhearted and deserve to feel love."

"They are no different from you."

Her eyes rose to mine, and any softness on her face disappeared.

"There's a crater full of difference between us," she scoffed.

"But if you're so bad, don't you think they would know it? Within that innocence and need to feel love, they're sensitive to others around them. If you were so evil . . . those children would sense it, don't you think?" I didn't mean to sound harsh, but I wanted—no, I needed—to help her understand and to work with her on changing her sense of self-worth.

"They know I love them," Ella agreed. "And yes, they are pure. But that love would disappear the moment they found out the truth. I'm not blind to that. It hurts, knowing even they would turn their backs, but . . . it's what I deserve." Her shoulders hunched, turtlelike, over her chest. "Ava says that it won't always be this way. She says one day we'll find a child in need of love that we can raise, together. She's waiting to find the perfect one, she says." There was an innocence to Ella's voice, a naivete that wasn't like her.

What story was she living now to think that could happen?

"How is Ava going to find you a child?"

I fully expected Ella to dive into a book she'd been reading about an orphan child or something remotely similar.

"By finding one that needs to be loved. One who has no one else left." Her guileless eyes blinked with innocence.

Fear grabbed a choke hold on my heart and squeezed.

"How . . ." I swallowed hard, desperate for water to coat the sandy texture of my throat. "How is Ava going to do that?"

I was afraid to hear her next words, and yet I already knew what she was going to say.

But I didn't want to hear it, regardless.

Was that wrong? Cowardly?

"Ella." I changed the subject, based mainly on fear. "Tell me more about Ava. You started to, the other day in the park, but I don't think I have a full picture yet of who she is to you."

If she was about to say what I thought she was going to say, I needed more information.

I needed to understand how Ella could find herself mixed up with someone like Ava.

I needed clarity on Ella's involvement.

I needed . . .

Shit, what I really needed was to wake up from all of this and start the day over.

~

Rather than respond, Ella asked for a break. While she composed herself, I swallowed Tylenol and realized the bottle was almost empty. Damn. I'd gone through that bottle too fast.

When Ella rejoined me in my office, I was ready to find out more about Ava and her influence on Ella's life.

I was ready for whatever truth Ella wanted to share.

I had to remind myself that Ella was mentally unwell, and it was possible that whatever truth she shared was a fabrication, part of a story, a dream world she lived in.

I needed to remember that.

It was my job to help her navigate from that dream world, from the story of her own telling, to reality.

I'd forgotten for a moment, but Tyler's session yesterday had sparked the idea.

It was entirely possible Ava wasn't even real, when I thought about it.

Until the other day, Ella had never mentioned a roommate or friend from prison. I would have thought that in all our sessions together, especially in the beginning, when I'd asked a plethora of questions to get to know her, a roommate would have been mentioned.

She wasn't real. She was Ella's comfort blanket, her imaginary friend. I was able to breathe better now that I'd wrapped my head around Ava.

Ella sat cross-legged on my couch, her knee-length skirt tucked around her legs, her hands folded in her lap.

"Ava is like me. Sometimes I think we're sisters or even the same person, though she's so much older than I am." She sighed and breathed in deeply.

Her words confirmed my suspicions.

"Ava was my cellmate in prison. She was the first person I met, and she was a bitch. I hated her at first. I wanted to stab her in the heart so many times that first year. I used to dream about strangling her in the middle of the night, shivving her in the shower, doing something, anything, to get her in trouble with the prison guards."

Ella sounded . . . foreign. Unrecognizable. A stranger on my couch.

"Why did you hate her so much?" I picked up my notepad. Much of what Ella was about to share would mirror her own life and would hopefully reveal more than she had in the past.

"She reminded me of myself. Her anger was so powerful, a pungent aroma that poured out of her until it became addictive. She did the one thing I had been too afraid to do."

"What was that?"

"She accepted who she was. Embraced her destiny and never faltered. *Fear* was a word she never knew. Fear, for me, was all I ever knew."

The words rested there between us, and their power and strength in that moment said more than any other confession she'd made during our previous sessions.

Her pupil size decreased in both eyes, and her nose flared until her facial features were unrecognizable. The glow of hatred that surrounded her physically pushed me back in my seat and attempted to flatten me.

"Ava castrated her uncle." Ella's lips slithered into a smile. "She castrated him while he was drunk and high and then fed it to him before slashing his throat."

I tried hard to hide my recoil.

"All I did was stab my parents. What she did was . . . beautiful. Poetic. I was jealous, and that jealousy ate at me for that first year. But then something changed. She caught me crying one day in the shower, and rather than feel naked and vulnerable, I felt understood."

For a young woman sentenced to prison, the need to be wanted and loved would be overpowering. For a young woman who had been sexually abused for years, to find a way to survive in prison, where she would either continue to be abused or become the abuser . . . it could be destructive.

The woman in front of me wasn't someone I would classify as an abuser, and yet that's exactly who she'd become, according to the notes I'd received from her therapist during that time.

"Ava taught you how to survive." I filled my voice with understanding, with sympathy, with forgiveness.

Ella nodded.

"She did more than that, though. She gave me strength to not only become a survivor but to also discover a better person in myself. It's why I got early parole. I was able to let go of that anger, that hatred, and find a way to survive and thrive." Ella leaned forward and reached for her now cold tea. In three gulps she emptied the cup.

"Ava needs me as much as I need her," she continued. "I'm her yin. I soften her rough edges and calm her when life gets too crazy for her. I help her focus and find purpose in life."

Ascribes unwanted attributes to Ava, I wrote.

The more Ella described Ava, the more certain I was she wasn't real.

"What is Ava's purpose in life, then? What does she do?"

I could have thought up numerous responses to this question.

Ella was a complex person with a history so destructive it was a wonder she was able to find healing. The therapist she'd worked with previously had spent a lot of time on self-abusive behaviors, and if ever one had a success story to tout, it would be Ella.

Attributing her unwanted emotions and expectations to a persona of her own making made sense. We've all done it in one form or another. We all wear masks, hide our true selves, present the versions of ourselves that we need to be in order to be accepted.

That's exactly what Ella had done in this scenario.

I wrote this down in my notebook, only half listening to Ella as she continued to talk.

"Ava's purpose is to protect those who can't protect themselves," she said.

I leaned forward to grab my cup.

"She watches out for the children who need to be loved."

I brought the cup to my lips and looked toward Ella, ready to listen.

"I find the children, and she protects them."

The grip around my cup loosened, and it fell onto my lap, spilling my tepid tea all over my notes and my lap and staining my soul as I realized what she'd just confessed to.

I jumped up and grabbed a handful of napkins to clean my mess while Ella sat there, calm, as if she didn't have a care in the world.

I didn't want to believe Ella's confession. I didn't want to hear what else she had to say. I wanted to remain in my own little reality, ignorant of the truth that had been staring me straight in the eyes the whole time.

All this time, I'd been wrong. Wrong about Ella. Wrong about the serial killer. Wrong about everything.

Ella's mind was fractured, and in her brokenness, she'd destroyed lives.

And in my own blindness, I'd allowed it to happen.

Whoever had left me those notes, they'd known. They'd been right to blame me. But they were just as guilty. They could have gone to the police.

So why hadn't they?

Why come only to me?

And what did I do now?

Chapter Thirty-Eight

PATIENT SESSION: SAVANNAH

It was too beautiful a day to be cooped up inside, and I was too antsy, so when Savannah arrived, I talked her into joining me on a walk.

I was a little surprised she didn't fight me on the idea.

I needed a distraction. After yesterday's session with Ella, I'd called Dr. Brown to see if I could get in today to see her, but she was out of the office, and the earliest appointment she had available was for tomorrow. I knew I needed to act fast. Stalling could mean another lost life on my conscience, but I also needed to talk the situation through with Dr. Brown first. It was possible I was misinterpreting things, and I needed a second opinion before I potentially ruined Ella's life.

Between Ella's confession and the fact Tami had gone radio silent on me, it didn't surprise me when I'd woken up this morning outside in my backyard, listening to soft classical music via headphones, curled up in the lawn chair with my comforter wrapped around me.

The last thing I remembered was leaving Tami a voice message to let her know I'd left a plate of food in the microwave for her before I went to sleep in my own bed.

The circles beneath my eyes were more pronounced, and the stabbing pain in my head had grown from the dull throb I'd woken up with.

I'd been tempted to hunt Tami down, to go to her place or even the police station and find out why she'd ghosted. If it weren't for the fact I was exhausted, had Savannah's appointment, and knew that Tami must be in the middle of something huge to not return my calls, I would have.

"Hellooo. Earth to Dr. Rycroft." Savannah faced me, walking backward. She'd lifted her large heart-shaped sunglasses up so I could see her eyes.

"Sorry, I must have been daydreaming," I said.

"You haven't heard a word I've said, have you?"

"I'm sorry, Savannah. Can you tell me again?"

"I just admitted to being the serial killer, that's all." She twirled around so her back was to me. I picked up my pace so I was walking beside her. "It's not nice to ignore people when they're talking, you know," she continued, sounding hurt.

"I wasn't ignoring you. I was just . . . lost in my own head." Spaced out, exhausted, should have been in bed . . . I could describe it any way I wanted, but truth be told, she was right.

"My dad would say that's the same as ignoring someone."

"Again, I'm sorry." We walked side by side. "My mom would have called it maudlin."

She paused in her stride. "Maudlin? That sounds old-fashioned. What does it mean?"

"Sad. Sentimental. Self-pitying." Take your pick. It was a word she'd used whenever she'd been drinking and wasn't paying attention to me when I was trying to talk to her.

"Why are you sad?"

"More like emotional. Or just overly tired."

She nodded. "That would explain those dark circles. You should try wearing some makeup when you're in public." She sipped the smoothie I'd bought her earlier.

"You didn't admit to being the serial killer, did you?" I brought the conversation back to what she'd just said.

"Guess you should have been listening. Now you'll never know," she quipped with a saucy grin on her face. I couldn't see her eyes, covered by the dark lenses, but from the way she jumped ahead and spun around so she faced me once again as she walked backward, I knew she was in a mood.

A good mood.

She was dressed in cutoff jeans and a snug black T-shirt that showed more belly skin than was appropriate and had a plaid shirt wrapped around her waist. Her braided hair was decorated with tiny little skull bobby pins, but her face was devoid of makeup.

"I haven't seen this side of you in a long time." I liked it. It was exactly what I needed today.

Savannah laughed.

A real air-filled-with-the-trill-of-birds kind of laughter. Laugher that was infectious.

"I'm good. I'm happy even." She stuck her tongue out. "There, I said it. Are you satisfied?"

My brows arched as high as my smile was wide.

"Satisfied? With one measly little happy? Come on, Savannah. I need a few more emotional adjectives than that," I teased, enjoying the sparkle in her eyes.

I was thrilled, more than I would ever let on.

"So what brought about this . . . happiness?" I tempted fate by asking, but I figured it was worth a shot.

"Why do you have to push? Push push push push." Savannah twirled one more time. "You know, I think I kind of like you." She gave me a sidelong glance, and her lips hinted at a smile.

I shrugged. She laughed again. I liked the sound.

We crossed the street and headed into Wonderland Park. Savannah led the way, and I had a feeling I knew where she'd take us.

After a few right turns, we sat down in the Red Queen's courtyard, surrounded by red rosebushes. Not only were the queen's guards standing at the entrance of this garden, but there were also smaller statues along the walkway, hidden among the bushes. The queen herself stood in the middle, surrounded by a variety of flowers at her feet.

"Doesn't it look like she's watching us?" Savannah walked around the statue, at times looking over her shoulder as she passed by. "I swear her eyes move."

"Neat work of art, for sure." I settled down on a bench.

"Don't you wish that these stories were true? I think it would be cool." She plopped down beside me, one leg resting on the other, and leaned back in a completely relaxed pose.

I would have bought it, except she drummed her fingers along the top ledge of the bench, and the muscles in her thighs remained taut.

"You would want to live in a world where a queen chops people's heads off for little reason?"

Her lips quirked. "As long as it wasn't my head, I'd be fine with it. But come on, a rabbit that hops everywhere wearing a clock, a cat that materializes out of thin air, and a place where everyone wears outrageous hats? I'd be down for that in a heartbeat."

"Some days it would be nice to live in a fictional world—I get that." My world would consist of a beach, a cabana boy, and endless books to read.

"Did you know there's a librarian who dresses up as Alice? I saw her the other day."

I'm pretty sure she was talking about Ella.

"It was neat. She was reading the kids a story and had the best voices too."

"Did you go and listen?"

One brow rose. Her nose wrinkled. Her lips turned down in a frown. But her eyes twinkled. She was still a kid at heart.

"I bet you sat in one of the chairs close to the children's section, didn't you? Close enough to listen in but not close enough to be noticed." I twirled the straw in my own smoothie cup and tried to cover the laughter she no doubt caught in my voice.

"Maybe." She tapped the top of the bench even faster. "She was really good."

I glanced at her tapping fingers, making it obvious that I'd noticed she was antsy.

"So?" She sat up straighter, removing her hand and placing it in her lap.

"So . . ." The word lingered between us.

Savannah let out a very long and exasperated sigh.

"Fine." She worried her lip for a bit before turning toward me. "My uncle is staying longer."

"For how long?"

I wished I had my notes right then.

"You got me. My parents decided to extend their vacation, something about visiting friends." Her fingers started their drumming action on her thigh.

For someone who appeared quite happy, she sounded anything but.

"Does it bother you they haven't come home yet?"

She snorted. "Like I really care."

"Did you ask to join them?"

"Why would I do that?"

"Oh, I don't know," I said. "Seems to me like you might miss them or something."

"Miss them? Are you high? This has been the best summer ever. For the first time in my life, I get a break from their crazy shit and endless lectures."

She lied, not with her words but with her tone.

"How are things going with your uncle?" I still hardly knew anything about him, and I wasn't comfortable with that.

She shrugged. "He's been away for a few days. He'll be back tomorrow, when we thought my parents would be back. It's been . . . nice, to be on my own. You know? I'm old enough."

I agreed with her. She was old enough to be on her own.

"Are you looking forward to him coming back?"

She tried to hide it, but there had been a flash of angst in her gaze. Not just regular teenage angst, but something more . . . I was on alert now.

"Sure. He's cool. I'm good being alone, though. It's nice. No one to clean up after, no one to tell me what I should or should not be doing. I've waited for this freedom forever, and it's finally here. I just wish it could always be this way."

I wished I had my notepad.

"One more year and you'll be off to college, and you'll have your freedom then." I needed to drive this point home, that this aspect of her life was only temporary.

"One more year of living in hell? No thank you." She flicked a piece of hair off her face and arched her back, her face turned up to the sun.

"If you had to choose, would you rather live with your parents for the next year or your uncle?"

From the look in her eyes, I could see her trying to figure out where I was going with this.

"How about none of the above? Honestly, Doc. You seem off today. What's going on?" She angled my way, one leg tucked beneath the other, fingers tap-dancing on her knee.

"We're not here to talk about me, Savannah."

She snorted. "Whatever." She planted both feet back on the ground and bent forward, elbows on knees, head cradled by her palms.

"I want to be free. Of them all. I don't need them in my life. I don't want them in my life," Savannah said, her voice lower than the growl of an uneasy dog.

My heart twisted and turned for whatever trauma she'd experienced but never admitted to. From all outside appearances, her parents were a loving couple, devoted to their daughter despite how hard she'd made life for them lately.

"Why do you hate your mom and dad so much?"

"Because they deserve my hatred." The words flew out of her mouth like a butterfly escaping its cocoon.

"But why?" All I wanted to do was help her get to the root of that emotion, to understand where her strong response originated from. If she could hate them with so much passion, she could love them just as much.

Savannah's leg bounced, and she played with the cup in her hands before she jumped up and faced the Red Queen.

"They don't know how to love. Not real love. Not love that children deserve. Don't you get it? They're selfish and judgmental and expect me to bend to their will without being aware I might have a will of my own. Did I tell you I used to pray for their deaths? I would beg and plead with God to kill them, whether it was in a car crash or some type of accident. I thought God loved me . . . and if he did, he would save me from them. But there's no God." She spat on the dirt to the side. Her back was rigid, her shoulders tensed, her hands fisted. "Which means I need to take care of it myself."

There was an aura about her that swirled with anger and frustration, and it scared me.

"What do you mean by that?"

I hadn't helped her. Not one bit. From the time we'd started meeting to now, the anger and hatred she'd felt toward her parents had only grown, not diminished.

"When I realized there was no God, I knew I'd have to take control of my own life. Of my own happiness. And I will. I have a plan, and Uncle is going to help me. I don't need my parents in my life, and by the time I'm done, everyone will finally believe me that they weren't good people." Her voice broke, and she tried to hide the swipe of her hand against her cheeks. But I saw. I noticed the tears.

My heart burst with tears I couldn't shed, because all those feelings in her voice—the loneliness, the sadness, the frustration and emptiness—they were in my soul.

I pictured a little girl who sat at a table with a deck of cards, waiting for someone to play with her.

A little girl curled up on the couch, watching a movie by herself, while her parents argued about something inconsequential.

A little girl like me, but not like me, who just wanted to be loved.

Why was it whenever I spent time with Savannah, there was this yearning for the little girl of my soul to come out? To be felt and heard and loved?

"You must trust your uncle." It wasn't a question. It was a statement. Confirmation of what I heard.

"He's the only one I like in my family. He gets me. He loves me, and he doesn't just say it, you know? He shows me. My parents, they might say it, but I know they don't mean it. But him . . . whenever he's around, I feel loved."

"Feeling loved is nice." I needed to be careful how I trod these next few minutes. "Everyone shows love differently, just like everyone needs to be loved in different ways. Maybe when your parents return, we could have a session with them about this?"

Savannah snorted. "Like that will ever happen. I'd rather they just didn't return. Maybe their plane will crash, or . . ." Her eyes lit up as she talked.

I leaned forward, elbows resting on my knees, and looked at the girl in front of me.

There was something off about her today.

For all her laughter and happiness earlier, I caught the anxiety she tried to hide.

For all her talk of love and dreams of being free, I heard the panic in her voice.

For all her bravado, I saw the little girl who wanted to be loved.

"How about we get off that topic"—I gave her my gentle smile along with my accepting voice—"and talk about the next few weeks. What are your plans? Will you go back to the library?"

"My uncle wants to go on some day trips, even camp for a few nights. Do some shopping and just have fun. He likes to spoil me. When I was younger, he called me his princess." She grabbed one of her braids and tugged. "Those are probably the only good memories I want to keep from when I was little."

"Being his princess?"

She was saying all the right words to raise my alarms.

I really hoped his treating her with so much love was just that—an uncle loving his niece. A familial love between two family members.

My stomach clenched, the smoothie rolling around in endless waves.

"My uncle loves me. What's wrong with that?" She jutted out her chin in a challenge.

I leaned back on the bench. "Absolutely nothing." I hoped I read too much into her words, that her uncle was as amazing as she thought he was. But I couldn't shake the dread inside me that he wasn't.

She turned her back, ran her hands along the queen's voluminous dress.

"I wish I was the Red Queen right about now," she said. "Off with your head," she shouted, her arm slashing in a hatchet movement. She glanced over her shoulder, her eyes narrowed, and she waited for my reaction.

I shrugged.

She *tsk*ed me, her finger wagging while she shook her head in mock dismay.

"Now, now, Dr. Rycroft. That's two shrugs from you already. How unlike you."

I went to shrug again but caught the movement in time.

"Why don't we head back, Savannah," I said, making my voice light. I grabbed both our cups and tossed them in the garbage on our way out of the courtyard garden.

Savannah walked two steps ahead of me.

I didn't mind.

By the time we reached the edge of the park, she'd slowed until we walked side by side.

"I'm still going to the library," she said out of the blue.

"Is that right?"

"I'm learning a lot. I'm beginning to understand how the mind of a killer works."

My brows arched like the McDonald's arches.

"All from reading a few books?"

"I'm a quick study," she shot back. "When I want to be. You know what they say, right?"

"No, what's that?"

"Practice makes perfect."

My stomach churned at the implications of those words. I smiled at people we passed by and waited till we were out of earshot before asking the question I knew she was dying for me to ask.

"So how does the mind of a killer work?"

She twirled again, her face as bright as it had been when she'd first arrived, but this time, the joy in her eyes was real.

"It's fascinating. It's like they shut off all emotion and only focus on themselves. Nothing else matters, only whatever plan they concocted in their mind. Their focus is everything. Most of them are brilliant. Did you know that? They had to be to get away with all the murders they did. And it wasn't like they knew how to kill at first. They had to practice. To learn."

"I wouldn't call that fascinating, nor would I call them brilliant. They eventually got caught, didn't they?"

"Everyone makes mistakes."

There was no disdain in her voice, no reproach, no disgust.

Instead, I heard respect, admiration, and praise.

"Savannah, killing a person is never okay. You know that, right?"

"Why? Because society deems it so? Fuck, even in the Bible, God demands retribution and death."

"You are not God." I shouldn't have had to remind her of this.

"Yes I am."

I waited for her to clarify.

"My father says we were made in the likeness of God. So if I look like God, if my faith can move mountains, and if my tongue holds the power of life or death . . . sure sounds like I'm God to me."

I stared off to the side. The need to control my facial features, my eye roll, and even the sigh that wanted to come out were strong.

"I think you're taking the scripture and what your father said out of context, don't you?"

"Ask me if I care." She pulled at both her braids, taking one of the skull bobby pins out and handing it to me. "My mom almost threw these out, said we don't worship the devil in our home. Can you believe that? I found her in my room, holding a bunch in her hand."

"How did you feel when she admitted that?" I was used to Savannah changing the subject on me, so I just went along with it.

Her forehead wrinkled as she thought about her answer.

"I hate when you ask me about my feelings. You know that, right?"

I nodded. "That's kind of in the job description, though. Hate to say it."

"Whatever." She stared straight ahead. "I was mad. She had no right to be in my room and take what wasn't hers. It wasn't right." She crossed her arms over her chest.

"Did you know your mom would feel that way when you bought the skulls?" It was important to get Savannah to stop focusing on herself all the time and start thinking about how others around her felt and were affected by her decisions and reactions.

"I really don't care." Her lips pushed out in a pout. "But you're going to make me answer, aren't you?"

Why say anything when she said it for me anyway?

"Fine. Yes, I knew she wouldn't like them. And yes, I bought them in spite of it."

"Or maybe because of it?"

"So what if I did? Do you really think I care what she thinks or believes?"

"I'm curious—does your uncle like skulls?"

She gave me an odd look. "He has a few tattooed on his body. Why?"

"I just wondered if he knew how your mom felt about them, that was all."

She snorted. "He doesn't care what she thinks. He only cares about me. His princess."

Chapter Thirty-Nine

MEMORY

I can't stop the shaking no matter how hard I try.

Mind numb. Heart racing. Body on fire.

Uncle's fingers tap-dance along his steering wheel while I bury mine beneath my legs.

We're on the run, but we're free.

Free.

I don't even . . . My mind can't . . . What does that even mean? Free?

"Breathe, princess, just breathe. We'll stop at a secluded beach tonight, sleep under the stars, just you and me, and celebrate our new life. Trust me, okay?"

His fingers leave the wheel and reach for mine.

His thumb runs along my skin. Focusing on his touch calms me.

He calms me.

I breathe. Deep.

We did it.

I did it.

OH MY GOD. I did it. I made them pay. I—

"That's my girl." Uncle winks as he squeezes my hand. "The hard part is over. You did great, Firefly. I couldn't have done it better myself."

The praise goes straight to my heart.

"*How many times have you—*" *I choke up, unable to untangle the word from around my tongue.*

"*Killed?*"

I nod.

"*Say it.*"

What does he mean, say it?

"*I want you to say the word. You need to say it for yourself. Make it real. Don't degrade the memory of what you just did. Take ownership of it—be proud of it.*"

He speaks to me as an equal; I hear it in his voice. He doesn't see me as a child who needs tutoring but an equal who has to get over this mountain, the mountain of my first kill.

"*How many times—*" *I clear my throat, forcing the knot around my tongue to relax so the word can slip free.* "*How many times have you killed someone?*"

His nod tells me how proud he is of me.

I've never felt that sense of pride from anyone other than him. I can't remember the last time anyone else said they were proud of me or loved me or even believed in me.

Not like he does.

"*Between us, three people. They all deserved it too. I've never been caught, so when I ask you to trust me, I mean it. We'll be fine.*" *He stares straight ahead into the night, his truck lights on the dirt road the only things illuminating our way.*

Those lights, the brightness staring straight ahead, pushing back the dark night as we race along the road, they give me hope. Hope that no matter how dark things seem, no matter how suffocated I feel, there will always be a way out.

"*How many people have you killed?*" *he asks me in turn.*

"*Two.*" *The words aren't pulled out of me. They don't cut my throat into shreds as I admit the truth. They slide off my tongue with ease.*

The raw honesty of that one word breaks something inside me. It breaks and births a new being with a need for room to grow.

"That's right," he says with pride. "You've killed two people who didn't deserve to breathe the same air as you. Two people who didn't love you and only used you for their own purposes. Two people who were already dead inside."

"I hated them." Is it just me or does my voice sound different? More mature. "I hated them," I repeat. I like how it sounds, the emphasis placed on I and the H and how the words all ring together. Three words become two become one as I accept the feelings for what they are.

"They didn't deserve your love or hate. They don't even deserve to be a memory for you. Wipe them clean from your mind. Create your own memories if you need to. Fill in the blanks with what you believe you deserved. No one will know the difference."

His words make sense. I'll take the good parts, like when I was younger and my father was my daddy. A daddy who loved me, protected me, paid me attention, rather than the man I killed tonight. The man who was raping my mother, who called her a whore even as he degraded her and their life together.

"Is that what you did? Created your own memories?"

He nodded. "People say everything in life is dictated by your surroundings, what you were born into, how you were raised. That all that psychology crap is built into your DNA, and you can't help but react based on those imprints. I call bullshit. Life is what you make it, Firefly. There is no predestination mumbo jumbo, no afterlife, no God you have to pray to for forgiveness. Life is about choices. Your choices. You get to choose who you will be, where you will go, who you will love, and what memories you'll take with you."

I think about that.

I hold the power to change my life at any time. Become someone new. Create a new life with a different history, one of my own making.

"Any regrets? From any time you killed someone?" Deep inside, I know the answer, but I want to be sure.

"Not a single one."

"She was your sister." The words are whisper loud and mixed with a little bit of sadness.

He squeezes my hand hard.

The Patient

"She stopped being my sister the day she stopped protecting and loving you." The finality in his voice takes away any misgivings I might have been holding on to.

"You are the only family I have or need," he says. "We are all we will ever need. You and me. Together, we can do anything."

The shaking disappears. My head clears. My heart calms. My body changes.

"That would have been my only regret," I hear myself admit. "That I took the sister you loved away from you." I don't say that my biggest fear has been that he would resent me, blame me, turn from me because of that.

"Hear me when I say this. She would have been dead whether you cut her throat or not. She was a shell of a person. She deserved everything that happened to her tonight."

He's right. I wanted her—no, I needed her to know the pain I've lived with for years. She deserved to feel the pain of my knife cutting through her skin, tearing past the muscles and tendons and veins. There was no way in hell I was going to let her gently fade away, never to wake up again.

No way in hell.

"Don't call me Firefly anymore." I'm not that little girl anymore.

I stopped being her the moment I held the knife in my hand, I just hadn't known it.

His Firefly was the teenage girl who hated her parents but was too scared to do anything about it. She had no hope, no future. Her narrow-minded worldview consisted only of how much she hated her parents and wanted to be free.

Except she never thought she'd ever be free.

I'm not her anymore.

I'm the one strong enough to grab hold of that knife.

I'm the one strong enough to live with the decisions I made.

I'm the one strong enough to take control and keep it.

"Fair enough. What should I call you, then?"

My name has to be worthy. It has to be one I wear with pride. It has to be deserving of what I just did and what I will continue to do.

"Call me Ava."

It rolls off my tongue with ease. It holds the taste of melted chocolate. It sounds like the name of someone who knows exactly who she is.

Who she is.

This time, it's me who squeezes his hand. Me who runs my thumb up and down his, feeling his skin beneath mine.

This time, it's me who unbuckles my seat belt and moves across the seat until I sit next to him.

"Well, hello there, Ava. Nice to meet you." There is a gleam in his eyes I've never seen before.

Before, he always looked at me with such tenderness. His touch was gentle, as if I were as skittish as a newborn bunny. He coddled me while loving me at the same time.

I don't want that kind of love anymore.

I curl up next to him, my feet up on the seat, my hand on his thigh. I play with the zipper on my sweater, slowly undoing it, knowing he's watching.

"New name for a new life. I like it." This time it's his tongue wrapped in a knot, his voice hoarse, his pulse rapid.

"How much farther to the beach?" I ask.

It's pitch-black out. After midnight. No one will notice our absence, not for a long time.

My father had been fired from his job, his company truck taken from him. He'd been dropped off at the house, on the side of the road, like an unwanted pet. No one knew he'd come home.

No one ever visited the house. We were loners. Secluded by design. I'd quit school a year ago and was homeschooled by my uncle. My mother had quit her job, only announcing it that night before my father's abrupt return.

No one will notice their deaths.

There's no rush. We're not running for our lives. We can take all the time we want, enjoying the summer air, the warm evening breezes. We don't have to decide right away what we want to do or where we want to go.

We have the rest of our lives ahead of us.

Lives with no regrets.

Chapter Forty

The heat of the day lingered in the evening hours. It hung in the air like a wet blanket, the pressure weighing me down in my lawn chair.

Following Savannah's session, I'd shut my phone off and taken a nap, due to a vomit-inducing migraine that hit me hard.

My body held that heavy feeling associated with waking up from a deep sleep too quickly. I could barely lift my arms, let alone push my legs over the edge of the chair so I could sit up. I was dizzy, light-headed, and I staggered like a drunkard when I finally managed to head into the house.

There was a sweating pitcher of iced tea left on the counter with a glass covered in lipstick stains. I rubbed the back of my hand over my lips and was surprised to see the red-tinted smear left on my skin.

I didn't remember putting lipstick on, much less making a pitcher of iced tea.

I poured myself a glass, cleaned up the liquid I spilled because of my shaky hands, and collapsed on my kitchen chair. I was exhausted and glad no one was there to notice how pathetic I looked.

Unable to handle the mugginess inside, I headed back out, where at least there was a bit of a breeze to cool the sweat on my brow. We didn't get a lot of these sweltering days in Cheshire, but when we did, I regretted not installing an air conditioner.

My mind was quiet for once. As I lay there under my outdoor umbrella, my body relaxed to the quiet evening sounds of birds, soft laughter drifting over the wind from the park, and the mundane sounds of everyday life around me.

It was all so perfect. Perfectly mundane, with the grill smells from my neighbor's yard, the squeak of an outdoor laundry line, the barking from the dogs down the street, the hum of vehicles as they drove by.

This was the life I'd dreamed of here.

Minus the headaches. I knew that people who lived in higher elevations or near mountains experienced climate migraines, but that wasn't the case with Cheshire.

There was a slam of a car door in the distance followed by pounding on a door.

The pounding was in rhythm with the pulsing in my head.

"For Pete's sake, answer the door," I muttered, my eyes still closed.

"Dr. Rycroft?" a voice called out.

Tyler? What was he doing here?

"Dr. Rycroft?" he called again, his voice insistent and even a little crazed.

I struggled to push myself up from the chair.

"Out here." My voice broke. "Tyler, back here," I tried again.

Footsteps scuffed against the rocks in my driveway before the gate opened.

"Where have you been?" The gate slammed into the fence with a bounce. "I've been calling you all day." He stood above me, his eyes wide.

"What's wrong?" The frantic way his pupils darted every which way had me gripping the armrest of my chair. I pushed myself to my feet. "Tyler? What's wrong?" I asked again.

He rocked on his heels.

"I can't find her."

"Can't find who?"

"Her." He rocked back and forth, almost bouncing as he stood there. "I can't find her. She's gone. Missing. I can't find her."

My heart vibrated with alarm. I reached out instinctually to offer comfort, but Tyler stepped back, almost stumbled, to get out of my reach.

"I thought she'd come back. I thought she'd stop. I thought I could stop her," he mumbled, before he turned and walked away from me, from my deck area to the grass, then turned back my way. He rubbed his hands together, and the friction of his dry skin sounded too much like sandpaper. The sound scurried up my skin like a trail of red ants.

"Stop what?" I pushed out a lawn chair for him to sit.

"I thought you'd help me," he said, his fingers pushing through his messy hair. "You said you were always there for me, but you lied. You weren't there. I called and called and called—" He dropped his head, linking his hands behind his neck.

"We didn't have a session today, did we?" I tried to remember, tried to see my calendar in my head, but the headache was there, pushing everything else away.

"You said you'd be here," he pointed out, his voice muffled from the way his head hung.

"I'm sorry, Tyler. I'm not feeling well today." I rubbed my right temple area and closed my eyes for a brief, blissful second. "If I missed our session, I apologize." I needed to get my head in the game, to hear him, to read behind his words, but in all reality, I wanted him to leave.

"I . . . I'm sorry." His voice remained muffled as he spoke into his T-shirt. His curved back grew in width as he inhaled and then stood. "I didn't realize you weren't well. I'll . . . I'll figure it out." He rubbed his forehead, his first two fingers digging deep into his skin.

"Sit down, Tyler." I added some oomph into my voice, hoping I sounded more in control than I felt. "Talk to me."

I couldn't even watch him as he paced back and forth. Five steps to the left and then back. Then five steps to the right and then back. He did this at least three times before my eyes felt like they were on the twirly cup ride at the county fair.

"How about I grab us something to drink?" I didn't even wait for his answer. I headed back into the house, careful to keep my steps small and my back straight.

I swallowed a couple more Tylenol, prayed for strength, and did something I hated to do. I turned on the record app on my phone. My head wasn't as clear as it needed to be. If I recorded the conversation, I could listen to it after the migraine was gone and add the notes to his file.

Back outside, I placed his cup down in front of his chair, sank down in mine, and waited some more.

"Tyler." I didn't bother to keep the exasperation and frustration from my voice. "Would you please sit down? You're not helping my headache any."

He returned to his seat and sat like a scolded schoolboy.

"Sorry," he muttered.

"Please tell me again, slowly, what's wrong." I sipped at my iced tea and was surprised to see Tyler reach for his cup and take a long drink before placing it down and wiping his lips.

He just drank something without thought, without question, without accusing me of poisoning him.

That was huge.

"My girlfriend is missing. We had a huge argument because she's been . . . she just hasn't been home." His face tightened, the vein along his jawbone pulsed, and I watched as the color of his skin changed from a light tan to a dark shade of red within seconds.

"Breathe, Tyler. Breathe."

Small tremors rippled through his arms. He was struggling to contain his emotions, and the last thing I wanted or even needed was for him to explode.

"When did you last see her?"

"Two days ago. We had a huge fight after I saw you, and she left. She said she wasn't coming back, that she didn't need me anymore . . ." His body shook, and what I took for anger was actually tears.

They streamed down his face, streaking his skin until they pooled beneath his chin.

"I'm sorry, Tyler." I softened my voice. "What did you fight about?" He wiped his face, then took another drink from his glass.

"She said I told you too much. She said that I couldn't be trusted, that you weren't to know anything, and I broke that trust." He stared at me, a look of helplessness in his gaze. "I just wanted her to stop. I don't like where she's headed. It's a dark place, and I won't be able to reach her if she does this anymore." His head dropped. His fingers tightened around the cup until I thought for sure it was about to break in his grip.

I reached over, gently pried the glass from his grasp, and set it out of the way.

"Tyler, what was—is—she doing that I'm not to know about?"

He scratched his neck, leaving white claw marks on his skin. He started to say something, then stopped.

"I'm scared, Dr. Rycroft. I don't know where she is, but I have a feeling I know what she's doing, and it's not good. It's not good." He covered his eyes with his hands and rocked slightly in his chair.

"I'm too weak. Too weak to help her. Too weak to understand. It's all my fault. I could have stopped all of this right from the beginning if I'd only stood up to her," he mumbled behind his hands.

One minute he was crying, the next he was as solid as a rock. He pushed himself from the chair and stood.

"I've got to find her and stop her. I thought maybe you were strong enough to do it, to see behind my words, to understand what I wasn't allowed to say, but—" His face tightened, his hands fisted, and that pulsing vein was beating even faster.

What was I supposed to have caught? What didn't I see that I should have?

"Tyler, maybe we can call the police and—"

"NO!"

I jumped, my hand clasped tightly to my chest at his shouting.

"Why don't you understand?" He lowered his voice, but the intensity was still there, stirring the swamp of emotions beneath the surface. "No cops. I thought you could help me, but you're useless. Ava was right," Tyler mumbled as he glanced around my yard with a wildness in his gaze. "I should have listened to her. This was a mistake, and she knew it."

"What did you say her name was?"

I couldn't have heard him right.

There was no way I heard him right.

It just wasn't possible.

"Her name is Ava, and I should have listened to what she said about you all along. What she's doing is wrong, and you aren't helping, so I have to stop her myself."

With a look of disgust cast my way, Tyler left my yard, his heavy footsteps harsh on my driveway before I heard his car start and squeal away.

I sat there in stunned silence.

What had he meant? What role was I playing?

What was this about Ava? Ella's Ava? No. She wasn't real. It wasn't possible.

But what if it was?

Ella had said her Ava wanted a child. Tyler's Ava wanted a child. And a lot of children in our town were suddenly without parents.

Chapter Forty-One

Guilt is like a worm, vile and wretched, working its way into the hidden parts, the secret parts, the ugly parts of your soul. Slimy tracks of guilt cover every hidden crevice until it oozes out of you.

I hate worms.

The silence in the small therapy room was heavy. I looked everywhere but at Dr. Brown, who watched me, studied every movement, dissected every eye dart, muscle twinge, and jerk of my lips until I felt like a laboratory rat.

I needed to share the recording with her, but the moment I'd arrived, desperation had turned into fear, and I wasn't sure I could go through with it.

I needed to tell her about Ella. About Ava. About Tyler. I needed to tell it all, so I didn't understand my hesitation.

"What happens if I cross a line with my patients?"

"Who are you trying to protect?" Her chest rose up and down with her breaths, and her fingers twitched in her lap, but the look on her face never changed.

Questioning. Inquisitive. Hungry.

"Them." She should have understood that, right?

"What is it about protecting them that is causing you so much stress?"

My thoughts were all random, like a dozen helium-filled balloons floating above the outreached hands of tiny children. I wasn't sure which one to pull down and pop.

"I want to shield them, their emotions, their . . ." I couldn't find the word to describe the need inside me.

I was drowning in a sea of uncertainty, and I needed her to throw me a lifeline.

"They need you." She reread her notes, not necessarily agreeing with me, but repeating my earlier words.

"Or maybe I need them?"

"Maybe. But I don't think that's it. I think you're feeling an over-whelming sense of guilt, and you need help walking through what you think is a minefield."

"Isn't it?"

"I don't think so."

She sounded so sure that it made me pause.

"It's okay to want to look out for them, Danielle." Dr. Brown relaxed just enough that her back wasn't ramrod straight. "I find myself wanting to do the same with you." The words were soft, tender, and barely loud enough to hear, but I did.

But why would she want to protect me? From what? I recalled Tyler's words, how he'd said something similar about Ava.

What did I need saving from? What was going on that I couldn't see?

My brows knit together like a handmade sweater with the tiniest of stitches.

"I think I know who the killer is." I threw the words out, like dirty camping dishwater. I needed to get it off my chest. Share my fears, my suspicions. Have someone else carry the burden.

"Did you get another note?" Her body was at attention.

I didn't answer. Not because I couldn't but because there was a feeling I got from her, a vibe that came across as too much.

"Danielle? Is everything okay?"

There was a war going on inside me. One part of me wanted to trust her, needed to trust her, but there was another part that pushed me away from that need, that warned me she had ulterior motives.

"Okay, how about we backtrack? How are your sessions with Ella going?" Dr. Brown changed the subject.

She turned a few pages in her notes, perhaps pretending she was reading over them.

We both knew she wasn't.

She gave me the time to think about her question.

What about Ella?

Ella wasn't who I thought she was. She was more damaged, more burdened by her past than I wanted to believe. It hurt to realize I'd been wrong about her.

"Ella isn't the one who's killing the parents." I let that drop like an open bottle of glue. It spread around us, between us. Our feet stuck to the floor.

"But you know who is? Or she knows who is." It didn't take her long to look behind my words.

My brain hurt.

"She . . ." I tried again. "It's her . . ." I couldn't quite put it into words. They were there, letters wanting to be grouped together to tell the truth, to share what I knew, but I couldn't get them out. They'd been locked in and the key thrown away. My mind was blank. When I thought about her, all I saw was a faceless figure in the distance, half turned from me, only her outline visible.

Everything felt like that lately. Blurry. Uncertain.

"You want to protect her."

My head snapped up.

"It's okay," Dr. Brown said. "It's okay to be hesitant with revealing truths we know from our patient sessions. Let me ask you a few questions, and maybe that will help. Do you believe she's a danger to herself?"

"No."

"Do you believe she's a danger to others?"

I hesitated to answer this one. Danger as in how? Did I believe she was physically going to hurt another person? No.

"Danielle?"

I sighed, and the wire of my bra dug into my ribs as my chest expanded.

"It's Ava." It felt like a brick had been pushed off my chest, freeing my lungs to breathe easier the moment I said the words. I felt lighter.

"Ava?"

"Tyler's girlfriend. Ella's roommate."

"Danielle?" Dr. Brown licked her lips and tilted her head. "Who is Ava?"

I forgot I hadn't told her about the woman. Everything I'd learned was new to her.

"Ella's roommate and previous cellmate. She's also Tyler's girlfriend. I think. Or maybe there are two Avas. I don't know. Honestly, at first I thought Ava was made up, Ella's imagined friend, but . . ." I dropped my head into my hands. I didn't know anymore. It all felt too . . . convoluted.

"I have a recording. From Tyler. He dropped by the house last night, frantic, worried, even slightly crazed, and I had a migraine. He didn't know I recorded him. I should have told him, but I didn't think it would be an issue. I just wanted to make sure I didn't miss anything, and with my migraines, I do. All the time, I miss things." I babbled, like a speeding car along the freeway, weaving in and out among the slower vehicles, never headed in a straight line.

She was not following me. I could read it in her eyes, her confusion, in the way she squinted at me, how her pen was poised above her notepad but she wasn't sure what to write.

I fumbled with my phone and found the recording.

"Danielle—"

"Let me play it," I interrupted her. "You'll understand better once you hear him."

I played the recording.

"My girlfriend is missing. We had a huge argument because she's been . . . She just hasn't been home." Tyler's voice was loud and clear. I peeked up to watch Dr. Brown's reaction.

She had an intense look on her face. Good—she was paying attention.

"Can you start it over, from the beginning?" Dr. Brown asked. This time, her pen furiously scratched her paper.

I started the recording over again. By the time Tyler admitted he was scared about what his girlfriend, Ava, was doing, she asked me to stop.

"When did you record this?"

"Last night. I was trying to fend off a migraine when he drove up."

"Tyler?"

I nodded. "Yes, he's the only male patient I have."

The way she studied me, I felt uncomfortable. I looked away, down toward my phone.

"I don't know what to do with this," I confessed. "I need to tell Tami. I know that. I should have told her a long time ago. About the notes, about Ella's roommate, about Tyler. She warned me he wasn't who he pretended to be, but . . . what if he's mixed up in the murders? What if he's helping her? Tami mentioned it could be a team, which would make sense. Tyler has been so desperate for Ava to love him, accept him, that he would do anything for her."

I looked up then with alarm. Fear flooded my body as I realized what I'd just said.

"I thought it was Ella. I've been so afraid that the notes were about Ella. I thought in our last session that Ava, her roommate, was made up, and I've been afraid . . ." I couldn't continue, so I buried my head in my hands, my fingers lightly massaging my temple.

"I can't help her," I finally managed to say. The knowledge hit hard. It was devastating. The truth had eluded me for so long because I didn't want to see it, to acknowledge it. But I couldn't help her.

"Can you?" I lifted my gaze to hers and wiped the tears that beaded on my lashes. "Can you help her? Please?" My soul fractured into a million pieces at my admission, and I wasn't sure I could ever fix myself.

I couldn't read Dr. Brown. She was a blank slate. I had no idea what she thought or even felt. There was absolutely no vibe coming off her. "I think I need some time off. To start focusing on myself," I said to fill in the silence. "There's a reason I'm sleepwalking. A reason I have all these migraines. A reason I'm failing my patients. I need to heal myself before I can help anyone else." I swallowed hard, not giving Dr. Brown a chance to speak. "Can you, I mean, will you take on Tyler, Ella, and Savannah? Can you help them? Find them someone they can trust? Someone who can help them better than I have?" I begged, unashamed. She nodded, and a sob jerked from my chest, the pain of that ball of emotion tearing me as it came out.

"Of course, Danielle. Of course I will help. I'll make sure they're in the best hands." Dr. Brown cleared her throat and looked toward her office window.

"Thank you. Thank you, thank you, thank you," I choked, the tears flowing down my face, the pain inside me a mixture of relief and guilt. "I feel like the lid on everything I've been afraid of—everything I've pushed away, pushed into a box so I wouldn't have to deal with it—has come off. Everything wants to come out, and it's too much. My natural response will be to box my emotions back in. I need you to help me not do that." I couldn't believe how much poured out of me. A waterfall of words and emotions cascaded down to the rocks below. Without Dr. Brown's help, I'd smash to my death on those rocks.

Where she had frowned before, now she smiled.

"I'm here. I will do everything I can to help you and the others."

Her words eased something inside me.

"Danielle, can you send me that recording? And any others you've made with your patients?"

I nodded, relief flooding me, knowing I didn't have to do this alone anymore.

"For the rest of our session, would you mind if we focused on you? I know you want to talk about Ella and Tyler and Savannah, but right now, you're more important. Is that all right?"

I nodded.

"I find your choice of words interesting. *Boxing your emotions in.*" She outlined a box in the air with her index finger. "Do you feel you do that, or is that a term you use with your patients?"

I shrugged, which was followed by her come-on-now-Danielle-you-know-better look.

"Yes," I admitted. "I do that. It's not healthy, I understand that, but it's a process I learned early on from my father. It's something he used to say to me, to put those feelings into a box and move on. It's ingrained in me." It was basically a do-what-I-say-but-not-what-I-do scenario.

"Is there anything else you place in that box, Danielle?"

I shook my head.

"I wonder, how many boxes do you think you have?"

Interesting question, one I'd never thought about.

"After all these years, probably a lot."

In my head I pictured one in particular. It was tiny, pink, and trimmed with a white satin ribbon. Almost like a coffin, except the more I focused on it, the more it looked like a canopy bed, one of the old Victorian ones you'd expect to find in a Southern plantation home or in a palace.

It was the type of bed any little girl would want. It must have been my bed as a child, except I was pretty sure my bed was just white.

"What are you thinking, Danielle?" Dr. Brown asked, her words coming through the fog I'd found myself in.

"You'd think I'd have a lot of boxes, right? For my emotions, for my patients, for my own personal life. But when I think about it, all I see is one little box that is more girly than anything I've ever had in my life," I reminisced under my breath.

"Describe it to me." There was a hushed level of excitement in her voice. When I looked at her, her eyes were lit with interest, her lips pursed as if in thought.

Why did she care about it so much? What did it say about me? About my emotions? About what I was going through?

Was there some hidden Freudian euphemism I didn't know about?

"It's a box fit for a little girl. Pink, with ribbon, pretty and soft. Something that would be used for dress-up clothes or special childhood items." I swallowed, unsure if I really wanted to admit the rest about the bed.

I knew the first thoughts that came to mind when anyone brought up images or memories pertaining to beds or bedrooms, especially for children.

"Where was this box?"

I didn't want to answer, and she knew it.

"I'm really not sure," I hedged.

"Why don't you try to focus on it," she suggested. "Maybe look at the lid. Does it have a lock, or can you open it easily?" She leaned forward even more, as if she were about to catch her toddler from tumbling after their first set of steps.

"Danielle, work with me, please?" She tempered the excitement in her voice, but it was still there, in the way she smiled, the grip on her pen, the sway of her shoe as she recrossed her legs.

I closed my eyes.

Dr. Brown would take that as a sign that I'd focused on the box like she requested, that I'd attempted to take off that lid and peer inside.

I only closed my eyes because I didn't want to see her face, to feel the pressure and the guilt of doing something I knew could be both helpful and harmful at the same time.

Nothing good came from opening boxes hidden away in the recesses of your mind.

Nothing.

Chapter Forty-Two

THURSDAY, AUGUST 29

For the first time in a long time, I felt at peace. It didn't feel real, like at any moment that blissful, relaxed feeling would disappear. Logically, I knew it would, but for the next few minutes, I'd live in the moment, embrace it, and maybe collapse on the couch to sleep.

I sent Tami a quick text to let her know I was home and to update her on the new direction I was on. I was taking a leave of absence from my practice, and Dr. Brown was taking over my patients. Things wouldn't be official until Monday, but I'd already left messages for Tyler, Savannah, and Ella, explaining what was happening.

Tami texted back, telling me how proud of me she was for making that choice.

Dr. Brown just wanted me to focus on me. It would be hard but, in the end, worth it. It had to be worth it.

I curled up on the couch and closed my eyes, waiting for the blissful darkness to take hold.

∼

A while later, my eyes popped open, and I sat upright, my heart pounding. I was in a brain fog, searching the room for what had startled me until I noticed a face pressed against my window. Wild eyes stared back at me before a solid pounding on the glass had me bolting to my feet.

My hands shook. My heart was about to push out of my chest. My nostrils flared as I was about to—

"Dr. Rycroft, I need to talk to you." Tyler pounded his fist on my window again. "Please let me in."

For the love of . . . Tyler?

It took me a moment to find my breath. I waved him toward the front door, where I waited for him, my heart still pounding, my hands still shaking. It was late. Why was he here?

"Dr. Rycroft, thank you." Tyler ran up the steps to my door and squeezed past. "I won't stay long, I promise."

"Next time use the doorbell, please." I sounded harsh, but he was lucky I didn't box his ears for scaring me.

I followed him into my office and sat in my chair with as much calmness as I could muster.

"I . . . I wanted to talk with you before I did something." He leaned forward, elbows resting on his knees, hands together, while he looked me directly in the eyes.

His gaze wasn't steady. It was frantic, shifting, and his legs bounced. He was on edge, and I needed to calm him down.

"Tyler, it's okay," I said. "You're in a safe place now."

His eyes blazed bright, cheeks crimson, and his lips cracked like dying leaves.

"You don't understand. It's not okay. It hasn't been for a long time. I've got . . . I've got to stop her."

"Ava?"

"I can't let this continue. It's not right."

"What do you need to stop her from doing?" I was asking a question I already knew the answer to. It was all clear to me now.

"Tyler, do you mind if I record this?" I asked a lot, I knew, especially after leaving that message on his phone that he was being transferred to another therapist.

"Yes. Yes, that's a good idea. You can use that when the police come. You have my permission. Wait"—he reached his hand out—"should I repeat that on the recording?"

"What do you mean, when the police come?" I looked up, out my office window, as if they were there.

"You don't know? Haven't you figured it out yet?" He leaned forward to hit the record button on my phone. "Hurry up, before it's too late."

"Tyler, I'm going to record everything you tell me today. Do you agree?" The words were a little hard to get out, like my tongue was swollen.

He nodded. "Yeah, it's fine. If the police need this as proof of what I've told you, use it."

There was a look on his face, like he was waiting for something.

"Tyler?"

He nodded. "Okay, okay. Good. Hurry."

Why such a rush?

I rubbed an area at the top of my neck where an air bubble pulsed in my head. There was a pressure point at the back that, if found, could help negate headaches. I pushed as hard as I could because I knew any moment the sharp pains would begin.

"Ava." He swallowed. "Ava is . . ."

I didn't find the pressure point in time, and a jackhammer went off in my brain, the entry point right in the center of my head, and everything turned black, silent, and for a brief minute, I was adrift, floating in an oasis of nothing.

Bang. Bang. Bang.

There was a loud pounding on my front door that brought me back into the moment.

I stood shakily.

"No, don't. Please. Please don't let her in." Tyler blocked the door, hands spread wide, pleading with me.

"Tyler, please move."

Bang. Bang. Bang.

"Let me in, you little shit. I know you're in there." The doorknob jiggled, then turned, and a woman I'd never seen before barged her way in.

Tyler stood in front of me as if to shield me.

"Ava, don't. Please."

This was Ava? Tall, dark hair pulled into a messy bun, ripped jeans, and a black tank top over a solid body. For some reason, I pictured her more . . . rough looking.

"Danielle." Ava pushed past Tyler, forced him out of the way, and pulled me into a hug. "I can't tell you how long I've waited for this day." Her smile was warm, welcoming, and her eyes scrutinized me as if reading my reaction.

Tyler stumbled to the couch and sat down with a thump, his body trembling with earthquake-strength tremors.

"Please, Danielle, sit." Ava indicated toward my chair as she joined Tyler on the couch. She placed her hand on his leg, and he stilled. Instantly.

"Ava." I struggled to get her name across my lips.

"Yes. I know. This is a surprise. It's not how I thought we'd meet, but I figured this would be easier. And less messy. Tyler," she said with a tight smile, "doesn't know how to keep his mouth shut."

He blanched at her words, and real fear entered his eyes.

"I'm not sure I understand." My throat dried up, my lips were parched, and my hands shook like leaves in the wind.

"Don't be scared, Danielle. I promise, I'm not here to hurt you. I just thought we should talk sooner rather than later."

I watched Tyler from the corner of my eye.

This wasn't just a little chat. Not by the way Tyler acted. Something else was going on. Something that scared him.

"Are you here to kill me?" The words came out calm, collected, clearer than I thought they would.

"Kill you?" She laughed.

I noticed the way Ava squeezed Tyler's knee, how the muscles in her arm tightened. And yet her smile, her eyes, showed none of that tension. She was good.

"No, Danielle, I'm not here to kill you. I'm here to protect you. Mistakes have been made. Mistakes"—she turned to Tyler and snarled—"that I will rectify soon, but to do that, I need your help." Her snarl disappeared, and a simplistic smile appeared in its place. "I made a promise to El—" She stopped at the same moment I stood.

The sky outside was painted in a blaze of red and purples. That wasn't what had caught my attention. It was the fact that those shades were due to the half dozen police cars lined up outside my house. Their lights reflected against every surface until, even with my eyes closed, it was all I could see.

"Danielle, please, wait." Ava stood with me and reached out as if to stop me, but I stepped away from her reach, eager to place as much distance between us as I could.

I headed toward the front door.

I listened to Ava berate Tyler as I walked down the hallway. She tore him apart, blamed him for everything, and it made me feel sad for him. For her. For what it meant to have the police outside my home.

I should have been in full panic mode. Flight or fight. Run as fast as I could. And yet each step was precise. Measured. Careful. Each breath was too. Controlled. Slow. Full.

The police, they were here for Ava. Possibly Tyler too.

I opened the door to my home as an officer walked across my lawn toward me.

Behind him, squad cars blocked off the street and the park, and I noticed all my neighbors rushing to the other side of the street for safety.

That's when it hit me. My body shook. My legs could barely handle walking down the steps as I faced the officer with a gun trained on me.

"Hurry, she's inside," I said, my voice wobbly under the strain.

I had just sat and talked with a serial killer and made it out alive.

I inhaled deeply, my lungs aching as I realized how close to death I could have been.

"Stop where you are." The officer's voice was harsh, cold, dominating.

I stopped.

"Place your hands above your head and kneel."

What? Wait. No. They thought I was Ava? *No no no no no no no no no.*

I fell to the ground, my hands lifted high.

"She's inside," I said again. "She's in my front office along with her boyfriend, Tyler." There was a misunderstanding. They were just being safe, cautious . . . right?

I looked beyond the officer in front of me to those behind him, and never had I felt so much hatred directed toward me, but it was there, in the eyes of all the police who stood with their guns pointed, assessing me, condemning me.

"You don't understand. I'm Danielle. I live here. Ava's inside my house. She's the killer." I spoke up, my voice clear as I tried hard not to show my panic.

I looked around for Tami. She should have been here. She needed to be. Why wasn't she? Why couldn't I find her?

The officer in front of me motioned to others to head into my home, their guns in front of them as they opened my door and disappeared inside.

"Where is Tami?" I couldn't hide the panic. It was in my voice. It was all I could do not to fall apart.

Why were all these guns trained on me?

"I need Tami. Detective Tami Sloan. Where is she? She'll clear this up."

"What you need," the police officer said as he approached, "is to be silent." One step at a time, pistol in one hand, cuffs in the other.

Tami would help. She knew me. Sure, things had been weird the last few days with her not returning my phone calls or chatting before she left for her shift, but she was just stressed.

The officer looked up as the screen door to my home opened and slammed closed.

"All clear. No one in there."

My head whipped around. "They must have left through the back. There's a gate in my backyard." I was desperate to help, for them to believe me. The serial killer, the one they called the Cheshire Mad Queen, had been there, in my office. I'd spoken to her.

"No evidence of anyone going through the back either. Grass hasn't been cut in a while, so we would have seen if someone had gone through." The death glare from the cop to the side sent a tremor of fear down my body. "The house is cleared, but you'll want to see the basement. Lot of bloodstains by the look of it."

Bloodstains? Basement? I never went down there. What was going on? Where was Tami?

"Danielle." She was there, on the sidewalk, off to the side. I let out a tortured breath. She was there. "Danielle, it's okay. You're going to be okay." She lowered her voice until it was soothing, calming, reminding me of someone attempting to approach a wild horse. She moved slowly toward me, her steps careful, measured, her breathing in check.

Tami was calm, which helped to keep me calm.

I kept my hands behind my back, unfisted, despite the tension coiling through my muscles. I wanted to scream, cry, beg for her to understand.

"I'm okay, Tami," I reassured her. "You'll help sort this out, right?" I smiled, my voice light but not airy, not unsettled. Firm.

A loud murmuring erupted from the crowd that had gathered.

I looked at Tami in alarm.

"I'm trying, Dani. I'm trying." Tami was close to me now. "I've done everything I can. Now it's your turn. You need to go with the officer, okay? There's some things we need to clear up, if that's okay." She spoke to me as if we were the only two in my yard, as if there weren't multiple officers behind her listening in to every word, as if the street weren't full of reporters and cameras and people who knew me.

Sabrina was there too, in the crowd. Hands covering her mouth. She was shocked. I could read it on her face, even from across the street.

"Ava was inside. She came to me. She wanted to meet with me."

She nodded. "Dani, don't say anything more, okay? I need you to remain calm and quiet."

"I don't understand what's happening." Tears fell down my cheeks as I was hauled to my feet.

"We just need to clear some things up, okay? Come to the station, where we can talk and where you'll be safe. Please?" She held out her hand, and I was surprised to see it tremble. She was just as scared as I was.

"Dani, please?" Her voice shook with unshed tears.

The officer behind me wasn't gentle as he cuffed my wrists. The click of them closing rang in my ears. The heaviness against my wrists, the weight on my arms, made it all the more real.

I was scared.

The glares from the other officers didn't go unnoticed.

I dropped my head and focused on my feet as she walked with me to the back of a police car and helped me in. She spoke to someone outside the car before placing her hand on my shoulder and squeezing.

"Danielle, I . . ." She paused, choked up and in pain. "I'll see you at the station, okay?"

Tears ran down my cheeks as I nodded, too afraid to say anything.

I knew I wouldn't see her. We were too close. She was too close to the case. To me. I would speak to a million other people before they'd even consider allowing her to talk to me.

The car door slammed shut, the sound reverberating throughout my body.

Throughout my soul.

Chapter Forty-Three

I was exhausted. Weak. Fragile. And my head was two seconds from explosion, like when you open a bottle of carbonated soda that's been shaken.

All I wanted to do was curl into a ball, pull a blanket over my head, put on noise-reducing headphones, and sleep. Sleep and never wake up.

I sat in a cold and sparse room. One single table. Four chairs. Three were empty at the moment, but they hadn't been earlier. I was alone. I stared into a large, thick window, where I knew an audience watched me.

Last night, I'd been read my rights and told I was suspected of being the serial killer Tami had searched for. No one listened when I explained it wasn't me. That it was Ava.

They had placed me in a jail cell, provided a thin blanket, and left me alone for the night.

I hadn't slept a wink. I'd refused to close my eyes and waited all night for Tami to come and make things right.

She never came.

When they brought me to this room, they gave me some water to drink and said someone would be in to see me soon.

That felt like hours ago. No one came. No one checked. No one wanted to listen to my explanations.

In their eyes, I was the criminal. The murderer. Whispers followed my steps until the door closed behind me. Haunting whispers I would never forget. I'd never met such hatred before, and I didn't understand it.

"Why am I here?" I repeated my question over and over and over again. Someone was there, listening to me. I just needed them to believe me, to understand. "Tami knows. She knows me. She knows about the notes, about my patients. About Tyler. She can clear this up." I rested my head on my forearms, exhausted.

Several more hours passed before the door opened.

I straightened right away with tension but relaxed with relief when Dr. Brown walked in. She wore a thin cardigan over a camisole and capri jeans with ballet slippers. She looked comfortable, relaxed, whereas I shivered beneath a sweater, thick socks, and sweatpants. I was a mess compared to her. The cold had seeped into my bones from this room, and no amount of layers would warm me.

I was never going to be warm again.

She set a bag down on the floor and pulled out a thick wrap. She arranged it around my shoulders, over my arms, tucking the ends in, and an immediate warmth covered me.

"I placed it in the dryer for a few moments. I figured you'd be cold."

If my hands had been free, I'd have launched into her arms and hugged her. But I wasn't free. I was chained, handcuffed, and treated like a criminal.

"Dr. Brown, please, talk to someone. Tell them it's not me. Please?"

She remained silent as she shuffled papers on the table. The silence between us grew. I was terrified but tried not to show it.

When she finally looked at me, I could tell she was gauging my reaction. "Danielle?"

"What's going on, Dr. Brown?" There was a desperation in my voice that pleaded with her to be honest with me.

"I'm going to ask you some questions. They may seem weird at first, but I promise to explain myself, okay? I need you to keep an open mind and to trust me. I promise you, we will get through this."

She pulled out a notepad from a file and uncapped her pen. "Just think of this as one of our regular therapy sessions."

I wanted to tell her okay, but nothing about today was similar to our regular therapy sessions, and she knew that.

"In our last session, you mentioned you've been having a hard time sleeping." She paused, and so I nodded. "Not only are you sleepwalking, but you've been having bad nightmares, right?"

I swallowed hard and nodded again.

"You look exhausted."

I was so tired that my body ached and my skin tingled with each movement, and even the thump-thump of my heart hurt my chest. I didn't know a body could be that weary.

"How about you tell me about the latest one." Her pen was poised to take notes.

I didn't want to. I was afraid that whatever I said would be used against me.

She must have sensed that. She pointed to the camera that had blinked red the whole time I'd been there.

We watched it together. Blink. Blink. Blink. Then the red light disappeared.

"You're not being filmed. We are alone in here, just the two of us."

We were not alone.

"What about that room?" I motioned to the one behind her. "Who's there?"

She looked over her shoulder and dipped her head, and the mirror disappeared. Two people stood on the other side, arms crossed, intent looks on their faces. I didn't recognize them.

"They're with me, Danielle. They are both psychologists. Try to ignore them if you can. I need you to be honest with me, as honest as you, Danielle Rycroft, can be."

Psychologists? I didn't feel comfortable with that or with her wording. But I was no longer in control, was I?

"I'm not a killer. I'm not." It was important that someone believe me.

Dr. Brown dropped her pen and looked at me. Something in her gaze wormed into my soul, and I knew that whatever she was about to say, it wouldn't help.

"Your blackouts, they were increasing, weren't they?" The words sounded simple, innocent, but they were heavy with doubt.

"I never came to covered in blood, if that's what you're asking. Not once." But even as I said it, I struggled to recall all the times I'd blacked out. Sometimes I'd be home in bed, or I'd be in the kitchen pouring myself a glass of orange juice, or in the bathroom stepping out of the shower. Other times I'd be outside walking through the park or down a quiet street.

But never, never had I been covered in blood. That much I knew.

"I know it's bothered you, when you realized you were sleepwalking. Have you thought about those missing hours? Where you were? What you were doing?"

My head shook back and forth, back and forth. Not because I didn't agree with what she said but because my brain was on overload, too many thoughts, too many memories being revealed.

"Talk to me, Danielle. Please."

"I was just walking . . . that's all I do is walk . . ." My childlike voice was filled with those deep needs that rushed through me. The need to retreat, to hide myself, to escape the life that had become my nightmare.

"How many times did you wake up wearing different clothes?" she asked, her voice full of something between a question and an answer.

I swallowed hard. Why did it . . . then it hit me. *No. No. NO! No no no no no no no no* . . . It was not possible. I would know. I would *know*.

My fingernails dug into the palms of my hands. "I'm not the killer. I wouldn't—" The pain in my chest and the thump-thump, thump-thump, thump-thump of my heart intensified until I swore it was about to pop out of my chest. I wanted to rub the skin over my heart with the palm of my hand, but I couldn't. I lifted my gaze to the ceiling with a desperate need to not cry.

"It's going to be okay." Dr. Brown reached out to me with her arm, offering a lifeline. I grabbed hold, unable to let go. "Of course I know you." She squeezed my hand. "You, Danielle Rycroft, would never harm a living soul. Deep inside, you know this too." She handed me a tissue.

Tears flowed down my face, but they weren't strong enough to wash away the fear inside me.

"I followed him," I whispered. She was going to think I was crazy.

"I'm sorry?" She struggled to grasp what I'd said. It was written plain on her face.

"I followed him. Tyler. I . . ." A bag full of rocks lodged in my throat, impeding the words. "I was worried." Those three words didn't adequately convey my reasons for following him, but they were the only ones that came out.

Dr. Brown's head tilted to the side. "You . . . followed . . . Tyler?"

I felt like nodding my head would be the wrong response.

"I'd like to focus on this for a bit, if that's okay?" She set her pad of paper on her lap. "Let's start with why."

"Why? You mean why did I follow him?" Stupid question, because of course that's what she meant. I worried my hands together. "Tyler, the things he said to me, about his girlfriend, they . . . they weren't adding up, and I . . ." I swallowed past the shards of glass in my throat. "I was afraid he was involved in the murders somehow."

"Why would you feel that way? Did he give you any indication he was?" Her pen hovered over the paper. "Did you share this with Tami?"

The Patient

Not sharing with Tami was something I was going to regret for the rest of my life and then some. Maybe all this could have been prevented, maybe those other murders could have been avoided, if I'd only said something.

But I never did. I was too afraid, and every time I tried, I'd get hit by a migraine. My body had been trying to tell me sharing would be a bad idea, and I'd listened.

Obviously, I shouldn't have.

"I need my phone."

"Why?"

"Tyler, he came to see me, before . . . before the police came. And then Ava came in. You'll hear her. You'll see that she's involved. It's all there."

She glanced behind her, at the people I'd tried to forget were there.

"Are you sure you recorded it?" Dr. Brown asked.

"Of course I'm sure. I had his permission to."

A knock on the door interrupted us. It was loud. Jarring. A police officer stepped in and handed Dr. Rycroft my phone.

She placed it on the table. I punched in my password and then found the recording.

I played it. I didn't watch as she listened. Instead, I closed my eyes, remembering the scene in my office before Ava came in.

The sound of her voice, how she spoke to me, so different from how she spoke to Tyler. Goose bumps covered my skin.

"What am I listening to, Danielle?" Dr. Brown's words were measured, carefully constructed, though I could see a myriad of thoughts as they raced across her face.

Somewhere, somehow, I had lost confidence in myself, and so had she.

"My conversation with Tyler."

"Tyler." One word. One sigh.

"And Ava. She's the real killer."

289

She looked at me with a mixture of pity and . . . understanding?

"Let's go back to what you mentioned earlier. You said you followed Tyler. What did you see?"

I wanted to wrap my arms around myself, to hug myself, but instead I played with the edges of the wrap, twisting the fringe with my fingers. Why were we back to this? Why weren't we following up with the recording?

"Danielle, trust me, remember?"

My thoughts raced. I wanted to trust her. I had no choice but to trust her.

"Nothing. I saw absolutely nothing. One minute he was there, and the next minute . . . I know it sounds weird, but he disappeared. I don't know if he knew I was following him or if I just lost him in the crowd." I scrunched my face at the memory. A dull throb started between my eyes. I pressed my index finger into a pressure point where the throb had settled and pressed hard.

Lights danced before me, even with my eyes closed. Little star formations against a black backdrop, and as I focused on those brilliant stars, a soft ringing sounded in my ears. It reminded me of a wind chime my mother used to have outside the kitchen window when I was young.

"Danielle?" I heard a voice in the distance, like a rolling summer thunderstorm coming in off the distant lake. I tried to find the voice, to see who called, but I couldn't.

Something touched me, and I jumped. My eyes burst open, and I was afraid of what I'd see.

Dr. Brown half knelt in front of me, her hand on my knee.

"Danielle? Can you hear me?" Her lips moved, but the sound didn't sync. It was like watching a delayed newscast on the television.

The pounding in my head intensified; the pressure from the pain pushed against the skin covering my skull until I thought my head would explode. My hands were pressed tightly against my temples, and a low moan escaped from deep inside my soul.

And then it was gone.

The pain. The pounding. The pressure. Gone.

"Danielle? Danielle?" She added force to her hand on my knee. "Are you okay? What's going on?"

"I'm . . . I'm okay." My mouth was dry, and my voice sounded like a frog in heat, but the dancing lights, the paralyzing fear, and the intense pain in my head weren't there.

"Where were you just now?" Dr. Brown straightened, poured water into a cup, and handed it to me. "What just happened?"

"I . . . I got—" I tried to think back to what had happened. "I got dizzy, and there was a ringing in my ears. Another migraine." I shook my head, an attempt to grasp my thoughts. They flittered about like moths escaping from a closet.

My shoulder muscles were as hard as boulders, and I felt like I was going crazy with all the thoughts that raced in my head. Thoughts I couldn't grasp. The only one that stuck was that I had to clear this up—I had to get out of here.

Chapter Forty-Four

FRIDAY, AUGUST 30

My heart beat to the cadence of a drum. The thumping picked up pace as I sat there, so confused about what was happening.

"Please tell me what's going on." No more questions. No more therapy session talk. I just needed the truth. I was exhausted, bone weary, and I couldn't do this anymore.

"Danielle, how much do you know about DID? Dissociative identity disorder?"

My forehead crinkled. Multiple personalities was how it had been labeled when I'd studied to be a therapist.

"I don't know much, to be honest. I've read up on it a little, but I've never had a patient diagnosed with the disorder."

Dr. Brown nodded. The kind of nod you'd expect from a therapist.

"I've worked with several patients diagnosed with this, which is why certain aspects from our therapy sessions stand out to me." She lifted a file from the table and flipped it open.

"Wait." I stopped her from saying anything more. I didn't want to hear it. I didn't want to hear what she had to say.

She must have sensed my fear. It had to be on my face, in my voice, because she placed her hand on mine and squeezed.

"I can't imagine how you must be feeling right now. But I want you to know I'm here. We're going to walk through this together, okay? I promise you, I will not leave you."

I pulled my hand from hers. What the hell did she mean?

"I am not crazy."

"Danielle, when you played the recordings for me, what voices did you hear?"

"For the first one? Mine and Tyler's. On the one we just listened to? Mine, Tyler's, and Ava's." I was angry, and I didn't bother to hide it.

"Do you know what I heard? Your voice. Your voice in three different pitches. Your voice lowered when you spoke as Tyler, and it had an edge when you were Ava. But each and every time, it was your voice."

"No. Not possible."

She just looked at me. Didn't say anything. Just waited. Waited for me to come to her realization. Except I wouldn't. I couldn't.

"What about the notes? Do you have them? I didn't write them."

"I have them. I also have journals from your office." She bent down and pulled out notebooks from the bag she'd brought.

I recognized them. They were the notebooks I'd given to Ella, Savannah, and Tyler. Notebooks I'd wanted them to write in, to journal their thoughts. Except there were two other notebooks. One was mine, where I'd kept track of all my blackouts, and then there was another I didn't recognize.

"This was Tyler's." Dr. Brown flipped open one of the covers. His name was written on the front page.

She then flipped through a few pages. There were dates on each page. Dates identical to our sessions.

Dr. Brown then pulled out the notes I'd received.

I looked them over. And noticed something I didn't want to accept.

"We believe these were written by the alter called Tyler."

I tore my gaze from the notes and caught the compassion in her eyes.

She then opened each notebook and showed me all the different handwriting.

"So you see, then, I couldn't have written those." Even as I said it, though, the truth slowly trickled in.

If I had DID, if there were alternate personalities within me, then it was entirely possible it had been my hand that wrote those notes, but when I was in a different personality.

My stomach lurched as I realized the truth. I leaned to the side and threw up.

"They're real. I see them . . . I hear their voices . . . I . . ." I started to cry, and tears rolled down my cheeks as my heart broke into a million tiny pieces.

I was broken. Broken, and I couldn't ever be fixed.

"I believe you are suffering from both auditory and visual hallucinations and delusions. Your blackouts, your migraines, everything you've been dealing with lately, it all adds up."

Nothing added up.

"But they're real. I know they are," I argued, not wanting to accept her truth. "They have lives. Ella works at the library. Please, can you get Tami for me? She'll tell you . . ." My voice trailed off because of the looks thrown my way every time I asked for Tami. The whispers as Tami helped me into the car. The way they called me crazy, mental . . .

"There's no detective named Tami that works in this unit. They also checked with the library. No volunteer or hired employee by the name of Ella."

She flipped open to a sheet.

"Does the name Anna Danielle Rycroft sound familiar?" She pointed to a photo on the sheet with a name, my name, beneath it.

"I don't . . . that's me, my full name, but I . . . God, this can't be true." My head pounded. The intensity of the pain grew until I wanted to crawl out of my skin.

"Danielle? It's okay. If this is too much, it's okay." Dr. Brown's voice was meant to be soothing, but it wasn't. It hurt me, the sound of her voice, the squeak of her chair, the clink of the chains around my wrists. Everything hurt.

I rested my head down on my arms, the need to sleep so overwhelming that I no longer cared about who I was, or who I could be, or anything else.

"Stay with me, Danielle. Please? Just for a few more moments." Her hand touched mine, and I lifted my head slightly.

"Your head hurts, doesn't it? I think that's the tell for when one of your alters wants to take over."

Alters? Tells? This couldn't be happening.

I shuddered. My body felt foreign.

"Your other patients who have . . . this . . . are they okay?" I whispered.

"They are. It has taken time, but they've accepted their family. It's not something to be scared of, Danielle. I promise to be there with you, with all of you, as we figure it out."

When she said the word *family*, my headache dissipated a little. Not much, but a little. There was also a feeling inside me, a sense of rightness.

It was as if there were a thin layer of mist in my head covering the truth, and little by little, Dr. Brown was helping to clear that mist.

I didn't like it.

I didn't think I had a choice, though.

"Think of it as a puzzle, Danielle. Your life, everything you've experienced, is one section of the puzzle. Tyler, Ella, Savannah, Tami, and even Ava are all other sections."

I understood puzzles.

"You'll help us put all the pieces together?"

"I'll try."

I saw a mental video of lives being played out in my memories.

Savannah's truth of her childhood, the abuse from her uncle. I understood where her desire for death came from. I watched Ava come to life as Savannah's parents were killed. I saw the hard life Ava lived in prison and how she created Ella to help her survive. That was where I came in. I was the glue that held us all together. The knowledge that everything I'd ever believed about my past was a lie . . . it tore me into pieces. And yet, I realized, these pieces, if put together again like a puzzle, would form one life. One life with different chapters.

Just like Alice as she tumbled down the hole. Nothing was as it seemed.

"What about the murders? Do you still believe that was me?" *Please, God, please let her say no.*

"Not you. I can say with every certainty that Danielle Rycroft did not commit any murders."

She was trying to make me feel better, but I heard the words she didn't say.

It was too much. Too much for me to process.

"You want to speak to the others, don't you?" I asked.

She shook her head, which surprised me.

"Just Ava. I think she's the dominant one. The one who can answer our questions. Will that be okay? If I talk to her?"

I shrugged. I had no idea.

"If Ava comes out, what happens to me? Where do I go?" So many questions with no answers. Who could answer them? Dr. Brown? Ava?

A serene smile softened Dr. Brown's face even though I caught the excitement as it rose inside her at the mention of Ava's name.

"I'll speak to Ava, but I think you'll be fine, Danielle. She needs you. Every alter within a family plays a role. I believe yours is to be a helper, like you've told me. You're there to help Savannah and Ella and Tyler, and by the sounds of it, you've done a fabulous job in helping them grow to be stronger individuals. You should be proud of yourself."

I doubted I'd ever feel proud of myself again.

"How do I give Ava permission to take control?" I said this in a whisper that I was surprised Dr. Brown heard.

"It's okay. Just close your eyes. Ava will know what to do," she said.

There was understanding, compassion, and acceptance in Dr. Brown's eyes, and I knew I could trust her.

I closed my eyes, accepting a vision that filled my mind.

One of a soft bed with turned-down covers and silk pajamas and my favorite book waiting to be read.

Chapter Forty-Five

AVA

I pull my hand from the good doctor's and look around. I am thirsty as hell and could use a stiff drink, but it looks like all I'll get is water.

"Ava?"

I want to raise my arms high, stand on my tiptoes, and stretch my body as far as I can. Instead, all I can do is wiggle my fingers and lean to the right, then to the left in order to stretch.

"Is there any more water? My throat is dry."

I catch the way her eyes light up before she tamps them down. She doesn't want me to know she's in the game now.

She's ready, but so am I.

If she expects me to give up all my secrets, it needs to be a two-way street. I need some assurances, some favors, and I have no problem letting this linger as long as necessary.

Where else do we need to be? We're going to be stuck in this hellhole for the rest of our lives unless I can figure out a way to get us out.

It might take time, but I will. One way or another. We will get out. I've done it before. I can do it again.

She pours me water and waits till I guzzle it down.

"I think we need to set some rules, don't you?" I want to be the one in control. Not her. God, I wish we were on a couch in her office and not in this room. It's cold. And it stinks.

This isn't my first rodeo. I've done this way too many times to let the head shrink be the one to set all the rules.

"What do you have in mind?"

Good. I like how this woman thinks. She's going to let me lead the way, hoping that I'll start to feel safe and share our secrets.

She may work with DID patients, but she's never worked with me.

I'm not like most hosts. I keep a firm hand on everyone. We all have a purpose, and I make sure we all serve that purpose.

"First, you only talk to me. Danielle, Tyler, Savannah, and Ella won't be coming out to answer any questions. They are all freaked out by what's going on, and I've had to figure out ways to calm them down. Ella is a wreck. She's closed in, and all the progress she made with Danielle is gone."

When she nods, I take it that she agrees. She could be nodding to say she understands, but I could give a rat's ass if she understands or not. This is the way things will be if she wants any answers.

"What about Tami?" she asks.

I scoff. "Tami's busy taking care of Danielle. She's her friend. I let Danielle create her because she was lonely. Since you won't be talking to Danielle, you won't be speaking to Tami. Understand?"

Tami was a mistake. One I sure as hell won't make again.

"Second?"

I shrug. "I'll let you know the other rules as we need them."

I never said I'd play fair.

"In order for that to work, I need two promises from you." She leans back, taps her fingers along her thigh.

"What's that?" Now I'm on guard.

"I want you to promise me everyone is safe and they won't be harmed."

I almost jump out of my skin.

"Who do you think I am?" I barely keep my voice level. Fury fills me so fast my hands shake. "They are my family, bitch. Of course they will be safe and unharmed. They're all resting. I fixed up their rooms special, just the way they like them. I know how to take care of my own." I want to spit at her, slap her, shut this shit down, and say screw it all. How dare she accuse me of hurting them?

All she does is nod her fucking head.

I breathe in a few deep breaths, knowing I need to remain calm. If I don't, she'll have the upper hand.

"What's the second promise?" I force the words out with a snake smile.

"That you won't lie to me." She doesn't even skip a beat, blink, or pause.

"Done. Why would I lie? Serves me no purpose." Talk about a waste of a promise. If I want this to go smoothly, then I need to cooperate, which I have no problem doing.

"Where's Danielle now?"

It takes everything within me not to roll my eyes. I thought she understood how these things work. Does she understand how families of alters work?

"Danielle is in her room," I repeat, a little more slowly to show how insane I find the repetitive question. "She's getting comfortable, relaxing. Tami's with her, like I said before. Tami turned out to be smarter than expected. She's going to explain everything to Danielle." My foot is itchy.

I jiggle my hands, the handcuffs hitting the table with a bang. "Any way I can get out of these? I promise I'm not going to hurt you. My foot itches like a bitch."

She shakes her head at me, and I swear there's a bit of a smirk she tries to hide.

"You're going to ask about the rest of them, aren't you? Ella is already gone, as in she's lost within her own world, drinking tea with the Mad Hatter. She's fast asleep and won't awake till I tell her it's time. Tyler, well . . . Tyler is in a time-out for a while. He broke some major rules, and now I can't trust him. He's going to need to earn that trust back." Just the thought of Tyler puts me in a black mood. Now isn't the time to deal with that.

"You're upset."

"Wouldn't you be? You get betrayed by someone you love, and we all end up in here, in prison." My knuckles crack in my attempt to calm myself. "You'll try to get us into a psych hospital, right?"

"You blame all of that on Tyler?" She ignores my request.

"We would have gotten away if it weren't for him."

She picks up a file, our file, and flips through a few pages. "He was the one who left the notes, wasn't he?"

"He's never done that before. He was sneaky, and it took me a while to figure it out. Otherwise, I would have stopped that shit from happening a long time ago. But then he had to go and tell Danielle about me. Again, something he's never done before. If he hadn't, then I wouldn't have had to stop him, which means I wouldn't have come to her house. She could have been kept in the dark, safe from all the ugliness." One plus one equals two. "So, yes, Tyler's the one to blame."

"He's the reason you were caught, is that what you're saying?"

I nod.

"You're the Cheshire Ma—"

"The Cheshire Mad Queen," I interrupt her. "Yes, I knew what they called me. Me. Not anyone else. You understand that, right? Danielle had nothing to do with any of the children we protected."

"You seem to be wanting to protect Danielle right now?"

What is it with the stupid questions?

"Of course I want to protect her. She's innocent. Haven't you heard a word I've said? All I've done since we moved to this stupid town was protect her. She's obsessed with Alice, so it made sense to move here, where she had good memories. Plus there's that park with the statues from her books." It feels like I'm talking to a teenager. I'd forgotten how tedious this could be. "I didn't want to take that from her. Which is why I protected her from knowing anything. Whenever Tyler or Ella said too much, I stopped them."

The look on the doctor's face hasn't changed.

"Do you think it's possible you were so focused on protecting her that you made mistakes that indirectly ended up linking Danielle to your murders?"

"What the hell are you talking about?"

"The police found the stack of wrapped books in the house. The same books you left in the children's rooms after you killed their parents." She flips through her file and places her finger somewhere on the page.

This is where I'm supposed to give a reaction, but I don't. I won't.

"Still had nothing to do with Danielle." I give her a smile, a Cheshire Cat smile, knowing I'll win this argument. "In fact, I'm not sure how they managed to connect any dots to her." I watch her, searching for the answer to a question that's nibbling at the back of my head. "Unless it was you," I say, laying out my accusation as if it were plain for all to see.

"I called the police, yes," she admits. "I gave them the notes too. But it wasn't until after hearing the first recording of Tyler, I started to piece together things that were bothering me and realized Danielle might have DID."

It's like she's gauging me, testing me to see how far she can poke. Am I supposed to be surprised at her admission?

"So what, you called the police. There's still no way you could connect the murders to her."

She turns the file in her hands around so I can see what's on the paper.

The leaflet.

The same one Danielle had in her rare Alice book, the one I found for her in an old bookstore years ago. Hidden among the pages, probably used as a bookmark, was this leaflet that was produced for children who read the story. There aren't many out there anymore, and Ella thought it would be a nice touch, so we had a bunch of them printed out.

Damn it.

Only Danielle had the original leaflet. There was a slight tear that I couldn't hide in the photocopy.

"They found this in the house you were living in. Although, from what I saw when I walked through it, it wasn't the best living conditions. This, along with the books . . ." Her voice trails off as if that should explain everything.

"Okay, but that's only one item, and I could have stolen it from Danielle like I did the books. There's no other way to pinpoint her. She was never there."

The good doctor shakes her head and gives me a smile full of pity. Too much pity, if you ask me.

"If you were there, she was there."

"No, she wasn't." I can't believe I have to spell this out for her. "Sure, we all share a body, but we are all different. I speak differently than Danielle and Ella and even Savannah. We all have different pitches, different ways of speaking. Our mannerisms couldn't be more different than a roomful of complete strangers. My eyes are wider than hers, I smell different than her, hell, our palms are even different."

"And yet your fingerprints are the same, just like the DNA of your hair."

Fine. Okay. I blow out a puff of air but don't bother to respond. I can argue this all I want, but she's right. The bottom line is if I was there, so was she. So were all of them. Which means we all have to suffer together, even if I give them a respite and live this part of our life for us.

That much I can do.

"Can we move from this topic, please?"

303

Dr. Brown nods. Her fingers continue their tap dance along her leg. "Can you tell me a little bit more about your family? How you all came to be?"

"That fascinates you, doesn't it? How many patients have you worked with that have alters?"

She smiles, a little more condescending than friendly. "There's more families like yours than you'd expect."

"Huh."

Interesting. I've only ever met a few, during our early years, following the death of Savannah's parents.

"There's about a dozen or so of us. Everyone but me is resting, and I only allow a few up at a time. Too many gets overwhelming, and since I'm the strongest one, I'm also the matriarch of our family."

She takes notes while I talk. She's probably trying to build a family tree or something. It won't matter, though. I don't trust her enough to let her talk to any of the others, and they sure as hell don't need to experience life in this hellhole.

"Have you always been the host, Ava? Since you're the most dominant one?"

"Can I please get these off? I promise I will not harm you. I'd be stupid to. I know how this works—if I play nice, you'll help us. All I want is to be sent to the psych ward. I don't want us to be in prison. I'll tell you whatever you want if you can promise me that."

"I can't promise you anything, Ava. I'm sorry. I'll do the best I can to help you and the others, but what happens is up to you, your lawyer, and the judge."

"So that's a no?"

"Until I know you better, I'm sorry."

I knew it. She has the power to release me from these cuffs. Damn it.

"Ask me anything. I said I wouldn't lie."

"Then answer my question."

I have to think for a minute, recall what she asked. "No. I didn't come until after Savannah . . . well, let's just say little Sav had a breakdown and couldn't follow through with killing her mommy and daddy, so I . . . helped her."

The doctor nods her head while her pen furiously writes across the page.

"No, Savannah wasn't the host either. I know you're going to ask. The real host, the real us, she's a precious little girl we all work hard to protect. Anna Danielle Rycroft. Danielle recognized the name earlier. We all love her and take turns reading her stories. She has the best room out of all of us. It's all pink with ruffles and lace and teddy bears and a table where we all sit for tea parties." I let the image of Anna and her room fill me until the smile on my face is as wide as the love in my heart for her.

"She has no idea how awful life can be. No idea. To protect her after her uncle . . . Well, Annie was the first one to protect our little Anna. Annie sleeps all the time now. She . . ." I'm getting all emotional, and I don't like it. "Annie deserves all the rest she needs after everything he did to her." I drink in the anger I feel toward that man, the hate that rages through me every time I think of him, the satisfaction of what I did to make him pay.

"I'm so sorry." Dr. Brown looks at me, her eyes full of sorrow and sympathy. Real sympathy.

Maybe I can trust her. Maybe she does understand.

"Savannah came after Annie when it got to be too much. Savannah is weak. There's too much love inside of her mixed in with the darkness. She wants to hate, she wants to kill, but she can't stomach the idea of doing it. He"—I spit at the idea of saying his name—"he brainwashed her into thinking he was the only one who truly loved her, but even he couldn't kill for her. I did that. Me."

That's why I'm the host. That's why I'm the one strong enough to do what needs to be done. That's why I'm the one who continues to do what needs to be done. No one else can. No one else is strong enough.

"I killed him, you know. Add that to my list of sins. One night, after we'd been camping close to another family with a little girl, I knew what he was going to do. I was getting too old, you know? I waited until after he'd passed out from drinking, went and warned the parents, who immediately left. Then I cut off his dick and stuffed it in his mouth." I feel a bubbling well of laughter rise, and I try to squash it, but a little giggle escapes. "That's how I was caught. My own fault. The father called the cops, who found me washing all the blood off my hands." I shake my head at the memory, my smile still plastered on my face.

I will never forget the look on that monster's face when I held his *thing* in my hand before forcing his mouth open. I'd already tied his hands behind his back, so there was nothing he could do.

"As much as I'd love to dive into all of that, would you mind telling me about Ella, Tyler, and Danielle, and any of the others, first?"

I wrinkle my nose at being forced to move past that memory.

"Prison life was hard, but I was just as hard, so it didn't matter. Until I realized that if we ever wanted to get out, we had to change. I couldn't do that, but Ella . . . she could. She worked in the library, she changed the direction we were headed, got us out of fights, and shaved time off our sentence. She practically lived in the little library in prison. She read every book they had and even managed to convince the padre to bring in more for her to read."

Dr. Brown nibbles on her pen for a moment before she realizes I'm watching. "So Danielle came into being after prison, I take it? You utilized all the learning from Ella and—"

"And"—I decide to finish for her—"realized that we really are a screwed-up family and need someone to help us navigate the real world. So in comes Dani. She's only here to help us, to help us deal as much as we can. The next time she wakes up, she won't remember any of this or Cheshire. I created a whole backstory for her that is different from anything we've lived. We all have different backgrounds, but I wanted her to have a happy childhood, one where her parents really did love her. That's what she'll remember. I keep her and Savannah on a loop, I guess you could say."

I can see the doctor wanting to interject, to ask a question about that, but honestly, who has time for that? I'm getting tired. I need to pee, and I'm hangry.

"Tyler is someone I created because I needed help. He was my watcher. He kept an eye on things, showed me things I'd missed. He's actually really smart, but you wouldn't know it from his behavior lately."

I can see the questions swirling in her brain. I've given her so much to go on already. But I need time to focus on what she said earlier, that I'm the reason we're all in here.

Shit.

"Listen, I promise, I'll tell you everything, explain it all. Even the murders and how we picked the children to save. But"—my foot starts tapping with energy I need to expel—"I gotta get out of here, okay? Please? Just a break?"

Dr. Brown looks at her watch. She'd better not ask for only a few more minutes.

I breathe a silent sigh of relief as she nods.

"I'll have someone escort you back to your cell, Ava. Now that we've met, I'll see about getting you moved to a different location. For the time being, we'll be meeting a few times a day. I'll make sure you get some breaks, though." She pauses, the look in her eye as if gauging how much to tell me. "The police have a lot of questions they need answered. You understand that, right?"

I nod, eager to get out. I stand and glance at the ankle bracelets I know I'm going to be wearing for a long time. Again.

She sees what I'm looking at and frowns. "Do you plan on hurting any of us?"

"No." I add as much conviction as I can into my voice. "We're here to stay—I know that. I made the mistake. I'm the one who has to pay. *He* says so."

Her forehead wrinkles in confusion. "Tyler?" she asks.

I snort. "God no." I don't know how much to tell her about *him*. He scares me, truth be told. Maybe . . . maybe she could help me with that.

"Listen," I say, "there's a long road ahead of us, one I need to figure out how to navigate. One you can help me with." I don't mean it, not truly, but I need her to trust me. I can't do it alone, and hopefully they won't put me on strong meds that will dull my senses. They shouldn't if I can show I'm safe and willing to work with them.

As much as I hate it, I'll work with them. With her. We did it before; we can do it again. *He* warned me I'd have to pay for the mistakes I made, for placing my needs ahead of the family.

Everyone else listens to me. But I listen to him.

"Then I'll see if we can forgo the ankle cuffs. Are you going to be okay?" She places a hand on my arm, a friendly gesture that I appreciate more than I'm willing to admit.

I swallow back a ball of emotion and just nod.

I need to think about who I can awaken, someone I can trust enough to share this space with me, someone who will let me take the lead but can help me navigate the paths. Someone who can help me figure out how to get us out of here, so we can continue helping children who need us.

I know who that someone will be.

It's time to awaken a member of our family who has been asleep for a very long time.

ACKNOWLEDGMENTS

Dear, dear! How queer everything is to-day! And yesterday things went on just as usual. I wonder if I've been changed in the night? Let me think: was I the same when I got up this morning? I almost think I can remember feeling a little different. But if I'm not the same, the next question is, Who in the world am I? Ah, THAT'S the great puzzle!

—Lewis Carroll, *Alice's Adventures in Wonderland*

With every story I write, there is always a team alongside me, and without them, without their support, I wouldn't be who I am, and this book wouldn't be what it is.

Pamela Harty and Danielle Marshall, I can't thank you enough. Pamela, thank you for always listening and being there for me. Danielle, from the moment I met you, you have encouraged me to follow my heart. This book wouldn't be what it is without you or Alicia Clancy— not just because you both are brilliant editors but because your belief in both me and my career has been life changing.

Tonni Callan, where have you been all my life? Your enthusiasm for this story helped me over the mental and emotional bumps. Thank you for loving the concept as much as I did. Special thanks to Kristy

Barrett at the Novel Bee Facebook Group for your support, your help, and all your ideas.

Margie Lawson, my tribe, my friend, my writing coach. You deserve a huge bouquet of thank-you balloons and an extra-large hug. I've never had someone push me to honor my readers more than you. My brain is mush; otherwise, I'd write something outlandish, off the wall, and offbeat, so instead you'll have to accept this ordinary expression of love from me.

Kelly Charron, Laura Lovett, Abby Roads, Trish Loye, members of my Secret Society FB Group, my girls who text with me every day and help me through plot points (Elena, Dara, Trish . . . here's to more conferences, more bottles of wine, and more writing sprints), all those in the FB group called Readers Coffeehouse, and so many others, I would willingly share my chocolate with you any day!

I couldn't end this without thanking my family. While I was writing this story, so many things have happened to us, and yet we've made it through it all because we remained together. I will always remember this as the book I wrote when two of my daughters moved out and became adults and when my husband and I decided to get off the crazy cycle and I fell in love with him all over again. So, with that in mind, thank you to Jarrett for taking on the role of chef, and to my kids, who put up with my blank stares as I rethought a plot point . . . let's do it all over again, shall we?

ABOUT THE AUTHOR

 Photo © 2013 Vanessa Pressacco Studios

Steena Holmes is the *New York Times* and *USA Today* bestselling author of titles including *Saving Abby*, *Stillwater Rising*, and *The Memory Child*. *The Word Game* was named to the "20 Best Books by Women in 2015" list by *Good Housekeeping* and *Redbook* and won the USA Book News Award, and Steena won the National Indie Excellence Award in 2012 for *Finding Emma*. Steena lives in Calgary, Alberta, and is a self-proclaimed "travelholic" who can't resist a good cup of coffee. To find out more about her books and her love of traveling, you can visit her website at www.steenaholmes.com or follow her journeys on Instagram @authorsteenaholmes.